WOLF'S HEAD

J. K. MAYO

FAWCETT CREST • NEW YORK

A Fawcett Crest Book
Published by Ballantine Books
Copyright © 1986 by J.K. Mayo

First published in Great Britain in 1987 by Collins Harvill, London.

Library of Congress Catalog Card Number: 86-28704

ISBN 0-449-21549-0

This edition published by arrangement with The Atlantic Monthly Press

Manufactured in the United States of America

First Ballantine Books Edition: October 1988

Also by J.K. Mayo
Published by Fawcett Crest Books:

THE HUNTING SEASON

*Under old English law 'Wolf's head' was the cry
for the pursuit of an outlaw
as one to be hunted down like a wolf.*

Autumn

1

IN THAT FORGOTTEN PART OF FRANCE BELOW SAVOY AND above Provence—north of the olive groves and south of those long plantations of walnut trees—which lies between the Rhône and the Alps, a man sitting at his fireside looked up as the dog lying on the hearthrug lifted its head and whined.

The man closed his book. "Bayard," he said, "that's the third time in an hour. If you think there's someone out there, say so and be done with it."

The dog heaved itself on to its front legs and sat with its chin on the man's knee, gazing into his eyes. The man put a hand on the dog's head and they exchanged looks with one another. What the man saw was a liver-and-white spaniel that stood more than two feet high, well into its middle age but only a little stout, panting and with its eyes bleary and bloodshot from sleeping so close to the fire.

The dog saw a small man with no spare flesh on him, a man well past sixty whose head was bald except for the close-cropped hair that ran round his cranium from ear to ear, and whose face was cast in severe lines emphasized by the clipped moustache, black and grey like the hair, but softened by the full-lipped mouth and the kindly expression in the dark brown eyes that met the solemn stare of the dog.

Now he said: "I think we have a visitor, and you think so too, don't you?"

The dog lifted its chin from the knee and looked expectant, since it knew the man was about to go outside.

"You've been restless all day, and so have I," the dog's master went on. "He's been keeping an eye on us, hasn't he? A careful one, this visitor. Let's go to meet him." The two of them stood up and the dog became enthusiastic. "Ah, but quietly!" the man said. "Quiet, and stay to heel."

They left the sitting room and went next door into the salon. With the door between the two rooms closed behind them they were in the dark, save for the moonlight which came through four tall windows. The man opened the nearest window and they stepped on to the terrace. It had been one of those October days in that high corner of the Dauphiné when the sun's heat was still strong, but now the freshness of the night air said that winter was near. It was a clear night with the stars high and bright. Thirty thousand feet up, an airliner made its way to the Mediterranean.

Man and dog passed along the terrace, through a gateway cut in a beech hedge into the kitchen garden, and walked familiar paths to the sundial in the centre. Here the man sat on a stone bench and had the dog sit beside him. He took a pipe from his pocket, and made a long-business of lighting it. The flame from his gas lighter illumined himself and the dog, and the curved stone benches that surrounded the sundial.

"If he's ready to come in," he said in a conversational tone, aware that he might have another listener than the dog, "that should fetch him."

A pair of owls were hunting the garden and the field next to it. One of them hooted every now and then while it quartered the ground in its slow flight, and the other called encouragement from a beech tree. Up in the hills a vixen let her eldritch shriek into the night and somewhere a farm dog on its chain yelped in answer. The spaniel trembled, but kept its silence.

Then the man put his hand on the dog's collar as a figure emerged from the darkness of the beech hedge and came down the path towards them.

The newcomer walked into the circle where the garden paths met round the sundial, and said: "That's a good dog you have there."

"I am Paul Adhemar," the man sitting on the stone bench said.

"How do you do?"

Adhemar took his hand from the spaniel's collar and stood up. "Let's go into the house."

"All right."

Once they were inside Adhemar led the way to the kitchen, a long low room with a solid fuel stove at one end, the windows set in deep embrasures in the thick walls. Wooden shutters on the outside were closed, but Adhemar drew curtains across as well.

"Now," he said, "Bayard, look about." The dog went off to roam the house and Adhemar closed the kitchen door.

"I've been out there for two days," the visitor said. "There's no one around."

Adhemar shrugged. "Who knows?" he said. "Go on, sit down. You're on your last legs."

"My legs will hold up a while yet, thanks. On his birthday last year you and David lunched together. There's a photograph."

He stood against the wall, a tall man in a shabby black suit worn over a dark uncollared shirt, black hair tangled, black stubble on his face, the face browned by sun and weather, lean and close on its bones and strong-blooded too. A Celtic face if ever I saw one, Adhemar said to himself: and the eyes, eyes of a deep blue, a dark surprising blue, brilliant and hard and passionate. One of those damned wilful intelligent high-handed Celts who carry their own law in the genes got from their barbaric forebears. No wonder Louis XI made them his bodyguard.

"I'll bring the photograph," Adhemar said, "but for God's sake sit down. You're my guest, in my house."

"I don't know that yet. I don't know it's your house."

"Ah, you don't believe I am Paul Adhemar."

"No. Not yet."

Adhemar rubbed his moustache with the knuckle of his forefinger. He nodded slowly. "Wait," he said, and went out.

The man left alone in the kitchen propped himself on the big elm table and let his head droop. He put a hand to the back of his neck and probed at the tension knotted there, digging at it hard. He felt some relief and stretched to ease himself further. "Might get a sleep tonight," he said out loud. "Might get a good sleep."

Then he looked up and sniffed—and on the long grim mouth a private smile broke out, a smile as open and pleasured as a schoolboy's—listened a moment, put a handkerchief in his hand, took one stealthy stride to the stove and opened the oven door and looked in. A big Le

Creuset cast iron pot sat there. He heard bubbling from within. The waft of meat cooked in burgundy wrapped itself round his face.

"Oh, God!" he said. "How good!" and tenderly closed the oven door.

He was leaning against the table again when Adhemar came back to the kitchen, and handed him a small coloured print. He studied it under the light. Two men sitting at a restaurant table with a background of green leaves, the scaled trunk of a plane tree behind them: one of them the major, David Marsham; the other this man beside him.

"Thanks," was all he said, and gave the print back to his host.

"Now," Adhemar said, and pointed to a battered wicker chair at the end of the stove.

The man took off his shabby jacket and threw it on the floor beside the chair, revealing the Walther PPK in its shoulder holster, and slumped thankfully on to the worn cushion, the chair creaking as he settled himself, legs stretched out straight.

Adhemar had not brought only the photograph back with him. He was at a cupboard getting glasses, and the man's eye caught the label on a bottle of whisky that now stood on the table. "Dear God," he said. "The Lagavuillin, in the middle of France!"

"From David," Adhemar said. "It is what he always brought when he came here."

The man, whose face had begun to relax into that exposed nakedness that comes with remission after long strain, felt the bleak mood cast its shadow on him again.

"David's dead," he said.

"I have had a month to expect that," Adhemar said. "His letter prepared me for it, that if you came it would

mean his death. So I have known it now for two days since
I first knew you were out there.''

''You saw me? Heard me?''

''No. I sensed you out there watching me the day before
yesterday, and the night before that, about two hours after
midnight, I woke up because my house was being watched.
I knew then you had come.''

He saw the other accept this slowly and with trouble.
''There are not many like that,'' Wolf said at last.

''No,'' Adhemar said, not many.'' He held two glasses
with whisky in them. ''We shall drink to David, but first,
since you have assured yourself of who I am, assure me
you are who I think you are. Where was that picture taken,
of David and me?''

''Yeah,'' the man said. He was taking his time now,
forming an opinion of this small nut-brown man in front
of him, this man who would wake from his sleep because
there were eyes watching from the darkness outside.
''Yeah—it was in the Square Montfort at Vaison-la-
Romaine.''

''Good,'' Adhemar said, and passed him the whisky.
''Now we shall drink to David Marsham, wherever he may
be.''

The visitor came to his feet. ''To David,'' he said and
looked into the deep colour of the spirit cupped in his
hand. ''And death to all traitors!'' he said gently, and
drained the glass, and set it quietly on the table.

Adhemar looked up and was surprised at the serenity
that had now settled over the young man's face. ''All traitors?'' he asked, wondering what the boy was talking
about.

''Oh, yes. Every single damned one. They sent David
and the rest of us to die, you know.'' Adhemar had poured

more whisky into the glass, and the man sipped at it now, taking the taste of it. "So, every single damned one."

"It seems you are at war then," Adhemar said lightly, but disliking the fanatic glow in those strange, over-alive blue eyes, which belied the nonchalant tone the young man had used. "But at war with whom?"

"Yes—who are the enemy? Where are the enemy? That's all to be found out still. Who would arrange such a thing, who *could* arrange such a thing? Sometimes my suspicions are enormous and seem lunatic. Above all, don't you see, *why* would they arrange such a thing? To send twelve men on such a mission, and plan for them to be killed—for what reason?" He spoke with a particular note of frustrated anger that Adhemar recognized: it was the pent-up mixture of exhilaration and fear that invades men when a desperate enterprise still somewhere in the future, and still to be prepared for, throws its shadow on to the present. "For what possible reason?" he said again in a low voice, the exasperation gone as the energy it had called for drained away.

He stood hunched over now, brooding on his questions, staring at the stone-flagged floor. Adhemar studied him, and wondered what it was all about and whether—if in the end he decided to help him—he would be an ally worth siding with. The man was wrought up to a point Adhemar could not like, but on the other hand, he was suffering from intense fatigue, and—David Marsham had sent him.

The Frenchman went to a drawer and took out knives and forks to lay the table. The bustle he made broke the spell and his guest straightened himself, and realized that he had withdrawn himself into a fit of abstraction.

"I do apologize," he said. "I'm being a wretchedly ungrateful guest. But you see the scale of the—the predicament.'' He spread his arms to suggest size and uncertainty.

''No, my dear boy, I don't,'' said Adhemar, and since he was holding a pair of oven gloves and had been about to take the iron pot out of the stove, he slapped them into the other's outstretched hands. ''I don't see anything of the sort, for the simple reason that I have no idea what has happened.''

He spoke with some asperity, partly because he was irritated and partly in order to get hold of the initiative, and put a stop to these pointless commentaries on a tale that had not yet been told him. ''For a soldier,'' he went on snappishly, ''you're a poor hand at making a report. By the way, there's a stew in the oven.''

The bright eyes went blank and still at this insulting, offhand style of speech; it felt to Adhemar as if time stopped while they considered him. Then a sudden smile of enormous charm transfigured the haunted wornout face, and the man stooped to the oven, took out the iron casserole and set it on the table.

''You'll have to excuse me,'' he said, ''I feel as though . . .'' He stopped and started again. ''It's as if I had come home.''

And as Adhemar watched he fell asleep on his feet and lurched backwards on to the wicker armchair, and lay there dead to the world.

Adhemar stared and shook his head a few times, then helped himself philosophically to the *boeuf bourguignon*. As he ate, he watched the tautness begin to leave the sleeping face.

''Traitors!'' he said aloud. ''What the devil! Traitors?''

SPRING

2

SEDDALL LIKED A LOT OF WATER WHEN HE SHOWERED. He paddled about in the middle of the bath with a hot spray hitting him from one end and a cascade of cool drops soaking him from the other.

He was splashing about in Beethoven at the same time. The deluge of piano sound poured over him from a speaker above the door and another on the lavatory cistern. He took his music at such volume that the whole house had been soundproofed to pacify the neighbours: one of them was given to Buddhism followed by bran at breakfast time, the other to Irish whiskey and a high cholesterol intake, and in the old days, with all these decibels of young Ludwig's hurtling through the walls from the hands of Vladimir Ashkenazy, before ever the aspiring sun had topped the trees of Holland Park, they would have beaten the door down by now.

When Ashkenazy lifted his hands from the keyboard Seddall emerged from the cataract and turned the water off. Wrapped in a bundle of white towel he went into the bedroom, but he had listened for a few moments to the silence first. It was a big silence.

Sacha the cat lay in a sun patch on a chest of drawers and gloried in the warmth. She was little, black, gleaming, self-motivated, content and evil. "There's a magnitude in music," Seddall said to her, and put his forehead down to meet hers. Because his remark was trite, or because he was all wet from the shower, after they bumped heads she bit him on the soft skin just under the right eyebrow.

"Well, damn it," he said. "There *is*. All that bigness, makes you small." Peering into the mirror, "Why'd you always draw blood? The only cat I've had can't nip a man without drawing blood."

He dressed for the interview panel. A Swiss cotton shirt with the thinnest yellow and red stripes on it and a soft collar; a silk Liberty tie like a herbaceous border at the end of the summer, nice colours; and one of the suits.

"Do I look like Pooh?" he asked the cat. "I feel like Pooh. Small in bigness."

With this parting shot he ran downstairs and into the drawing room where he stocked up with cigarettes, the wallet, diary and a couple of pens. On the way out of the house he took the mail and *The Times* from the letter basket. Strolling down Phillimore Gardens: you can't beat London in a good May. What I want is one of those old-fashioned showers, those pipes with holes belt at you from all round.

A nice, nice day. The wind blew seeds out of the high trees. The scent of wallflower, waxing in the growing heat of the day, caught him in the face and stupefied the olfactory nerve ends. Flowering chestnuts flowered like anything in the park, their crowns lifting high above the houses.

He went into the café and the girl who brought him croissant and jam and a double espresso told him: "You forgot to comb your hair again, Harry."

"I'm just not respectable," he said.

"It's a pity you're not tall and thin and prettier a bit. With your hair like that you'd look like Samuel Beckett."

"Who he?"

"You know who he."

"I'm not an intellectual."

She said: "You don't have to be an intellectual to know who he."

"Enough, for God's sake! Why are we talking pidgin at this time of the morning?"

"You've got jam on your paper again."

The paper was much taken with détente, as a subject for moody speculation, at any rate. The meetings between the Cowboys and the Russkis in Vienna, Geneva, Stockholm and, for some inexplicable reason, a palace outside Cuneo in the north of Italy, were investigated to the uttermost ramification, and the leader comment was dark with scepticism. *Où sont les diplomaties secrètes d'antan*, Seddall wondered vaguely and got another big cup of espresso. He wondered too if anyone had found out yet what the poet meant by *d'antan*. What a nice, nice day, he confided to the girl.

"It is nice outside. Why don't you take me somewhere beautiful in your beautiful Mercedes 500 SL?"

"I don't have a Mercedes whatever it is, and what's a nice French girl like you doing picking up strange men in bars?"

"You're not strange, you always come here. And it's not a bar." She had hair as black as Sacha's and dark eyes, almond-shaped, with that single fold to the lower lid orientals have, a notable feature on a pretty face. "You're a bit odd, though," she said, "and quite cuddly."

"I *feel* cuddly this morning, like Winnie the Pooh. It was all that music in the shower."

"Like who?"

Vienna, Geneva, Stockholm and Cuneo and a hundred newspaper and magazine and television men at each section of the talks. Napoleon and the Tsar had met on a raft in the middle of the River Tilsit to talk turkey. What had *The Times* done about that? Their man had hidden under the table at the Congress of Vienna.

He paid for his breakfast. "The thing is, Monique, you can't hide a journalist under a raft, not in the nineteenth century you can't."

"You are thinking of the Treaty of Tilsit?"

In Kensington High Street he hailed a taxi and was trundled across town with some diminution of the spirit. The things Whitehall can do to a man! He remembered: today was not Whitehall, it was the MI6 jamboree in Mayfair. Re-addressed, the driver became grumpy and made hay with the traffic. Seddall's spirits rose again. What a lot of pretty girls about the place, and what a lot of lovely women.

Mendham and the psychiatrist were there already. Mendham looked like a clothes horse from Austin Reed's window, face and all, and the psychiatrist was wearing the uniform of a wing commander in the Royal Air Force with a clerical collar.

"Morning, Seddall," Mendham said.

The psychiatrist said: "Hi, Harry."

"My goodness, Padre, I didn't know you chaps rose so high in the service."

The psychiatrist smiled, waiting.

"I've been feeling like Pooh this morning. Can you say anything useful about that?"

"The useful things would be said by you, Harry. You know where I work, call on me when you like."

Mendham made a note on his jotter. Seddall took the jotter and looked at it. The note was in shorthand. The blighter *had* worked his way up, hadn't he! He was still doing it. Seddall tossed the thing back.

"Tell me, Mendham, where would you have a hidden a journalist at the Treaty of Tilsit?"

"I don't understand the problem. What was the Treaty of Tilsit?"

Seddall's opinion of Monique continued to form.

Arkley came into the room. He moved like a man with intermittent toothache. Walking, he laid his feet flat and ducklike but delicately down, as if rough contact with the earth would awake pain in him. He reached the table without a twinge and standing beside his chair made it seem that he had merely paused. He surveyed the three men at the table, the table itself, and the room as a whole. "Dr Garven," he said. "Mendham. Seddall. Dundas is not with us today, so I shall exercise my casting vote as deputy chairman if the need arises."

The psychiatrist said: "This is all of us?"

Arkley, halfway to sitting down, stood up again, smoothed his hair, pulled out a folded handkerchief and, polishing his glasses, sat. "You feel we are not enough? Dundas is unwell."

"I think there should be a woman."

"A woman?"

"They have tits," Seddall explained, "and there's other differences." He watched Mendham, opposite, kill the incipient smile. One for Mendham. This lunch date we have, maybe it'll be interesting.

Arkley, Savile Row'd to the incisors, gazed sombrely at Seddall's suit, which looked as if its owner had been rolling on the grass with a labrador.

"If we can achieve decorum? You suggest a woman. Please guide me on this."

"A woman may notice what a man won't."

"I follow that. I had thought you would bridge such lacunae."

The psychiatrist nodded. "I can't react like a woman, not beyond a certain point."

Arkley thought into this. "You would observe her reacting to the applicant, and learn about him from that? You will observe reaction in each of us?"

"That's right."

Arkley, now furious, smiled. He was still smiling when Mendham brought in the new boy.

"Sit there, Gyseman," and Arkley came in fast. "The first recruitment committee were in two minds about you, Gyseman. Can you explain that?"

The silence that Gyseman let run while he considered the question was remarkably long. Arkley's smile went away and a choleric infusion glutted his face. It was an odd thing to see anger rush in to fill that schooled unmoving countenance. The face was broad at the cheekbones and curved like a shield to the point of the chin, but at the eyes it was suddenly narrow, as if the midwife had gripped the skull too hard. The force temper had brought to it did it good. With the dark hair and wide moustache both streaked with white, he looked like a *condottiere* ready to ride. Instead he was a civil servant with white linen at throat, wrists and breast, and with a gold pencil lying at rest on the table between his still hands.

"It was a big committee," Gyseman said at last.

Seddall had forgotten the question, but Arkley had not.

"You don't think their uncertainty may be due to causes in you?"

"Yes, some of it, but it's their job to recommend. If they have a doubt I'd expect them to say no, don't take him. You're telling me they're a hung jury."

Seddall thought there was something about Gyseman.

"A hung jury." Arkley allowed himself to be unsure; tasting strange wine. "A hung jury? But surely they are a committee of most able and experienced men," pausing, "and women."

"Yes," Gyseman said, inflecting the word with such suppleness of purpose that Seddall stared at him. At first he had thought the boy merely arrogant with youth, perhaps literalminded, but he had laid the insolence so ambiguously into his reply that Seddall doubted, briefly, what he had heard. "Of course," Gyseman said now, resolving with nice timing into the conventional response.

Neither Arkley nor Mendham showed that they had heard anything out of the ordinary, but when Seddall met the psychiatrist's eyes they were conspicuously bland. Arkley's careful skirmishing was likely to go on for some time yet, and Seddall found it enervating. Napoleon said "*activité, vitesse,*" he reminded himself, and opened fire on his own account.

"Where'd you go to school?" he asked.

Gyseman allowed himself an ironic glance at the folder in front of Seddall marked "Gyseman, Michael J.", which doubtless contained his own history from nappies to now.

"Bugger that," Seddall said briskly. "You're getting carried away, laddie. Answer the bloody question."

Gyseman turned to meet the direct attack as if this was what he had come for, and actually leaned forward across the table towards Seddall. He had a blocky head on a thick neck set on broad shoulders, fair hair brushed flat to the scalp and merry deep-brown eyes that the ladies would love. The mouth was long, straight, ungenerous. Now that he had woken up he looked a rough and ready piece of work, not an elegant youth, not what Arkley was accustomed to. And he was showing this to Seddall. He had come to the interview to show who he was: not bad.

"Rannoch School," he said.

"What's Rannoch School about?" Seddall asked.

"It's on Loch Rannoch in the Highlands of Scotland. Lots of outdoor stuff, mountain-climbing, canoeing, emphasis on self-reliance—"

"Did you *learn* anything?" Mendham interrupted him.

Gyseman moved only his head when he answered, maintaining his four-square stance vis-à-vis Seddall. "Learned a lot, history and languages mostly: French and German."

"Tell us about your life as an undergraduate," Arkley said brusquely.

Gyseman ran his eyes up the files on the table in front of each of his interviewers, an impudent turn on the hard mouth. "Went up to Exeter, got a second in history."

Seddall asked: "Exeter University?"

"Exeter University? Exeter College, Oxford? Be clear please."

Coming from Arkley, this was aggression. Gyseman turned his whole body to meet it, as he had with Seddall, and Seddall acknowledged Arkley's enquiring look with a sour smile.

"Red rag to a bull, isn't it?" Arkley said, and Seddall dipped his head.

"I'm not with you," Gyseman said.

"You may well be right," Arkley said ambiguously, and opening the file in front of him turned the pages over at random.

"Oh," Gyseman said slowly, "I see. That was my congé. Very well."

He pushed his chair back and stood up.

Arkley was delighted. "Congé!" he said. "Are people still using that word? Do sit down, Gyseman. We've not finished with you yet."

Gyseman stood, angry not irresolute, making up his mind.

"Be your age, Gyseman," Mendham said. "They were provoking you. This is MI6 you're trying for, not Marks & Spencer. Some of us may look like gentlemen, but we're thugs under the skin."

Arkley peered dubiously at Mendham, but it was not clear whether he would have preferred Mendham to claim more specifically association, or dissociation, with Arkley's peer group. Seddall was used to seeing Mendham fit Arkley's shadow. That was twice this morning he had moved out of it. Seddall began to think his lunch with Mendham might be more than just interesting.

Gyseman sat down.

"That's right," Arkley said. "Don't give up the ship." He looked round cheerily. "John Paul Jones, fighting one of HM frigates off Flamborough Head," he explained.

Gyseman took out a packet of cigarettes and selected one, examining it for imperfections as if it were a twenty-four-pounder ball, and put a match to it. "What Jones actually came up with, when the captain of the *Euryalus* invited him to strike his colours, was 'I have not yet begun to fight'."

Arkley blinked, but tacked adroitly and raked Gyseman's stern. "Your enthusiasm for the Communist Party—since you are here, are we to assume that it has waned?"

Gyseman was taken aback. "The Communist Party?

I'm not a Communist. I've no connection at all with the Communist Party. Where did you get that idea?''

Mendham, shadowing well, took this up. "It says here," he tapped his copy of Gyseman's file "that you became Exeter College representative of the Communist Party as soon as you went up to Oxford."

Gyseman was flabbergasted; hit between wind and water. "Dammit," he said. "This is rubbish. I was college rep. for all of them—Communist, Labour, Liberal and Tory. It was just a joke.''

They left him in the silence until, for the first time, the psychiatrist addressed him. "It does seem volatile, Mr. Gyseman.''

Gyseman looked at him, seemed about to speak, looked away and looked back again. "What denomination are you, sir?''

"Are you saying 'sir' to the cloth or the uniform, Mr. Gyseman?''

"To neither.'' The elusive tone of contempt that he had used before shaded his voice again. As if he had made a decision, Gyseman turned to face Seddall once more, and studied him quite openly. Studied yellow-brown eyes, the colour some cats have: studied the loose-lipped presently sarcastic mouth: studied the pugnacious jaw and the thinning hair: and studied, it seemed to Seddall, the very air around him as if to see what effect his sprawled, unorganized—perhaps to the spruce Gyseman, anarchic—body was having on it. For Gyseman was spruce, there was no getting away from it, even if he was dressed in one of the uniforms of the well-heeled travelling American: the dark blue blazer, grey flannels, white shirt and ill-widthed tie.

"You know what it's like," he told Seddall. "Your first day at Oxford, all these gung-ho types come round, asking you to be college rep. for their bloody societies, asking you to play soccer or rugger or cricket, to row in their bloody boats, to go bloody beagling and play squash and hockey and lacrosse and come to the Scripture Union on Sundays. I said no thanks to all the sporting types but by the time the politicos came round I was fed up and said yes, yes, yes and yes. It was just a bad private joke. Each and all of them told me it wasn't terribly funny when they found out. It didn't mean a bloody thing, being the Communist college rep. I never was anybody's college rep."

"Not at all the collegiate boy, were you?" Seddall drawled, not quite comfortable at being chosen as the one mostly likely to understand Michael J. (Mick to his friends—see file) Gyseman.

"How sure am I that I can believe this, Gyseman?" Arkley enquired gently. "That your recollection is correct, even. We tend to forget our youthful follies, do we not?"

"It can all be checked out," Gyseman said curtly. "If in fact you don't know it already, it can all be checked out. Find my relevant politically minded contemporaries and ask them."

"I can assure you we don't know it already," Mendham said. "It is perfectly credible and it makes sense. But it would be an arduous work to check it, you can see that."

"Ah," Arkley chimed in musically, alighting on the appropriate page in the Gyseman biography, "and it fits in with your character, does it not, Gyseman? It says here that you put up an offensive notice on your door, yes, an anti-social notice to warn people off. I wonder if you remember that now?"

Gyseman, whose face had not changed colour when he lost his temper a few minutes before, merely gone as still as a stone, now blushed for this particular youthful folly. "It was a quotation from Trelawney: 'Those who come to see me do me honour; those who stay away do me a favour.' ''

Arkley, who had elicited at one stroke a blush on the applicant's cheek and an allusion he recognized, was pretty well pleased. "Trelawney, eh? Do you think he meant it?"

"I think he would have liked to mean it. I don't know if he managed to."

"A hanger-on to other men's coat-tails—Shelley, Byron—I would certainly doubt that he managed to mean it. I am of your mind there. But as to going back over that old ground to verify your account of a passing jocular acquaintance with the Communist Party, well, we have been I think more than adequately thorough, and consider the man-hours that would take, and all on your behalf, in a sense, Mr. Gyseman. After all, we are talking of nearly ten years ago."

Gyseman did not at once answer. Gyseman had drawn into himself and was thinking about something.

Seddall watched him doing it. The others waited, as if allowing the applicant time to come to terms with the idea that there was an ineluctable flaw in his past. Seddall thought, watching Gyseman, that if that was what they were waiting for they had a surprise coming.

"I don't think," Gyseman said, to this newly patient and courteously attentive audience, "that it's safe to leave it there."

"Safe!" exclaimed Arkley, a moment before Mendham said it too.

I'm not going to believe this, Seddall said silently, and dropped a few inches more into his chair.

"If it's true what you have told me, it would be unsafe to leave it." Gyseman was as clear and passionless as an empty mirror. "By which I mean that if it is true that you have not taken a sample opinion of people who knew me at the time, but have by some random method chanced on the fact of my being college rep. for the Communists—by my telling on a facetious whim, but let that be for now— then who is it that would recall that now, ten years after, and not only recall it, but postulate that I am or was a serious Communist; and why would he or she do that?'' He let his regard move from face to face. "Why would someone in MI6 do that?"

Mendham spoke immediately. "It wasn't Six covered that. It was Five."

Arkley looked at him in surprise, and Mendham, realizing that he had been defensive, looked surprised too.

"Let me understand this," Arkley was unperturbed. "Are you saying that if we had taken a representative sample, as I believe the phrase is, of your acquaintance at Exeter of that time, it would have shown us that you were of no particular political mind, and were given to striking facetious attitudes?"

"No, not that. I'm suggesting that only someone with recollection of the event, and who also had a purpose to fulfil, would put it as a serious affiliation to the Communist Party. And also, of those who knew about it, that the person most likely to know of it as a joke on the Communist Party only, but declining to view it in that way, is one who was then and is now more seriously committed to the Communist Party."

"I see," Arkley said, and looked at him curiously. "You put it most clearly."

"Yes," Mendham came in, "that's all very well, but it depends on whether we believe your version of what you call the event. It really does all depend on that, doesn't it?"

"What does?" Gyseman asked nicely. "What depends on that?"

Mendham stared at him, and then at Arkley, who returned the stare benignly and then looked out of the window with a cold look in his eye.

"Dear me," Arkley said. "What do you think, Seddall?"

"Oh, Gyseman's got it in one," Seddall said, struggling his way up in his seat and reaching for the Gauloises. "He's put a fishy smell under our noses, and we're talking about security now, not about Gyseman. Maybe it's nice fat chicken that's been fed on fish meal, but maybe it's red mullet going rotten, and even on the hundred to one chance of that, we have to find out."

Mendham banged his knuckles lightly on the table. "Five," he said, a sigh on the outbreath.

"Quite so, Mendham," Arkley cut in. "But this is not a secure meeting," and he looked at both the psychiatrist and Gyseman, though longer at Gyseman. "I must say, Gyseman, you have given us something to think about."

"How am I to take that, sir?"

Arkley leaned a little down to show that he had heard the respectful form of address. "You can take it that you have answered my question to you, why the first committee were in two minds about you. And as to whether you hear that in a minor or major key, is up to your undoubted wits." He paused. "Nevertheless, however you hear it, you will understand that this committee must go to avizandum until we have carried out some research on the lines you so ably propose."

3

MENDHAM ON THE OTHER SIDE OF THE TABLECLOTH WAS a different being from Mendham in the conference room. Seddall, experiencing the throes of revelation, found himself looking at a boy let out of school. It was as if the departmental man, dressed in careful imitative ways, that he had expected to lunch with, kept part of himself on the far side of the bridge that crosses from childhood to maturity. They said Mendham was brilliant, Seddall remembered, listening with doubt and amusement to the exuberant speech and watching the energetic and gawky body movement that accompanied it. He had seen brilliant men, one or two, behave like this, but never a senior functionary of MI6.

Mendham's face was volatile and nakedly expressive, and his arms, head and even his legs jerked and gesticulated like a fledgling on the nest, desperate to fly but not getting airborne. Seddall wondered what the psychiatrist would make of all this.

His host, who was generating so much vivacity in himself that he was quite lost to the formalities of restaurant life, noticed at last the waiter, trying to manoeuvre a large and glossy menu into the possession of this human whirligig.

"Oh, good," Mendham said, taking the menu. "We'll have martinis. Cold, dry, ten-to-one. Real ones, American." The waiter went away and Mendham gave himself up to an intense study of the menu.

Seddall had the odd sensation that he was being given an insight, between acts, into a performer who was unaware that he was seen. Seddall was not all that hungry, he rather fancied *oeufs en cocotte* and gooseberry fool; they had the eggs but not the gooseberry fool. He expected Monique could turn out gooseberry fool if she was put to it. He was going soft. Perhaps it was time to change the tone of this little luncheon party.

"Mendham," he said, "are you popping speed, or something?"

He lost that round. Mendham kept his eyes on the florid script of the menu save for the moment when he shifted his head to flash a smile at the silver vase of flowers on the table. "I'd heard you were a rude bastard, Seddall. Do you know what Arkley would say if he were here?" he went on, as if reading off the words in front of him. "He'd say, 'I'm growing old, John. I long for a '55 Chambertin, and that dates a man.' "

So it's Arkley, Seddall thought. "So that's it," he said.

"Yes," Mendham said.

Seddall nodded into the space filled with rich napery, rich food, rich gourmets and rich gluttons, that was the Toison d'Or. "We can't talk about that here."

"That's why we are here," Mendham said. "So that by no stretch of the imagination can we be talking about anything more vital than the weather. Do you *mind* having a dry martini?''

The two glasses descended from a silver tray on to the table.

''No, it's a good idea. I'd forgotten they existed.''

The waiter arrived. ''There you are,'' Mendham said. He sat up and looked at Seddall. ''What are you going to eat?''

''Baked eggs,'' Seddall said. ''Cheese, salad, an apple maybe.''

''Good God! Are you a Buddhist?''

''For fuck's sake, Mendham, I kill people. Buddhists don't kill people.''

''Baked eggs?'' the waiter repeated.

''Mr Seddall doesn't speak French,'' Mendham said. ''He wants *oeufs en cocotte à la creme*. I'll have *tournedo Rossini, bleu, pommes frites, chou frisé de Milan*.

''It's a pleasure to hear English spoken,'' the waiter said to Seddall, and departed.

''This morning,'' Seddall said, ''why did you pretend to be stupid?''

''Doesn't fool the boss, you mean? I use that persona sometimes, though, and it keeps me in practice.''

''What good's that? Your brains are on record, on file, stored in the computer. And why want to seem stupid?''

''First question: clever fellows can be stupid, you know. Second: it can be useful in those interdepartmental, inter-service liaison groupings. It reassures people, actually. They relax, you can pick up things.

''That state you were in a few minutes ago, euphoric, excited—that's natural, isn't it? You don't control it?''

Mendham flushed. He looked candid and sly, both together. ''I'm still in it. I can stop it pretty quick. Wrap it up and lock it away.''

"It must be useful," Seddall said. "Mendham's secret weapon, better than truth drugs or truncheons."

"You're saying I prostitute myself for my art?" Mendham said coldly.

"We're all prostitutes in this lark," Seddall said.

"I've heard that about you too, that you despise what you do, what we do."

"I don't despise what we do. I just notice what it does to us. Are you in the right business, d'you think?"

"Well then," Mendham said, "this *is* something. I thought you were merely asked to sit in on our recruiting side because of the number of our boys who keep turning up in Horseferry Road Magistrates Court charged with treason. Are you vetting me, Harry?"

A beautiful girl with short curly hair and vivid blue eyes, wearing a yellow jump suit, approached their table, pulled out a chair and sat down, and leaned over to kiss Mendham on the cheek. "John, I'm sorry to be so dreadfully late." She smiled at Seddall, all those lovely white young teeth, and put out a hand. "You're Harry Seddall; I'm Sorrel Blake."

"You can't be," Seddall said as he took the hand.

"Yes, I know, it's a hard name to live up to. Do you think I manage it?"

"Can you make gooseberry fool?"

She looked at him thoughtfully. "I could learn to, if I thought I wanted to."

"What's up?" Mendham said into his napkin.

"Major excitement," she said. "Where have you got to?" She looked at their place settings. "You haven't even started. We'll have to eat."

"Dear me," Mendham said. "*That* major!"

"The most appalling discretion," Sorrel Blake said cheerfully, "is being displayed by everyone."

The waiter turned up. "Hallo," Sorrel said as he placed eggs before Seddall and steak before Mendham. "Can I possibly have some rare cold beef and a green salad quite quickly so that I'm not too far behind?"

"Give me a clue," Mendham said.

"Who," Sorrel said, "would have thought the old man would have had so much blood in him?"

"How old?"

"Well, probably only about fifty."

"Duncan was royal," Seddall said. "Not that, surely?"

"Oh, Lord no."

"Lord advisedly?"

"Yes."

"More," Seddall said.

"Your place, not John's," she said.

Seddall's place was the Ministry of Defence.

Sorrel's rare roast beef arrived. "New potatoes, tossed in fresh butter," the waiter said.

"How thoughtful," she said, smiling.

When he was gone again, Seddall said: "Give me a number, from the top."

Sorrel looked at the blood-tinged meat on her plate. "Nice and rare," she said. "Number two."

The spoon carrying its morsel of egg to Seddall's mouth did not falter. "What an extraordinary thing," he said. She had just told him that the Minister of State for Defence, who was a peer of the realm, had been murdered.

"There's more," Sorrel said. She looked at the rare beef again, obscured the meat with lettuce and chewed on the potatoes.

"What more?"

"Decapitated," she said. "Tell you later," she said. "The rest of it's definitely not a lunchtime story."

"Very well," Mendham said. "Do you know what happened to me last week? I was out to dinner and my hostess asked if I thought it was essential to understand Hegel if one was to have a full appreciation of Beethoven."

"Goodness, what a compliment, to be asked a thing like that," Sorrel Blake said.

"It was, in a way. She thought I was a music critic."

Seddall said: "I don't suppose we have a car."

"Yes we do, unless it's been towed away," Sorrel said.

Biffing the two-litre Alfa Romeo through the traffic, she said: "Shall I tell it, or do you want to ask questions?"

Seddall took off his left shoe and put a foot in a crimson wool sock up on the glove shelf under the dash. "Tell it," he said. "But first I must congratulate you two on a fine performance. I was close to believing it myself."

"Easy for me," Sorrel said. "I was expecting it, but Mr. Mendham wasn't."

"He's a dark horse, ain't you, Mendham?" Seddall pulled out his cigarettes and lit one.

"Ah," Mendham said. "It happens like that sometimes. We had never met, but as soon as you kissed me I felt I'd known you all my life."

"Have a heart," Seddall said. "She's only thirty-three."

"Nothing of the sort. I'm twenty-seven, Mr Mendham. Here's the story. Lord Blacklock was at home, which is a house called The Grange on the edge of a village called Mustell near Deddington in north Oxfordshire: also in the house middle-aged male housekeeper called Edwards and Special Branch man with another SB in the garden, both awake and on duty. Neither of them heard a thing. Lord Blacklock goes to bed. Edwards gets up this morning and bustles about in the kitchen doing breakfast—"

"You're driving too fast," Seddall said. "We're not on the motorway yet, we're still in bloody Kensington."

Her mouth flattened and she changed down and notched into the traffic.

"Damn you, Harry," she said. "Bugger you, in fact. Hear this. Edwards goes into the dining room to lay the table for breakfast. And there on the table, there on the table . . ." She threw a failed smile at the mirror for Mendham in the back of the car. "I'm stuck," she said.

Mendham leaned forward and put a hand on her shoulder, "What was on the table?" he asked mildly.

"The head," she said. "Blacklock's head, planted on a silver coaster to make it sit straight."

Mendham's hand came off her, a movement of revulsion, and he sat straight up in his seat. "Oh, Jesus!" he said. "Hell on earth!"

Seddall was massaging his toes. The car climbed the Hammersmith flyover and he looked down at the Odeon, just a glimpse of it on the left. "Edwards finds the head. Who does what then?"

"Edwards yells and has a kind of fit. Special Branch rushes in, brandy for Edwards, phones Kenna, Kenna phones Downing Street, and Downing Street calls you and I take the call."

"What's the scene at Mustell?"

"We're sitting on the whole thing. No police, no one's to know, Kenna is not going out there, nothing unusual's to happen, we're to go there and you're to speak to Downing Street when we get there. I knew you were with Mr Mendham and he is okayed to come with us but none of us is to tell anyone else, no one."

"No one at all," Mendham said with a tone like satisfaction in his voice. "Not even Arkley."

"I think it's time to start driving," Seddall said.

"Yeah," Sorrel said. "I think it's time. Can I have a cigarette?"

Seddall lit cigarettes. The car began to run.

Seddall said to Mendham: "You keep dropping crumbs about Arkley. We should talk about that. We should do it soon.

"Jane has eight for dinner on Thursday," Mendham said. "You come then, bring someone. She likes to have the numbers even."

"For God's sake, John, dinner's nice, but how do we get to discuss Arkley? We can't just withdraw to your book-lined study to talk business like a couple of entrepreneurs."

The big airliners travelled down the sky alongside the car, their Pratt & Whitney engines lowering them on to Heathrow slow and steady, but always faster than the Alfa. Sorrel took the car up to ninety. The competitive spirit, Seddall said to himself, all ironic. She felt him think it, and for three hundred feet of road those vivid blue eyes homed on Seddall's, then went back to the road and the traffic streaming out of London.

"What we shall do, Harry," Mendham said prettily, "is withdraw to the attic and play with my electric trains. This will be one of Jane's intellectual groupings. They won't want to play trains."

"Electric trains," Seddall said. "I didn't know that about you.

"There are gaps in every security service," Mendham said smugly.

"Yes, but I didn't even know you did things in the attic," Seddall said crossly. "That's MI5 for you."

"Intellectual groupings!" Sorrel said with wonder. "No wonder you get asked questions about Hegel!"

She hurt the gearbox down to third at sixty-five and

leaving the M4 turned north for the M40 to Oxford, entered it at seventy and moved over to the outside lane. They went down past High Wycombe at one hundred and twenty with the headlights on.

"I don't want to cramp your style," Seddall said, "but your best bet for Deddington is to turn off on the Islip road. It's not a fast road but you'll save time."

"How the devil do you know things like that?" Mendham asked.

"Harry knows everything he needs to know, don't you, Harry?" Mockery reciprocated, that was what that was.

"I'll tell you what I don't know," Seddall said. "I don't know for sure where the turn-off is. So when I start to look restless keep in touch with your brakes."

The motorway ended and turned into a trunk road, fields and trees closed in on them. "There it is, that's it up there, now, now, you're going far too bloody fast."

The Cinturato tyres burned on the road and screamed, the gearbox, mindful that Milan had been good with steel since the Renaissance, sang but took the strain, and with her heart in her throat Sorrel kept the car in third and held the speed up on the turn, so that the Alfa Romeo sheered across the bows of an oncoming truck being overtaken by a Ford Sierra red with rage, and ran up into the side road.

"Oh, boy," Sorrel said. "Oh-boy-oh-boy!"

"They don't drive me like that in Six," Mendham said.

"You wouldn't treat a horse like that," Seddall said when he was feeling better.

"That's what cars are for," Sorrel said.

"You were as scared as I was," said Seddall, watching her, and got a glance from the blue eyes, brighter than ever.

"You can just bet I was. You're navigating now, you'll have to give me helm instructions."

The car wore on into north Oxfordshire, between hedges white with May blossom, under tall beech trees, past orchards, dairy cattle on pasture, fields yellow with rape, villages and hamlets, all beneath a high blue sky with white clouds sailing across it before a bowling wind, and came to Mustell.

They began to look for The Grange.

"Just one thing," Seddall asked. "Where was the body?"

"That's just it," Sorrell said lightly, but as tense, suddenly, as a clock spring. "The body's not there."

"Oh, no," Mendham exclaimed. "That's totally unreal."

"It's something," Seddall said, thinking into it. "I wonder what. It sounds fierce, whatever else it is. That's the house, Sorrel, up there."

Up a short drive that wound round a stand of beech trees, to a house of pale Pirbeck stone. An old house, with ovolo-mullioned windows on the porch and above it, but with big astragalled Queen Anne windows opened into the rest of it, and heavy stone tiles moss-grown on the roof: not a huge house, four or five bedrooms and three or four other rooms.

"The house will be for sale," Mendham said reflectively. "No heirs."

"That's the spirit," Seddall said as he got out of the car. "But if I was Blacklock's body I'd haunt it, looking for my head. That might spoil it for you."

He stretched and looked up at the house, and a voice from the tail of the car, behind him, said: "Don't turn round, just tell me who you are."

"Colonel Seddall, Defence." He held a leather wallet, which had been ready in his hand when he left the car, over his shoulder.

"Thank you, sir," the man said and came into view.

He was one of the big ones, a heavyweight and tall with it, and a red face full of anger. He's finished and he knows it, Seddall thought, but the anger will take him through today. He won't start being confused about it till tomorrow.

"Let's see the card," Seddall said, "and what's your name?"

"Tumelty. Sergeant Tumelty."

Seddall gave him back the card. "You've blown it, haven't you, Tumelty?"

"That's what I've done." From a habitual reflex at the onset of menace, the big body poised itself into a threat. "Then let's see the damage," Seddall said, and walked into the house.

Through the oak-floored, oak-staircased hall, through the long low drawing room and into the room where the dead man's head sat mounted on a silver George III coaster, with only a little butcherly blood dried dark on the silver and the table's high polish.

Harry had known Kenneth Blacklock in life, or he might have thought the face was drooping regret that the life had ended; but the face had always drooped. Against that, the head had always been held mighty upright, as small men hold their heads, and now it tilted forward, ready to fall into the basket at the base of the guillotine. From some cause there had been bleeding from the nose, and blood had trickled on to the mouth and lay crisped between the lips, and this more than anything undignified the death. The head and face if clean, with the neck clamped like that into the coaster's silver collar, would have been ghoulish enough, ghoulish plain and primitive, but the streak of blood round nose and mouth summoned up the extreme contrast between the savagery that had executed this perfecting act upon its killing, and the pathetic—not only pathetic, Seddall found it degraded—state of death the victim had been brought to.

Having been used for a message, an icon, a symbol, the head was thus diminished to a toy for a child; or as if it had been actually shrunk by a tribesman in the Amazon forest, to the trophy of a savage.

An idea let itself be glimpsed at the back of Seddall's mind, like a speck flying into sight over a mountain ridge, and withdrew before it could be identified.

"Poor man!" It was Mendham, using surprisingly plain language. "And how foul to do that with him."

Seddall turned from the relic on the table. "I want a dog to find that body," he said. "Where's Sorrel?" And saw her at the far end of the garden that ran from the room's windows, picking flowers.

"Mr Kenna's sending a dog from London. To a layby on the Woodstock road." This was from Tumelty's companion in misfortune. "The sergeant and I thought the body might be not too far off. You think the same."

"Yes, I think the same." Seddall looked at the man, who had favoured him with no respectful form of address.

"The name's Linklater," he said. He showed none of Tumelty's anger at having failed on the job, been outwitted by the viscount's assassin, certain to be sacked from the Special Branch. Hard, confident and intelligent, in his mind he was already off the force and planning ahead.

"What about the alarm system?" Harry asked him. "Bypassed, or what?"

The man actually smiled. "By-passed, in a sense. The system hasn't been touched. He must have come into the house before we secured for the night, and left this morning after we opened up. He's one in a thousand, this fellow."

"What else?"

"He dropped the Minister's body out of the bedroom window." He nodded at the head on the table, the sloping, melancholy head. "He cut that off in the bath. Made his way out of the house and picked up the body and trotted off. I expect into the woods." He pointed slantwise out of the window across the garden past the back of the house. Seddall looked into the darkness of the trees. A forest, he thought, as much as you'll see one in England these days. Sorrel was standing with the flowers in her hand, looking up at the house.

Linklater showed him a door to the outside, in a short passage, a kind of pantry between the kitchen and dining room, and he walked round the back of the house, watching the forest, the sun striking into the leaves only so far, before the forest mystery shut it out.

Sorrel stood with her bunch of flowers in the middle of the lawn, unavoidably like a flower herself, sunlit in the yellow suit, with that shining hair.

"It's a good house," she said.

It was a good house, and wasted on the man who had died last night, he thought callously. A misanthrope, a politician to the eyeballs, a backbench MP for twenty years, a Minister for four, who had inherited his uncle's title two years ago.

"Should I look at it?"

He smiled sourly, watching her as he spoke, so that she would not suspect the feelings the house had raised in him. "I don't ask you to, Sorrel, but if you do go and have a look at it, then you'll know the first thing about the man we're after."

"It will be you, will it? Hunting him?"

"Oh, yes," Seddall drawled, "I do think you can say that." He put a hand on her arm as she moved to pass

him. Her face was tight against the skin and her eyes
stopped on his shoulder. "After that, you'll find Mendham
in the drawing room. He'll give you a drink, and then go
with him to get a dog. Kenna's sending it out. We'll be
sniffing through the woods there."

"All right," she said, and walked up the garden into
the house.

Seddall wandered round till he found a sunken rose garden with a seat in it, and settled there with the flowers
beside him and smoked some Gauloises while he thought
about the call he was going to have to make to Downing
Street.

THE DOG LED THEM TO A GRAVE IN THE FOREST, SHALLOW
but decorously finished into a mound, like the long bar-
rows where the ancients buried their dead. The viscount
had died as many of the ancients died, from a knife in the
heart, but the body was wrapped in modern plastic sheeting.

"Excellent," Seddall said. "No bullet to get rid of, no
earth to brush out of his clothes. Cover him up again till
dark, and Sergeant, lurk about. Tonight we'll burn him up
in a car crash."

"A car crash?" asked Tumelty, who was for the time
being, after all, still a policeman.

"Yes," Seddall said. "It's contrary to this Government's policy for Ministers to get their heads chopped off
and have them left on dining room tables."

On the way back to the house, Mendham said: "It's not
really my pigeon at all, this one, is it?"

Seddall picked him up at once. "You weren't here, you
mean."

"I'll make no record, open no file."

"I like that. But don't go away altogether. Do you know what I'm saying?"

"No, I don't. What's eating you?" Mendham asked.

"Don't know. My ears are pricked, that's all. There's a voice trying to tell me something. I'll hear it in the end. I'll hear it."

Mendham said, "It doesn't sound very systematic."

"No," Seddall said. "You couldn't call me systematic. I'll get Sorrel to take you up to London. I'll stay on for this car-crashing business."

"What about the head being separate from the body? Even when they burn up you can still tell a thing like that."

Seddall peered up at him with a crooked, cold-blooded sarcastic smile. "Seat belt done it. Bloody dangerous things, seat belts. Didn't you know?"

They found Linklater at the front of the house. "You're staying here with Tumelty a few days. I've fixed it with Superintendent Kenna. Have you seen Miss Blake?"

"Went into the garden, I think."

Seddall went to the garden and saw her, trudging back to the woods with the bunch of flowers in her hand. Mendham joined him. "A bit sentimental, isn't it?" he said to Seddall.

"You think she's a softie? Working for me?"

"You should know. How long has she been with you?"

"Not long, eighteen months. You don't know what she's doing, do you? Perhaps she doesn't know herself yet. She's responding to the man who cut off the head and made a grave for the body. She's getting in touch with him. That's why she works for me."

"I can't follow that."

"John." Seddall's eyes were sceptical, but interested to see what Mendham made of it. "You can kill a man and still close his eyes for him. You can play a trick with his head, and still placate the corpse. Who are you, if you do that? That's the question. That's why she's going to leave the flowers.''

Mendham shook his head. ''I don't hear what you're trying to tell me,'' he said. ''To cut a man's head off like that is simply primitive. It's atavistic.''

''So is laying flowers on graves,'' Seddall said.

The two men stood in the sunshine, and watched the yellow figure disappear into the trees.

4

"WHAT A BEAUTIFUL SMELL!" MONIQUE EXCLAIMED.

"Beautiful smell," Seddall said agreeably.

Brunswick Gardens, where the Mendhams lived, was refulgent and odorous with cherry blossom. They walked, under the trees that lined the pavement, below an ecstasy of pink.

"You look *very* smart," Monique said. "You're never like that in the café."

"I disintegrate as the evening goes on. You look pretty chic yourself."

Monique walked backwards in front of him. She was wearing the very latest in Paris couture, a tumble of clothes, some of it trouser, some skirt, sash here and scarf there, in a considerable palette of colours.

"Stop," Seddall said. "We've arrived."

She waited where she was. "You can kiss me if you like, for noticing that I am chic."

"Never on a first date, Monique."

39

The almond eyes looked up at him. "Why did you invite me?"

"Because you talk about Samuel Beckett and the Treaty of Tilsit in the same breath. At breakfast time too. This is a party of intellectuals." He opened the gate. "Why did you accept?"

She entered the path. "Thank you. Because you are cuddly as well as *séduisant*, and because you make jokes, and of course, because I like older men."

Jane Mendham had been a girl in the '60s, but she still shook her hair out of her eyes as if she had just taken her hat off after riding over the jumps.

"You must be Harry Seddall," she said.

"Why, are we last?"

"No, John described you."

Seddall introduced them.

"John's in there," Jane said, and went off with Monique.

As they went upstairs Seddall heard Monique saying: "But it was unkind to recognize him from a description. Usually he looks messy but tonight he is quite smart."

"John exaggerates," Jane said. "I discounted."

Seddall raised his eyebrows at these brisknesses and went into the drawing room, where he was introduced to an American publisher, a theatre critic, and an aspiring dress designer of Hungarian origin.

When they sat down to dinner, Mendham had Monique on his right and the Hungarian on his left. Seddall was next to the Hungarian, and so took his dinner in the company of Monique, which he thought showed particularly nice manners, from one who was a professional London hostess, on Jane's part. The critic, doubtless, was also pleased with her since he sat, lusting, next to Monique. Seddall watched Monique, and she watched him watching her, as she grew vibrant beside the critic's barefaced sexual homage.

The initial sociable sniffing-out having been accomplished, discussion escalated to the massive Vienna-Geneva-Stockholm-Cuneo talks between the United States and Russia, and the Hungarian turned to Mendham.

"Do you believe in this détente, John?"

"Good heavens, I can't speak on that, I'm at the Foreign Office. Ask Harry—he'll tell you détente is not susceptible to credo."

She turned to Seddall. "Is that what you would say? What does it mean?"

"It means that détente is just a move in a game of chess."

"But chess is a war game," the Hungarian said.

"Harry's a soldier," Mendham said. "His point of view is bound to be limited."

The critic pounced. "Your point of view doesn't count, does it?" he told Harry. "Your career really takes off in wartime.

"Quite the contrary," Seddall drawled. "I'm a defence planner. My career ends when war starts."

Between these contesting chauvinists Monique, the cause of it all, interposed French diplomacy. "Well, in any case," she said, "is not the question academic, since when the Great Powers meet it does the rest of us no good at all? Look what happened when we were the Great Powers, what a mess we made of Europe at Versailles."

"After all," Mendham began, "Clemenceau—"

"Clemenceau was as bad as the rest," Monique agreed rapidly, "but only as bad as President Wilson and Lloyd George, and that Italian."

The critic, as if intent on duelling his way to Monique's

heart and bed, tried to interrupt. "You French always pretend to forget Italian names. It's simply an—"

"No!" the Hungarian exclaimed. "Let her continue. She is quite right."

Monique flashed her a radiant smile that neither Harry, nor the critic, nor any of her swains would ever receive from her, because it was the smile from woman to woman.

"Look what they did to Hungary," she swept on, honouring with creditable versatility this obligation to her ally. "How they prevented the democrats from making a success, and then undermined their short-lived soviet."

"So that we fell into the arms of Admiral Horthy," the Hungarian said triumphantly, "and his fascist Iron Guard. And look how they carved up the Hapsburg Empire, so that now two million Hungarians are forced to live in Rumania—"

"—and however many Albanians are stranded in Yugoslavia!" Monique finished, with a flourish, their duet.

"That was an effect of the last war," the American publisher joined in from down the table, ready to be as dogmatic as any two women. "And your two million Hungarians are as well off in Rumania as they would be at home."

"Absolutely not, Joe," the Hungarian said vigorously. "The discrimination against them is appalling. Also they *are* at home, it is just that home is now incorporated into Rumania."

"OK. What about the Albanians in Yugoslavia? They can't be worse off in Montenegro or Serbia or wherever the hell they are—"

"Kosovo, mostly," Mendham said.

"Where's Kosovo, John?" Seddall asked him.

"It's a district, what they used to call a uniate, where

the mountains run across the Yugoslav—Albanian border.''

"Goodness!" the Hungarian said, and put her hand on Mendham's. "There can't be many people in London who have heard of Kosovo. All right, John, what can you tell us about this other little place—Geneva, Vienna, Stockholm, but what is it called—yes, Cuneo, where they are holding their great talks?''

Mendham said: "Not much, I'm afraid. I've heard it called the Wigan of Italy.''

"That's a grotesque slander," Seddall said. "Cuneo's not a big place, but it's got a fine piazza, for one thing.''

"Well, where is it, Harry?" the Hungarian demanded. "Nobody's ever been there.''

"I've been there," Seddall said, and put his hand on the table. "Does that rate a bit of hand-holding?''

She laughed and clasped his hand, while still holding Mendham's. "Already I have two men, and we are still in the middle of dinner. So where is Cuneo, Harry?''

Seddall watched Monique watching him. She had stopped vibrating to the critic, who had fallen into a perhaps poetic silence. She mouthed an infinitesimal kiss across the table, and Seddall half-closed his eyes to receive it. "Cuneo!" he remembered a little too late, for a glance had passed between Monique and her Hungarian ally, and the faintest ripening of peach happened on Monique's cheek. "If you cross from France to Italy over the Maddalena you'll find Cuneo at the foot of the Maritime Alps on the road to Turin.''

The Hungarian laughed, squeezed his hand and returned it to him.

"Thank you, *mademoiselle*," Monique said, and the women's alliance collapsed in giggles.

* * *

IN THE ATTIC, WHICH THEY ENTERED BY A HOLE IN THE
floor, the toy trains ran round the room at waist height,
so the two men did not have to scramble about the floor
to make the most of their brief truancy from the social
obligations of downstairs. The trains, and their operator,
had more space to display their virtuosity at the ends of
the room. At one end the tracks traced, complicated, and
retraced their course through a station to the sheds where
the engines slept and the yard where the trucks and coaches
were marshalled. Down the sides were viaducts, inclines,
level crossings, tiny mailbags suspended by the track, a
small town and two villages.

Turning round, taking off his jacket, Seddall stopped
with one arm still in its sleeve. "What is *that*?" he asked,
and the deep pleasure in the voice delighted his host.

"That is Carnegie's zig-zag," Mendham said.

The whole end wall had been hidden behind a steep
hillside, across which the rails had been laid in a series of
steps, embankments meticulously revetted with timber,
each length of track high at the ends and low at the centre,
in much the same curve as a strung bow. At first sight,
Harry's eye suggested that any train descending the hill
would be expected to round a succession of hairpin bends,
which he knew was impossible; and besides, the ends of
the tracks looked funny. He let his jacket drop on the floor
and walked up to the mystery.

"You're wearing a gun," Mendham said, and some of
the surprise in his voice was the shock of an affronted
host.

"Always. You didn't notice?" Seddall peered at the
slope. "You've been too long behind a desk, John. What
is this thing?"

Mendham explained. "Carnegie ran the trains for the Yankees in the Civil War—he was a railway engineer, you know. He met this problem, how to run track down a hillside too steep for trains to tackle, and too short to run the track gradually along the side of the hill. So he designed this. Look!"

Mendham collected a single coach from the marshalling yard at the other end, turned on the power, and rejoined his guest.

"You do it. Put the coach on at the top, there, and when I give the word let it run."

The coach was vintage, in the livery of the St Paul and Pacific Railroad. Seddall placed it on the track at the top of the hill, and took his hand off it when Mendham said: "Go!" The coach ran down the slope of the first bow-shaped embankment and up the other side where it slowed and stopped for a moment.

"I switch the points, see that?" Mendham was working a little console in the corner.

The coach began to run down again the way it had come up, but with the points switched over ran down into the hollow of the embankment below and up its other side, slowed and stopped.

"Again!" Mendham said. Seddall glanced at him. The face was eager and happy, a child's.

The coach ran from right to left, down and up, from left to right and right to left all the way down the hillside, where it ran smoothly on to the track on the level and set off for Bismarck, North Dakota and points west, but stopped in the middle of a viaduct to wait for an engine.

"That's bloody wonderful," Seddall exclaimed, and loosened his tie. "Can I try that?"

"It's very simple. Just go along the switches on the box

from left to right, and press one down each time the coach stops ready to run backwards again.''

''What a brilliant bloody man, your Carnegie! If the train can't get down in one piece dismantle it, send it down in penny numbers, and reassemble it at the foot, right?''

''Right!'' Mendham poised the coach at the top. ''Say when.''

''When!''

The coach began its run, and Seddall began flicking switches. The coach dipped and climbed, ran back and dipped and climbed, making and ending each traverse of the slope of its own volition and always descending the slope. On its fourth run Seddall did not switch the points. The coach ran back down the same track, climbed a little and returned, climbed and returned until there was no movement left in it. Seddall looked at it, poised, halfway along the length of track derelict now of meaning as of energy, and then at Mendham, and saw that he had spoiled the game.

''So what's this thing about Arkley?'' he said.

Mendham took his time, fetched a bottle of cognac and two glasses off a shelf below Beattock Summit (1089 feet) and poured, and moved to the other end of the room and made things happen. An engine came out of its shed, waited while a made-up train of four coaches was shunted on to it, nosed its way out of the yard on to the line and began its journey round the attic. When it came to the hillside that Mendham had built for his Carnegie zig-zag it vanished into a long tunnel. Mendham watched till it came out safely at the other end.

''I think Arkley's run an operation I don't know about,'' Mendham said.

Seddall felt a moment of disillusion.

"In heaven's name, John. He's head of section, and he's deputising for Dundas as well, so why shouldn't he?"

"I've been in Planning seven years; he's never done it before."

The train whipped up a mailbag and took it into the guard's van, and rushed on. Seddall blinked. He watched the train, to see what it would get up to next.

"Seven years, John, is a long time. I think you'd like Arkley's job."

Mendham had facial control when he wanted it. He picked up the bottle and filled Harry's glass till the meniscus touched the brim. "I would be good at Arkley's job."

"Arkley's not bad at it himself."

"He's not that good at it," Mendham said.

"Everyone's nervous these days, John. They know what to expect of Arkley. Arkley's safe. They're holding on to Arkley until they're ready to reconstruct. He's not making much profit but at least he's not making a loss, so to speak. He's not expected to be that good at it, he's not *wanted* to be. He'll be sinecured in two years, three at the most."

Seddall kept his eye on the train, felt Mendham watching him. Mendham let a container train pull out of the yard and follow on to the express.

Mendham said: "Two years is a long time for Arkley's section to be at half-speed. Well sure, it's far out on the south flank, but Albania's destabilized since Hoxha died, Yugoslavia's in the toils, political and economic. There are things to do there. If it were your section you wouldn't let it sit."

Seddall's eyes narrowed. The goods train was falling behind the express, which meant that sooner or later the express would catch up with it. No doubt Mendham would do something about that.

"It's not my section, it's Arkley's section. He's content
to let it sit. He's an old warhorse in Whitehall. He knows
what they want."

The express moved faster, Seddall felt a little run of
adrenalin.

The room went dark. Lights came on in the towns, in
the coaches of the express, and signals glowed along the
track. Harry shook his head and slowly smiled. The express was catching up on the red light at the rear of the
other train. He waited to see what Mendham would do,
but when Mendham spoke he was beside Seddall, away
from the control system.

"Arkley's content to sit, do you think? He might be,
now. Last year, though, I'm not so sure he was just sitting."

The express rushed up on the train in front and a signal
fell, then two more. The train braked and rocked, luckily—luckily?—it was on a straight or it would have come
off. No, not luck. Mendham knew the layout and had made
the calculations. Mendham was a dark horse. The container train was taken off the line, back into the goods
yard.

"Last year," Seddall drawled, "what do you think Arkley was doing?"

"I don't know what he was doing, but whatever it was,
I think it's gone wrong."

Gone wrong, hell. This language problem they had in
the bureaucracy. Gone wrong could mean a monumental
fuck-up or a broken ankle. "You can't just say that and
leave it there, John. You'll have to give me reasons."

Seddall sweetly reasonable. Can this be me? Is it because we're playing trains? Just how clever *is* this Mendham?

"Last summer," this Mendham said, "Arkley was away

a lot, I mean he really was away a great deal. In May he went to Washington and Langley for a sector information-share with the Americans, that was three weeks. The end of June he went to a chateau near Gien for a liaison week with the French. Then he was at his desk all July, and working a lot of extra hours at night, but never once asking Studley or his secretary to stay on. In August he went shooting as he always does, but he's invariably gone to a place near Dalwhinnie and this time he went to a CIA shoot in Yorkshire.''

"Yeah," Seddall said. "Well, the Scottish moors have been low on grouse the past few seasons."

"Yorkshire's not much better, and you know perfectly well what I'm saying to you, Harry."

Seddall lit a cigarette and studied Mendham's face in the flame of the lighter. It was composed, not anxious, not over-excited; not the face of a man making a play or a man playing poker, unless he was a better poker player than Seddall was: it was always possible.

"I know what you're saying, that patterns are being broken all over the place. But why not an information-share with the Americans or a liaison with the French?"

"Because what came to Planning from the American one was derisory, more like an attempt to justify his expenses than anything else. The French one was a bit better, but if you didn't like the American one then you saw the French report was lighter-weight than you'd expect. I mean Arkley's good, put him next to another intelligence service and in the normal way he mines miles deeper than they know he has."

Seddall examined the glow of his cigarette end in the artificial night of the attic. "Well, look here, if he knows they want him just to ride it out for a little while before they move him up to some nice sinecure, why wouldn't he give himself a few pleasant trips on expenses? And, if Arkley's so good, and if he's up to some skulduggery, why wouldn't he cover his tracks better?''

The express came to a halt, perhaps to keep Mendham's mind free.

''Because the first takes care of the second,'' he said. ''They cancel each other out.''

''If you're right they cancel each other out. If you're wrong he's been behaving in a perfectly explainable way.''

''Oh, exactly. That,'' said Mendham, ''is why I'm talking to you, of all people. That's why I'm not firing distress rockets all over the sky.''

''You're passing the buck,'' Harry said, who was already tasting very grim relish on this one. ''Because if *you* make the move and you're wrong, then you're out on your neck. And if I sort it out for you and you're right, you've a cracking chance of getting Arkley's job.''

''You don't sort it out for *me*, Harry. You sort it out for Queen and country.''

''It could be a coup, John. He could be about to put another feather in his cap. He's not ancient, you know, he's fifty-three. At that age chaps like to bring off another one, they get to feel kind of young and tell themselves they're full of experience to boot. What a combination, they think. It *could* be a coup.

''It could be a coup,'' Mendham said, ''but I don't think so.

Another cigarette, dumping the old one in an ashtray beside the street lights. ''Tell me the rest,'' Harry said.

''Shooting in August with the CIA, right? Then in the third week in September he goes to Lecce for a holiday. Now that's in the very south of Italy, no one goes there for a holiday, not to Lecce.''

''This time, John, I'm sorry, but a man of Arkley's generation might well go to Lecce for a holiday, just because hardly anyone goes there. It's a baroque wonder."

"All right," Mendham said, "I'll accept that." Without warning, the overhead lights went on. Suddenly Mendham was on stage. "I'll accept it because I went there too. And what I saw wasn't Arkley glorying in the splendours of Lecce, but Arkley getting into the captain's barge of the USS *Kearsarge* at Taranto and going off into the blue for more than a week—eleven days, to be precise."

"You went there to *spy* on him?"

"I went there to spy on him."

"Well, sweetie," Seddall said slowly, contemplating Mendham now with great care. "You really put it on the line when you get your dander up, don't you?"

"I put my job on the line that time all right."

"And you've got an informer in Arkley's section, right?"

"There's a very worried man in Arkley's section.

Seddall smiled. He felt it was not a very nice smile. Mendham's lips got thin, his face went tough.

"Why don't you tell me the rest of it? Give me the clincher," Seddall said.

"No clincher, you know that already. After Arkley gets back from his manoeuvres with the Sixth Fleet, nothing absolutely actual. Back to business as usual, except that his temperament takes a change. Don't grin at me like that. Temperament's informative. Early winter and the run up to Christmas he's up and down a lot, up for four or five days, down the same. Then recently, early spring somewhere, it's noticed that he moves into a new behaviour. Hardly any ups, now. Closes in on himself, gets jumpy, puts a strain on himself to keep up that urbane style. You saw him at the meeting on Monday. Ask yourself what you think."

"That's all of it?"

"That's all of it."

"Uh-huh. Gyseman, on Monday—will Six want him?"

"Not unless we clear that political stuff at Oxford."

"Why don't I give him a run?"

Mendham, for the first time since dinner, laughed. "He's not even trained yet."

"I dunno. He herded sheep in New South Wales. He can shoot kangaroo from the saddle. I call that trained. You can work it, so make it so, why don't you? Just keep me posted on the Oxford stuff."

Mendham said: "You'll have to do a whole lot of paper work. I'm not going to have him come to you from Six, as a not yet accepted recruit doing probation in the field, or any informal garbage like that. He'll have to come to you from outside. As far as we're concerned he's likely material but he's not cleared, and if he turns out to be somebody's plant I'll come to your funeral, but you won't see any egg on *my* face."

"Good. I'll take him."

"And if he's a plant?"

"Then he's better under my eye, isn't he?"

Mendham examined Seddall as if he were a difficult text in a foreign language, then shook his head slightly as he had done in the garden at Mustell.

"That's all of that then," he said. "So, where do we stand on Arkley? Are you going to sell me down the river, or what?"

"After I've eaten dinner in your house? I'll be talking to you about Arkley." Then, sheepishly: "I want to run the coach down the zig-zag one more time. Can I do that?"

Mendham laid the coach back on top and let it run. Seddall switched the points, and the coach swung back and forward across the slope, taking its patient, lateral course to the foot of the hill.

"I do like that," Seddall said as he put on his jacket. "Primitive man might have thought of that, if he'd had railways."

"What can you be thinking of?" Mendham asked indignantly, rising to the defence of his marvellous zig-zag.

"I'm thinking of poor old Blacklock's severed head," Seddall said, "and the *kind* of man who would do that thing to him."

"You're out of your mind." Mendham's forefinger ran lightly and with love along one of the rails on the zig-zag. It was the caress for a woman's back. "This is a brilliant piece of applied engineering. It's the nineteenth-century equal of hi-tech problem solving. It's state of the art."

"That's just it, laddie," Seddall said, and hoisted up the trapdoor in the middle of the floor. "Primitive man can be state of the art. It's a worry, isn't it?"

He went through the trap, down into the house, and Mendham put out the lights in the attic and followed.

5

HE CAME INTO THE DAY WITH HIS EYES ON THE WINDOW and the sky. He listened for what had waked him until a woodpigeon crooned and he saw its head bob up and down across the sill.

Then he stretched along the bed and finding his arms frustrated by the wall behind him, rolled on to the floor and extended himself like a cat in glory. Sinew and muscle found their length, eased and loosened. Peace of body overcame him and he lay, basking, limbs all anyhow, random as a child in those moments where its own world is all feel and seeing. A hand lay beside his face. He exerted the fingers and watched them rub the pile of the carpet. He cocked an eye at the bright blue day outside and met the woodpigeon's, one black orb peering at him sideways under the raised sash.

"That's noon out there, fellow," he said to it.

The bird flew away, falling into flight off the ledge, out of sight at once.

"Gun-shy," he said. "Wise bird."

He stood up naked, tall-legged and long in the back, his skin browned by sun with a bar of white at the loins. He took a towel from the rail and wrapped it round his waist as he went downstairs and out of the house.

The high sun was warm on his shoulders. He went back into the kitchen, drank orange juice, put coffee on to filter, and took a bowl of cereal out into the garden which he ate as he walked the lawn, skirting the shade of the 200 year-old beech trees to keep the sun's heat on him. He settled leaning chest-high on the garden wall, eating his breakfast while he looked down on the river winding through the valley. Poplar and willow lapped its banks with green paler than the meadowgrass, and here and there an aspen flickered silver as the breeze turned over its leaves.

Horses were out to pasture on the meadows that ran from the main house to the river, and his eyes crinkled as he watched them. He gazed steadily the whole length of the valley, long after the bowl was empty, until at last he eased his neck as if satisfied and looked over at the soft Cotswold hills that rose to make the horizon. He stood so still and scanned them for so long that a female blackbird settled close to him on the wall, a gleam of brown feathers.

"Hey, my pretty," he said, and they left the wall together. When he had showered and dressed, he looked at his wristwatch and took a cup of coffee into the drawing room. The room looked out over the valley, but a French window at the far end led to a rose garden. He opened this and stood outside, watching the sheep that grazed on the hilltop behind the house. The jackdaws in the elm trees at the foot of the rose garden burst into one of their parliamentary debates. He glanced up at them, squawking, hopping about with a great flurry of wings and sending chips of bark and broken twigs down through the leaves. The tumult and the shouting died and a thought touched his mouth. The sheep grazed, undisturbed. He looked again at his watch and went into the house.

The telephone rang. He closed the French window and put the coffee mug on a table, and crossed the room to the escritoire where the phone sat.

"C'est vous?" he said.

Then: "Rien."

Then: "Ça va. Demain."

Finally: "Au 'voir."

He went to the kitchen and made a picnic, which he laid in a basket in the hall. He returned to the drawing room, unlocked a drawer in the escritoire and took out a Walther PPK automatic pistol, three cartridge clips and a silencer. He screwed on the silencer, checked the action and loaded a clip into the butt. He went upstairs and came down with a bundle of dark clothes in one hand and a canvas bag in the other. In the bag were a Smith & Wesson .38 Special revolver and three fast-load cylinders, and a dagger.

He knelt on the floor of the hall, took the revolver, ammunition and knife from the bag and wrapped them in the bundle of clothes, and put the bundle in the bag. He wrapped the Walther in a linen napkin and laid it on the picnic basket. He left them in the hall and went through the kitchen into the dining room, opened a door and switched on a light, descended a stone staircase, opened another door, and entered a cellar.

The cellar was stone-floored, about twelve feet by ten, clean but dank, and absolutely empty. He walked round it slowly, inspecting the stone floor and walls and the brick vaulting overhead. When he was back at the door, he stood there and regarded the cellar for a full minute, then

climbed the stairs to the dining room, picked up the bag
and the basket from the hall, and left the house.

As he went round the side of the house to his car he
heard a horse's hooves on the road. He put the bag into
the boot, and the basket in the back of the car. The horse
had stopped. He took off his coat and slung it on top of
the picnic basket on the back seat, and walked to the gate.

"Well then," he said to the horse, and ran his hand
down its shoulder.

He looked up at the rider.

"Hallo," he said.

"Hi." She had chestnut eyes, matching the glossy coat
of the horse, and the face was a flat oval descending from
high cheekbones like a Slav's: a cat's face. She was as-
sessing him, as if her interest was in people, not neces-
sarily in the man who was renting one of her houses.
"You're just going out," she said.

"Nothing that won't wait. It's time for a drink, don't
you think?"

"Thanks, but I shouldn't let this fellow stand any longer.
We had a gallop up on the hill."

He held up his hand, which was moist from the horse's
coat. There was still a shine of sweat on the girl's face.
"I thought you might have," he said. "He's a good big
beast."

"Big beast for a big girl," she said, and if she was
conscious of the double meaning she gave no sign of it.
She was still meeting him eye to eye, still making that
open and rather pleasant assay. "He would carry you,"
she said.

He could not hide it. There was nothing he would rather
do than ride that horse on the hill. She laughed. "What
about tomorrow morning? We'll ride and go back to the
house for breakfast. Can you be awake at six?"

"Tomorrow?" Something extraordinary moved out of his face at her, and her spirit recoiled. Her eyes flickered to look down at the horse's head. "Oh, yes," he said. "I can be awake at six tomorrow."

"Good," she said, engaging herself with the horse, leaning forward to pat its neck, her eyes still down. "I'll be here then with the horses."

"No, don't do that. At six o'clock I'll come to your house." His voice was so curt and the phrasing so definite that the words were a command, and she turned her head to stare at him and sat up slowly in the saddle. Whatever had startled her in his face the moment before had gone from it. She confronted blue eyes, strangely dark and still, and the lean face set hard and taut with no more expression than if it were made of bone.

"I'll expect you," she said.

They parted for all the world like the emissaries of two armies who had failed to agree a truce, and would meet tomorrow on the battlefield. As she rode the horse down the hill into the valley she wondered what the hell she had got herself into.

WHEN SHE WAS GONE HE WENT TO THE CAR, TOOK THE Walther from the basket and fixed it in place in clips under the driver's seat, transferred the basket to the boot, and turned left out of the gate, up the hill to the north. The car was a grey Ford Sierra. When he reached the A40 he turned east towards Oxford and let the car run. Driving the Sierra, wearing white shirt and tie, he was a sales rep making time between calls. He stopped at a Little Chef at about two and asked for an American-style breakfast. He took out an imaginary order book, well filled, and made notes in it.

The place was busy. Since it was May there were holiday groups as well as solitary men like himself, some of whom he put down as "colleagues" on the road. He was perfectly inconspicuous. He ate his meal, drank his coffee, and left.

When he approached Oxford he followed the ring road and then turned north to Woodstock and began to look for a layby with no vehicle parked in it. He found one in about ten minutes and pulled in. When he was sure there was no one about, he took the silenced Walther from under the seat and put it in the canvas bag in the boot of the car. From the bag he extracted a navy blue sweater and put it on. It was oversize, and came down loosely over his hips. The bag then yielded a holster which he clipped on to his belt at the small of the back, and into that he put the revolver. He fished a thornproof jacket out of the boot and distributed ammunition among the pockets. Finally he hefted the bag, closed the boot, and put the bag and the jacket on the back seat of the car, climbed in and resumed his journey to Woodstock.

He thought the pistol in his back was pretty uncomfortable. He thought that while he was at Woodstock he would like to walk round the park at Blenheim. He smiled a little at the thought that soldiering had brought Queen Anne's General John Churchill to that palace, and had brought him on this road that would lead, in the end, to nowhere. He would have to miss Blenheim though. It was just the sort of place he might run into someone he knew, and he was dead, wasn't he? They had cut down the beech trees at Blenheim. Two hundred and fifty years, that was the optimum life for a beech tree, and they were past that. Why was he thinking about beech trees, what were beech trees to him?

He drove into Woodstock and put the car in a public car

park, slung the bag over his shoulder and carried the jacket on his arm, and walked east out of the town. His shadow grew longer on the road before him.

At a little after six he went to ground in a coppice overlooking the wood on the other side of which lay Mustell Grange, the wood where he had buried Blackstock's body. Along this side of the wood ran a minor road. He watched the wood and he watched the road, waiting for dusk, for dusk to turn into dark. This would be the fourth night he had watched and waited here. Something in his blood told him tonight was the night. This time they would come: whoever they were.

When a vehicle slowed and the headlights began to hunt along the edge of the wood he left the coppice and went quickly down the field to the road. The waning moon was no more than a white gleam among black cloud. He came on to the road fifty feet behind them and ran along the verge in their wake. The brakelights shone and he watched the vehicle turn into the wood. He ran on.

He came to a track between the trees, and started up it. He heard a pheasant cry out, roosting in the branches and disturbed by the intruders: and he heard the clatter of its wings, so it was not far ahead. He moved off the track, grateful for the wet spring that had left the floor of the wood soft underfoot.

He fell to a crouch as the moon won free of the clouds and cast a pale light down into the forest. Then he saw them, not five yards off, a group of figures beside a vehicle with a high profile. He moved closer, until he made out six of them standing round the bonnet of a Range Rover.

"Keep your eyes skinned!"

This in French, from a short man, the man nearest him. Short man with a broad back, no sight of his face. The man giving orders, and so, the man he wanted.

Then another voice, speaking American: "C'mon, Pruvot, for Christ's sake. If we're gonna do it, let's fuckin' go do it!"

"Keep your voice down, and be calm," the short man said, and with no more words walked off up the track. The American and three others followed. The sentinel leaned on the front of the vehicle and watched them go.

Get him now, before his ears are tuned to the night, while he thinks his job has not yet started; but let the others move further on their way first. So wait, wait: go!

He came feral and silent out of the wood. When he was at the rear of the car the sentinel stepped away from the radiator and scuffed the ground with his toe. In a moment the man would turn.

He made four steps down the side of the car and just as the man turned he struck hard in front of the ear with the Smith & Wesson. The man gave a small sound and fell to his knees, his head drooping. He struck again at the same place and the man slumped to the ground. He heaved the man over, put away the revolver and drew the knife. He measured the stroke and thrust the knife into the man's heart, pulled it out and wiped it thoroughly on the man's coat, and waited till the dying ended. Even then he waited, his back against a tree trunk, with his arms folded and his eyes on the vague state of the body whose life he had taken from it. He stood as if tranquil but aware, like a man seeking to come, with patience, to a judgement.

At length he sighed and looked upwards, where the wind moved across the roof of the forest though the trees around him stood still and silent: then he stooped to the corpse and closed its eyes.

He set off up the track, his eyes hunting into the night through which he passed as if he wondered what creatures watched him, out of the dark.

6

SEDDALL'S DISLIKE OF POLITICIANS WAS NO LONGER strongly felt. It had settled into him long ago and now it was part of his condition. He knew that some of them had virtues, that others of them liked poetry, climbed mountains, understood aspects of the world's predicaments, cherished their families or responded tenderly to Mahler's chord-endings. He knew that they were quite like people in general, except for being politicians.

He disliked them, that was all. They were not the sort of people he wanted to know, and now he was in among them. He counted between twenty and thirty, not a great many for a Minister of State's memorial service, but then the service had been arranged with that in view—Friday at two, when most members of Parliament were already on the way to their constituencies for the weekend. Even the peers, whose House Blacklock had sat in, were thin on the ground. He wondered to what lengths government might have gone to keep people away. Least said soonest mended, soonest forgotten.

The viscount was getting short shrift, too. It must be something like a record, a memorial service on the very day after the funeral, and only four days after the death. The charred corpse and its charred head had been put to their last rest yesterday in a churchyard in Derbyshire.

Seddall had come here early, to St Sepulchre-without-Newgate, so that he could watch the arrivals, but so far all he had done was lodge what record of them he could in his memory. Nothing had struck him about any of the depressingly similar, oddly less than lifesize, men—for there were no women—who had come in small groups into the church and formed into a large group a little uncomfortably, as if the pews were the wrong colour, not what they were used to. They had to sit up straight here too, unable to loll about as they did on their green benches at Westminster. They did this, they sat up straight, like interviewees for jobs, nervous candidates, perhaps, for mortality.

Nothing had struck him, either, about the civil servants or the soldier civil servants. None of them looked as if they had cut the Minister's head off earlier in the week, or as if they thought their own heads would be next for the chop.

Seddall sat at the back of the church, therefore, and almost wished he had not come: almost, because if he had not come, and spent that half an hour wandering about beforehand, he would not have known here was buried that Captain Smith whose life the Indian princess Pocahontas saved from her fellow savages. His scalp too perhaps, thought Seddall (heads being much in his mind), from becoming a warrior's trophy.

So Harry Seddall sat there in a dour mood, looking at

the Colours of the Royal Fusiliers ranged down the aisle, for this was their church as well as Captain Smith's, and watched the Secretary of State for Defence stride in manfully to take his place at the front.

LAST OUT, LIKE A MOVIE BUFF WHO LIKES TO SEE ALL THE credits, Seddall stood in the sunshine and received a card from an elegant youth with a nice line in unobtrusiveness.

"Sir," he said. "From the Secretary of State."

Seddall took the card and turned it over. "Yes," he said. "I'll be there at six."

The youth did not bow or duck his head, but he did something invisibly courteous and departed.

SEDDALL STOOD AT THE OPEN WINDOW AND LOOKED down on Vincent Square. The square was built, not round the unconvincing garden or arboretum of most city squares, but round the playing field of Westminster School. The wind ruffled the curtains at his side and the clunk of bat on ball nourished his ear as the boys practised at the nets. Relegated to a segment of the ground near him a miniature cricket match, played by extremely small boys, produced a good deal of sound but comparatively few clunks.

A schoolmaster, exhorting by example, pounced and plunged about the wicket, mimicking the arts of the game. While the boys bowled, batted and fielded, all within the small perspectives of their size, the man sprinted as if in pursuit of the ball that had in fact already been collected and thrown in by a miniature extra cover, and having reached the deep field checked his step to make five or six loping strides before delivering to nowhere an immaterial but palpably cunning ball which, changing his lanky frame into the stance of a batsman, he turned deftly away.

The boys meanwhile, cause and source of all this free display of energy, played out the immutable game. Their white and stylized figures stayed and sped, tripped and stumbled, stroked and stretched for the ball on the sunlit grass of their allotted patch, small humans playing out their destinies according to rule, while the schoolmaster reared above them like a god rollicking in the empyrean through his endless random dance.

A child brushed past Seddall and out of the window on to the balcony where she leaned on the wrought iron rail and pointed.

"I like that one," she said.

She was a girl of six or seven in pyjamas and a pale blue dressing gown, with a rabbit stitched on each pocket. Still pointing, she turned her head to introduce him to her eyes. He thought children were subtle, in their own ways. Her eyes were grey and the whites a wonder for their clarity, her face an oval with skin as fresh as the day and her dun-coloured hair, already long, shone in the evening sun.

"Which one?" he asked.

"The boy with fair hair. There, he hit the ball."

"The batsman," Seddall said.

"Yes." Earnestly: "The batman."

"Why d'you like him best?"

She studied the boy, three or four years older than herself, as he patted the crease and looked round the wicket like a test match player at Headingley, feeling himself already the cynosure of watching eyes. So young, and in that way aware: Seddall wondered if the little shrimp was already going places or if he was just a natural imitator.

"Because he's the nicest," the girl said, and turned again to face Seddall. "Do *you* think he's the nicest?"

Her hands held the railing behind her and she swung slowly from side to side, looking up at him. She was a nice kid herself. He liked her—and knew the tribute insufficient—more than anyone he'd met that day.

"Oh, he's the nicest all right."

She smiled now. "I'm Susan," she said.

"I'm Harry."

He left the next move to her. There were children who could stop a silence and move the scene on as competently as any film director, and she would be one of them. She was.

"We can *sit* out here," she said.

They sat on iron seats, one either side of the tall window, facing half outwards and half towards each other. On both sides of the street below them people walked home from work, and on this side they had begun to arrive, men and women in well-mannered clothes who carried, some of them, whatever they had promised to bring home for Friday night's dinner.

Nurses coming off duty walked in twos and threes to the nurses' home further round the square, cars nosed into the continuous traffic to take their owners wherever they lived across London, and other cars pulled in to take their places at the kerb. Mail vans, no doubt filled with the last of that week's office mail, went where mail vans go.

Friday evening, just after six, was a good time in a place like this, under such a sky. And in such company.

The boy with fair hair lofted the ball into the good sky and the good company said: "*That's* a good hit!"

"Excellent," Seddall said, lying whitely.

An infant, it seemed, no larger or less fragile than Susan, moved warily over the grass, his face to the lifting, turning, falling ball. His hands were together before his chest as if in prayer. The hands moved three times as if accepting a recoil and the ball dropped into their clasp. The infant threw the ball back to the wicket and gripped one hand with the other and blew on it.

Seddall clapped gently, an octogenarian at Lords. "Well held," he said.

"What does that mean?" Susan asked.

"The boy who caught it, that was a good catch." He mimed. "He held it, so you say 'Well held'."

"Well *held*," Susan said, and then, "Why is he stopping?"

The fair haired lad was making way for his successor.

"The unfortunate thing is," Harry said, "that if you hit the ball and another man catches it, then you're out. You don't get to bat any more."

"I know *that*," Susan said. "It's like French cricket. But I don't want him to stop."

Seddall grinned at her. "That's the way the cookie crumbles," he said.

Susan pouted, but not, it turned out, at him. She had heard the Summons. "Susan!" it called. "Susan, where are you?"

Susan made a face and sighed and rolled her eyes. "It's *early*," she told him earnestly. "I only have to go to bed early because we're going to the country tomorrow."

"Hell," Seddall said. "I do the same thing myself. Take care. I'm glad we met, Susan."

Susan looked at him. She heaved herself off the chair, climbed on to his knee and gave him a hug and a kiss. "Goodnight, Harry," she said, and slipped to the balcony again.

Her mother appeared at the window and said: "*There* you are, darling! I hope Susan's been entertaining you, Mr Seddall."

"No need," Seddall said. "We're both connoisseurs of cricket."

Susan's mother had every right to be Susan's mother, same hair, same eyes, a woman who gave off well-being as she moved. "Come and say goodnight to Uncle Tom, darling, and then off you go."

"Uncle Tom!" Susan exclaimed, and grabbed Seddall by the hand.

She led him back into the room, where a long man lay in an armchair having his face washed by a Cairn terrier.

"Uncle Tom," Susan said formally. "This is Harry."

"How do you do?" the long man said, past the dog.

"Hallo, Uncle Tom," Harry said, and received a strong look from the Secretary of State for Defence.

"Can I have Scruffy?" Susan asked her mother.

"For a little while. He'll have to come down again later." Susan kissed and hugged her uncle and Harry for a second time, and was taken off to bed.

The Secretary of State pulled out a handkerchief to wipe his face. "Bloody dog!" he said, then: "I think a drink would be in order, don't you?"

Seddall perceived that this was an instruction, not an invitation, but he answered: "Thank you. Scotch would be good."

The great man gave him another strong look, and raised his voice to make the vexed hacking sound of the English gubernatorial politician. "I don't suppose you know where everything is," the hacking voice said, and the Rt Hon. Thomas Glaisher came to his feet with a sigh.

He looked tired, as pale and empty of expression as an image in alabaster. Life showed only in the eyes, which were set in mournful hollows, shadowed with fatigue and cracked with blood at the edges. This exhausted monument was not yet sixty, and held to be in full career: he was paying a price.

Seddall accepted the whisky and Glaisher, once again in his armchair, waved him irritably to a seat. "Your request to see me was urgent," he said, the voice too big for the space between them, "and since I'm dining here I thought it would be an unobtrusive way for us to meet. What do you want?"

The man builds a wall around himself, Seddall thought. Is it an aggressive style to keep himself and his power remote, for certainly it seems habitual, or is there more to it in my case—a defensive rampart to keep me out?

"I want to know about Blacklock," he said.

"We have little time, Seddall. Can you be specific?"

The form of address, since it was not meant to be reciprocated, made Seddall smile. "I have that art," he said. "Here goes. Blacklock was pressed on you by the Prime Minister and your party chairman. He was your Number Two but he was not your choice. Why didn't you want him?"

"I thought we'd kept that dark," Glaisher said. "How these people talk in their cliques and cabals! Why do you want to know that?"

"Because I think it may bear on why he was killed."

"Surely he was murdered by terrorists? The IRA most likely? Is that not why Downing Street told you to cover it up as a car crash, so that they could not claim it as a coup?"

"No, it's not. If the IRA had done it they'd have claimed it anyway, whatever we did to cover it up. This was not a terrorist killing, it has absolutely none of the characteristics. Which leaves me to believe that unless it was a freakish act, say by a madman, then it was responsive to something Blacklock had done."

Glaisher made a scoffing noise, a laugh without humour in it. ''The idea of Blacklock doing something that could evoke any kind of emphatic response is absurd, far less something that would bring his death on him. I'll tell you about Blacklock. He was a long-time member of parliament and a second-rate junior Minister, and he was bloody lucky to be lofted into Minister of State at Defence, I can tell you. He was a party stalwart and I'm not, I'm my own man. I'm as loyal as the next man but I toe no line I haven't helped to draw. It's known; I'm known for it.'' This was more than vanity or self-confidence; it was hubris. ''I'll tell you about Blacklock. He was a politician who had reached his zenith a long way from the top. They put him in with me simply because I'm an individual, to reassure the rank and file. That cannon-fodder on the back benches want balance, they don't want government to be outright or downright, they're nervous of Ministers who are definite. I'm definite, and Blacklock was the balance. Whatever force he had once had, and that was never much, had already gone. He sounded in public like those former Ministers who are finished with power forever but keep turning up on TV and radio making obsolete sounds that they think are still whatever wisdom they had when they were in power.

Seddall, who had begun by wondering whether the man's arrogance was the product of nature or of practice, no longer cared. Whatever its cause, it had been so long in place by now that it had reached the status of the sublime: not only was it perfectly callous to the fact that the subject of its contempt had earlier in the day received the last ritual of his mortality; it also paraded itself naked in front of Seddall with the same indifference to his presence as that shown by the noblewoman of eighteenth century

France going naked before her servants, in the confidence that they were of the same order as the beasts of the field.

"Yeah," Seddall said. "Well, as the old line has it, such men are dangerous."

Instead of repeating the scoffing laugh he had come out with earlier, Glaisher was on the alert at once. Delivering the pompous devaluation of the late Lord Blacklock he had settled deeper into the comfort of the armchair, his jowl had puffed into a second chin and fattened his face. Now the strong plane of the jaw tilted upwards and the head took on a lean and questing look, putting so much attention at Seddall that it struck like a threat.

"Dangerous? How, dangerous?" Glaisher demanded.

"I think," Seddall said, "of the Blacklock you describe—a second-rater past his best. When men get like that and don't know it, and they're still in government, they sometimes forget the questions sensible men ask themselves, they shake all the doubts off their head like dandruff and feel miraculously certain and full of power, sure of their judgement. They can do some silly things, right then."

Glaisher climbed slowly to his height, a gradual aggrandizing movement which ended with him standing over against Seddall, the head still tilted upwards, looking at him down the slant of that pale, immobile face.

"Go on."

"It's possible that Blacklock was into something he'd have been wise to leave alone," Seddall waited, "or to bring to you.

Glaisher's chin eased down. "What sort of slang is that—'Blacklock was into something'? What do you mean?"

"That he took part in something, maybe authorized it,

maybe even originated it. I mean, something you might not know about."

"*Might* not know about?" The man heard overtones everywhere.

"Sure. I don't know how much autonomy he had."

"He had autonomy. I had better things to do than wet-nurse Blacklock. A mediocre man is *safe* in government, you know. He may be ineffective, but he's safe. He's hemmed in by committees, by the bureaucrats, and in his case by the soldiers, since he was an Army Minister. Plenty of bright boys to change his mind for him if he came up with a bad idea, if he ever *had* an idea."

There was something missing Seddall thought, said so aloud.

"What do you mean?" Glaisher was puzzled. "Something missing?"

"I don't know. We've left something out. Something we spoke about suggested . . ."

"I must say, Seddall, all these 'somethings' are rather unimpressive. Try to be coherent."

"I know—I was thinking to myself. I should leave now." He stood up. "I've taken up a good deal of your time."

He had been admiring the carpet throughout his visit, and wished he knew Susan's mother well enough to ask her where it came from. It was the colour of rowan jelly more than anything, a red haze at his feet. A rowan tree will keep the witches off—where had he heard that?—keep young Susan safe.

Into Seddall's irritated consciousness, which was anxious to be elsewhere, Glaisher's voice hacked its way. ". . . so I want a few moments of your time on my own account. You say it was not a terrorist killing, and yet at the same time you seem to resist attributing it to a mad-

man, and I don't see why you do that. What could be more
mad than to cut the poor devil's head off and leave it on
his dining room table? So what are you suggesting? You're
not suggesting some seedy sexual scandal? Do these people *do*, well, that sort of thing?''

Seddall was briefly despondent to hear a Minister of the
Crown draw so readily on the banal repertoire of the vul-
gar Press, and to recognize in him the politician's fear that
put the safety of the government before that of the State.

''I take it you're asking me if homosexuals cut people's
heads off more than other fellows do, and though it's not
my subject I think it likely that the answer is no,'' he said,
and despite himself could not keep the sarcasm out of his
voice. He looked Glaisher in the eye. ''When I saw that
head on the table it struck me that it was a trophy, and
that it was a message. Bear in mind also that the body was
buried in the wood, and that since there was no attempt
to conceal the killing, then the burial was a respectful act.
Add to all this that the man who did it neither meddled
with nor activated the night alarm system, and that therefore he hid himself in the house from the evening before
till the following morning and that the house was guarded
inside and out by Special Branch men, and you have a
picture of what? Of a capable, skilled and controlled assassin who behaves also in an atavistic way, a man part
modern part savage. What I can make of it so far, and in
this I am guided by instinct almost exclusively, is that
placing the head on the table was ceremonial, to state that
the killing was retributional. The question is, to whom was
it stating that? To the killer himself, perhaps, or to his
God. Or perhaps to others, who may now expect retribution in their turn.''

Glaisher, as if soothed by the language of factual report
and the rationale Seddall brought to it, attended closely to

the first part of this delivery, but towards the end of it Harry felt him withdraw not only understanding and belief, but part of his presence as well. He was too dogmatic and assertive a man to move away physically—to be manoeuvred into visible retreat by the alien and incomprehensible—but he fell back behind lines of scepticism long prepared, and watched Seddall from far within himself, and from a long silence.

"Savage?" he said at last. "Retribution. Messages *to his God*." As if to endorse the outrage which had emphasized the last three words the pale face twice leaned itself down towards Harry. "My dear Seddall, these are very strange expressions, and though I realize that on the recent showing the Prime Minister has good reasons for appointing you to deal with this, this tragic affair rather than the more established security services, I tell you directly I much dislike your line of thought."

"I don't have a line of thought," Seddall said mildly.

"That's just a form of words," Glaisher said, in a reasonable tone. "You know damn well what I mean, and now I'll damn well *tell* you what I mean, and it's this. If there's something more intricate to Blacklock's death than plain terrorism or plain murder, which I take from what you say to me and from the cover-up ordered by the Prime Minister to be the case, then in my view the man who did it, and whoever is behind him, should be caught and killed and the affair buried in the archive forever."

Glaisher finished this speech with his chin thrust out like a horse fighting the rein. Seddall turned away and went to stand beside the window, looking out at the sunlight low and bright on the grass and the long shadows of the trees. He looked back into the room sideways at Glaisher.

"Blacklock was killed for a reason," he said. "I'll find out the reason."

"Ha!" Glaisher, glowering from the hearthrug, used the full word, aspirate and vowel. "Do you think all politicians are so used to periphrasis they can't talk straight? Well, there's more. What I don't like about you, Colonel Seddall, is your habit of temperament which prefers the underdog to the topdog. I heard it five minutes ago when you allowed yourself the notion that this man you are after had the right to administer retribution, the right to a God. He has no right from us, except to be pursued to his death—to his silence."

"You've been sussing me out, haven't you?"

"You work in my Ministry, man, and you report to the Cabinet Office, not to me. Do you think I like that? Of course I've been sussing you out, as you put it."

Seddall smiled down at the square. The playing field was empty now except for one boy bowling to another at the nets. The two of them were indulging in those extra flourishes of bodily grace a pair of cricketers will use when they have been practising long hours together and are alone, without other audience.

"You've been reading the Special Branch report on me. Superintendent Kenna wrote that." Seddall nodded to himself. "Kenna's a pretty good man."

"Not only Kenna's report. I've read everything there is on you, from the SIS to the Joint Intelligence Committee. All of them recognize your track record, but Kenna's doubt of you is shared, it is not unanimously held, but it is shared. In principle I am not opposed to insubordinate men of talent when they are fortunate, and you are one of those, but here today you remind me of that doubt. Already you identify with the man you're after, are in some *sympathy* with him."

Seddall stuck a cigarette in his mouth and then put his hands in his pockets as if he'd forgotten to light it and walked down the room, pacing to his thought. "Sure," he said. "You're right. In a narrow sense I'm trying to be in sympathy with this killer, whoever he is. The hunter must get to know his quarry, try to feel his nature. He must make what intimacy he can over the distance between them. You say that can lead to sympathy in a fuller sense. I don't say you're wrong. But I'm a hunter, not a judge. If I were a judge, it would be time to worry."

"You're a killer, too, Seddall. Let's not mince words."

Seddall was looking at the surface of a library table which had two vases of roses on it and a bowl of last year's rose leaves. He stirred the pot-pourri with his fingers, and saw the movement in the mirror that hung above the table. He did not look higher in the glass, but he sniffed the roses before he turned.

He thought it was time to go. He crossed in front of Glaisher to throw the unsmoked cigarette into the fire, and as if he were alone in the room went to the door.

"I've known men like you," Glaisher said. "Men who took their guns back to Purdey's because they'd shot one bird too many, and wanted no more of it. I've been with men on the hill who wished inside themselves that the stalk was enough for them, but who shot the deer and were sorry for it after. That could happen to you. I think it will. And if it's thinking of happening this time, I warn you Seddall, I won't let it.

Seddall came away from the door and sat himself against the wall in a nice big upright Queen Anne chair beside a nice old black Jacobean dresser that should have been out of place in this room. He liked the deep shine in the assorted pieces of furniture that made the room what it was,

like the glossy coats on well-fed dogs that knew they belonged.

"I don't get much excited when I am insulted by men
like you, Glaisher," he said rudely. "And I've taken as
much as I'm going to take. So think about this: you're
afraid that what you call the established security agencies
have made another fuck-up and that Blacklock was in it
somewhere, and Blacklock was Ministry of Defence—
where the buck stops with you. You think you are next
in line for 10 Downing Street and that this thing could
stop you in your tracks. I bet you even think MI Five or
Six might have gone round the twist and topped Blacklock themselves—and the way your mind will be working
on how their minds work, I'm not at all surprised you
would think that. So you're afraid that if the worst scenario is the true one, you can't be sure I'll sweep the
dust under the rug, and you can just see yourself standing
there sneezing in a cloud of dirt. I'm a killer—sure. But
what about you? You're thinking about my memorial service already."

Glaisher stood in front of the fire with his hands behind
his back and his feet planted well apart and his chin well
up. He would have been looking down his nose at Seddall
except that his eyelids were lowered.

"What the hell!" Seddall said. He went down the room
and looked at himself in the glass. It was the same face
he had shaved in the morning, the skin toughened and
seamed and coloured by the suns of another time in another country, mousey hair and less of it than there had
been, yellow eyes that mistrusted their own reflection and
a loose-lipped mouth that even as he looked at it began to
mock its owner.

His right hand went out and took some of the dried rose

petals from the bowl of pot-pourri. He watched the hand. It put the petals in his jacket pocket.

He went to the door and opened it. "See you in church," he said, and closed the door and went downstairs.

7

" 'Auctioneers & Valuers'," Sorrel Blake read the
words on the panel of the van. "Appropriate enough, in
the circumstances. I wonder who they are."

"They claim to be Jas. Smith Ltd, of Aylesbury,"
Gyseman said.

Sorrel kept her eyes on the house with the van standing
at the door. "You're not as simple as that, are you?"

"No, I'm not. Whatever they're here to value, it's not
the paintings and the silver."

She looked at him. "I hope Harry's right about you,"
she said, and touched the handle of the car door. "I'll go
in. Drop me off and drive away, and come back through
the bushes. If they're dumb enough, you'll have the advantage of surprise, as it says in the textbooks."

"You're just going to walk into it," Gyseman said.

"I don't think it's bad," Sorrel said. "I think they'll
just be meddlers. A thing like this, meddlers are likely."

She got out of the car and opened the back door to take

her overnight bag off the seat. He turned to watch her and their eyes met. "I'm inscrutable and tense," Gyseman said, "and you're tense and inscrutable. If I come in the door with a gun in my hand, hit the floor at once, right?"

Sorrel nodded. "Bye-ee."

"See you later."

He swung the car on the gravel and went off down the drive, waving out of the window. She waved back and turned towards the house. Striding up to the door she found the heft of the bag gave reassurance. She had come to places like this before often enough; a guest arriving for the weekend, that was the frame of mind for this one.

A late Friday afternoon in May with the sun down on the treetops and the birds singing out the day, that was the stuff, jolly nice. The front door opened as she reached it, and she walked into the house.

The man who had opened the door closed it, and another man took her bag. Two men in suits, but not Linklater and Tumelty, not the Special Branch men who had been here the first time she came to Mustell, and who were supposed to hand over the house to her.

"Thanks," she said to the man who had taken her bag. "I'll go upstairs and pick myself a room."

The man set the bag down, however, and looked at the door of the drawing room. Tough eggs, these two. Special Branch were tough eggs all right, but they could look right in cocktail bars too. These two would not look right in cocktail bars.

A member of the officer class came out of the drawing room, not as big as the tough eggs, but big enough, strong and compact and with the hard eye, the policeman's eye. Sorrel wondered: has there been a change? Is this the local Police? Watching the new one arrive, she thought not.

"Miss Blake," the new one said. "My name is Dudgeon, Ministry of Defence police."

Meddlers, right enough. "This is a surprise," she said carefully. "Let us two go into the drawing room."

There was a small clutter of equipment against the wall near the door into the drawing room. She stooped over it. "I see," she said. "We plan a photographic session, do we?" There were three small cases, not heavy. She took them by their straps and carried them through the door into the long low room, and put them beside her when she settled herself into a deep chesterfield. "Photographs are not on the agenda, Mr Dudgeon. Neither are you, if it comes to that. I should ask to see your credentials, I think."

Dudgeon was not eager to please. He stood with his hands in the pockets of his jacket, thumbs outside, and looked at her calmly. "The high hand," he said. "Aggressive man management. Stuff it, Miss Blake."

She nodded. "Fair enough," she said. "Have we a drink here, or is it being valued for tax purposes?"

He went into the dining room and came back with a decanter and two glasses. "Sherry," he said.

"About right," Sorrel said. "Thanks."

"My ID," he said, and put a wallet on the table at her elbow. "My orders." He put down an envelope.

She opened the wallet and scanned the contents. "Major," she said, "if your orders were a *lettre de cachet* for the Bastille signed by Louis XIV, they couldn't mean less to me."

"They mean plenty to me," Dudgeon said, and suddenly he laughed. "This is like a scene from the Victorian history books," he said. " 'I command here, sir!' 'No, sir. I command here!' "

"It's a scene you'll be prepared for," Sorrel said. "You must have expected it."

"My orders are not to interfere, simply to be here and be a witness to what you find in Blacklock's papers. Ministry of Defence has a legitimate and essential interest to safeguard when one of its Ministers dies, which is quite separate from Colonel Seddall's interest."

"That's cute," Sorrel said.

"The Prime Minister agrees, Miss Blake."

"That's cute too," she said, "but it won't be cute enough for Seddall."

"My orders will be cute enough. They're not ambiguous. And we have been diplomatic, tactful enough not to outrank him. There will be no need for friction."

Outside the windows the last brightness was still in the day, but dusk had already entered the room. Dudgeon went about, switching on lamps. "When do you expect Seddall?"

"He could be here in an hour. The car's gone to meet him off the Oxford train."

"Ah. I had wondered about the car." He did not look as if he had quite stopped wondering, but equally it did not seem greatly to concern him.

Sorrel was wondering about the car herself: what Gyseman would do.

He would take what she had told him to do as an initiative test, he'd be a fool not to. The question was, she thought, whether he would feel he had to show initiative, or whether he would have the initiative to know when there was no need to show it. Like now, when these people were only meddlers, not hostiles.

Time would tell. Meanwhile, she had a ghost to lay.

She got up and walked into the dining room. No light was on there, and she stood at the window in the dusk and looked over the lawn to the darkness at the foot of the garden.

Out there day was almost gone, and shadow deepened to black where the reach of her eye touched the night. As Sorrel stood there something from inside her made her frown and shake her head. Her body made a movement of doubt and then took her to the door that opened on to the garden, and outside.

She crossed the grass in the cooling air until she came to the end of the lawn. The dusk, surrendering at every moment to the night, had taken the colours from the flowers, but she smelled the lilac that grew against the wall, and the honeysuckle. Beyond the wall loomed the trees, and beyond the trees the night itself reared up, and rose forever, unlit by moon or stars. Behind her in that house the killing had been done, the head hacked from the trunk like some stark deed of the Middle Ages and the headless corpse carried into the forest to be put to its rest; and in an act joining her to the wild spirit which had brought its mutilated victim to that woodland burial, she had laid flowers on the grave.

It had not seemed like this to her when she did it. Then, it had been a response to the dead man's dying, and a gesture against the furtive banality the State would bring to disposing of the body and hiding how it had died.

Now, out of the night towards her, seeking her own spirit as if she had offered it to be shared, she felt the movement of an intolerable communion reach to touch her, as her eye had reached to touch the night.

The strength of it held her poised, immobile on the margin of a precipice down which she might fall: knowing that near or far, the passionate being who had laid his enemy in the forest grave was alive and waking, there in that same night.

The alarm that struck her brought with it an awareness of the senses so acute and alien that she found herself listening to the dark within her and without, for some long-forgotten voice, silenced before she or her remembered ancestors were born, that she would recognize. Recognize, why recognize? And this question loosened the embrace of the darkness and the night, and the terror of the unnameable summons that had come out of them.

"I don't know that I liked that very much," Sorrel said aloud, in much the same tone she would have used if the night had made improper moves upon her person: and extended nevertheless all her senses to pick up any lingering echo of the call that had come to her out of the darkness.

She heard nothing but the sough of a rising wind in the branches of the trees and the squeal of a hunted rabbit in the meadow. She felt the wind cold on the back of her neck and saw a bat flitter erratically by, and realized that the moon was out, a pale quarter-moon which no more than weakened the dark.

She turned to go back to the house. Lights came on in the windows of the dining room and ran out on to the grass, and Dudgeon's broad stocky figure appeared in the doorway.

"Sorrel, it's me," Gyseman's voice said off to her left.

"Oh, hallo," she said.

"They're just security yobboes from the Ministry," he said.

"I listened to them talk a while. Shall I go and bring the car back?"

"Do that," she said.

They reached the terrace and Dudgeon came outside. "Hi," Gyseman said to him, and wandered off round the house.

"Who was that?" Dudgeon asked suspiciously.

"A man called Gyseman," Sorrel said.

She walked past Dudgeon into the dining room and straight over to the table where the head had been. It was only a shiny table, nothing to do with those trees out there moving in the wind. That ghost was laid.

It did seem just possible, of course, that another one had walked up to her out in the garden, but one thing at a time, Sorrel, she said to herself, one thing at a time.

She went into the drawing room and gave herself a glass of sherry and sat down. Dudgeon followed her. He looked strange, as if he thought she looked strange.

"What was going on out there?" he asked her.

"None of your damned business," Sorrel said. "The fire's going out."

Dudgeon made the face of a brother confronted with a sister in a bad temper, and knelt beside the fire. He put wood on it, placing it with care for the airflow; a man being good with fires. When he had done the log basket was empty.

He went to the door into the hall and shouted: "Reynolds, get some wood for the fire, will you?"

"For God's sake!" Sorrel said. "This is a house, not a barracks."

She grabbed the empty basket from the hearth and went through the pantry into the kitchen, where she found Gyseman laying out the food supplies he had brought in from the car.

"Who cooks dinner?" he asked. "The viscount's man being sedated in hospital and all."

"Not Major Bloody Dudgeon anyway. You can bet on that. Probably Corporal-Cook Reynolds, if he has his way."

"I say," he said. "You're all cross about something.

What happened to the Spirit of Woman communing with nature that I saw in the garden?''

"You were *watching* me?"

"Not in the least. I averted my eyes."

She let the basket to the floor and said, putting her arms round his waist: "I think you need this."

"I just do," he said, hugging her in return. "I really do. Why, you're all shook-up."

"We're doing this for you."

"Yes, yes. I understand that."

She was a good-looking girl and a splendid-feeling woman. He liked those jumpsuits she wore, he liked this burgundy one she was wearing. He looked down her back, and liked her bottom.

"I like your bottom," he said.

"Don't *say* things like that."

"Like what?"

"Like office chauvinism."

"Absolutely not, it's not. I'd say it to Major Bloody Dudgeon, if I felt the impulse."

Dudgeon's voice said: "You'd say what to Major Bloody Dudgeon?"

Sorrel's arms loosened; his didn't. "I like your bottom, Major," he said.

"You're an insolent bastard," Dudgeon said without rancour, "and I don't recall that you've had the opportunity to examine it."

"You see," Gyseman said, "I'm not an office chauvinist at all." He took his arms from her.

"Yes, I see," Sorrel said, "You're a good man, Charlie Brown. Now why don't you simmer down and go and find the woodshed. I expect you'll feel more at home there, and the Major needs logs for the fire, don't you, Major?"

Dudgeon picked up the basket and held it out. "Here," he said to Gyseman.

"Gosh thanks," that young man said and went out the back door.

"My name's Alistair," Dudgeon said. "We're being a bit formal, don't you think?"

"Quite right, and I'm Sorrel. Can you cook? I ask because Harry likes playing in the kitchen but the trouble with that is you never know when he's actually likely to arrive."

"I'll peel potatoes. Meet my eye, for Christ's sake, there's nothing wrong with giving a man a hug."

Warmth came up in her face and the brilliance of the blue eyes opened itself to him. "You never know where you'll meet a human being these days. You were so bloody stiff when I arrived."

"Sorrel," Dudgeon said, "I'm what they used to call just a simple soldier. Human beings need human acts. I'm a married man, so I know that. We can be human till Seddall gets here, and then I'll have to fight my corner according to my orders. And if half of what they say about him is true," he added with some seriousness, "I'll have my work cut out."

"Well, well," Sorrel said. "What half is that?"

"What do I know about him? Army family—erratic but for the most part successful Army family, and he's right in the family tradition—a born irregular. Wellington and Sandhurst, and then conned himself an attachment to Aden, got himself captured, off the map for three months, came out of it all decorated and smelling of roses. Been all over the shop on his own ever since, answerable to God knows who, and has hardly been seen in his regiment from that day to this. Anyone who's ever served with him—Cyprus, Trucial States, British Guyana, you name it—they always say that when the unit's going in one direction, Seddall's going in the other. Wouldn't see him for a month, till he turned up badly in need of a bath.

"To be perfectly candid, that's all I know in that line, but he does have one hell of a reputation for suffering no-one much very gladly. The mystery is, how he gets away with it—that and the way he goes down to that place in the country and doesn't turn up at the office—"

There was a thumping sound at the back door and Dudgeon opened it to Gyseman, whose well-organized expression was under strain from the weight of the logs piled high on the basket.

"Mick, we're on a new footing," Sorrel said pointedly. "This is Alistair."

"Terrific to know you," Gyseman said with a constricted larynx.

"Piss off," Dudgeon said, "and dump this somewhere." He slipped out of the coat of his tweed suit and threw it on top of the logs. "Watch out for the paintwork, there's a good chap." As he rolled up his sleeves and moved towards the kitchen sink he said: "I thought that, ah, Mick, had gone to meet Colonel Seddall."

"No. Harry's driving himself."

"Then why the charade?" He looked honestly perplexed. She thought he *was* honestly perplexed. She wished a terrible fate upon all heads of government departments who interfered in security matters.

"Major Dudgeon . . ." she said, and cocked what was, she hoped, a quizzical eyebrow.

"Got you," he said. "Where're the spuds?"

Gyseman came in. "Too many cooks spoil the broth," he said. "*I* am definitely in charge of the halibut."

"Halibut!" Sorrel said.

"It's like dining with the Hussars," Dudgeon said.

"Tell me, Alistair," Gyseman said curiously. "Do your chaps just sit and stand about? Is that what they're best at? I mean, they don't seem to prowl the grounds with catlike tread or anything, do they?"

"Not their style," Dudgeon said shortly, refusing to leap to the lure.

" 'There was a cobbler and his last,' " Gyseman sang offensively.

Dudgeon turned from the sink to face him, with a potato in one hand and the peeler in the other. "Stop being juvenile, laddie," he said, in an unimportant but remarkably effective way. "We're having an intermission with no aggro; if you can't handle that, go and play in someone else's yard."

"This *is* our yard," Gyseman said first. Second, he said gracefully, surprising himself as much as any of them. "However, that's not the point, is it? I regret my words, sir, and here's my manly hand on't."

"Get lost," Dudgeon said again, returning to his potatoes.

Sorrel sat on a chair and put her ankles up on the table. "This is the life," she said. "A woman's place is no longer in the kitchen."

Behind her head, the telephone on the wall began to ring. She twisted round and took down the receiver.

"Yes," she said, "Major Dudgeon is here."

Dudgeon dried his hands and took the phone from her. "Dudgeon here," he said. His mouth went thin. "Called off, yessir. When shall I report? *No* report," he said slowly. "Yes, got it. 'Bye." He laid the receiver gently on to its rest.

He sat himself down on the kitchen table, not even noticing when Sorrel moved her feet to make room for him.

Under the discipline, she thought his resolute soldier's face looked mutinous.

"What's up?" she said.

He turned to her. "Wild goose chase," he said. "End of mission."

His eyes were angry. That's good, she thought. Harry will want to know all about this one, and the anger might help.

"Just when we were getting on so well," Gyseman said prettily.

Fortuitous or not, the line was helpful. "Yes, exactly!" Sorrel said. "And the halibut, you can't miss that. Wait at least for dinner."

"Can't, thanks. Must get the boys back. They're actually due off duty.

"No problem," Gyseman said, as smoothly as a bridge player knowing all other clubs were out and taking a trick with the deuce. "Send the lads off in the van and I'll run you up to London."

Dudgeon studied him carefully and then, just as closely, turned the scrutiny on Sorrel. "Very friendly," he said. "I do believe I know, though, why you're asking me."

He beat the knuckles of his left hand on the table a good many times, and hard too. Sorrel had to keep meeting the rough, angry, calculating eyes, so she studied him right back. She saw that he was not quite focussing on her, the direction was right but the setting was wrong; it would have been right for the back of her head, if he could have seen through it. Watching his mind work and the emotion moving on his face, she thought he was a tough customer, and not at all the simple soldier he had claimed to be.

"Very well," he said at last, rubbing his knuckles in the palm of the right hand. "I'll see the men off and I'll stay for dinner. I'll stay to see Seddall too, which is what you want, isn't it?''

"Yes," she said. "It's what Harry will want."

Dudgeon went off to speed his men on their way, shirt sleeves rolled up and a tea towel tucked into the waistband of his trousers.

Gyseman said: "He doesn't stand on his dignity, does he?''

"No, he doesn't," Sorrel said. "But his dignity's just been stood *on*, don't you think?''

"Yes, it has. He looked furious."

"He did indeed." Sorrel watched Gyseman as he went to the refrigerator and took out the butter. "Why so strong a reaction? A soldier does what he's told, expects to be told, doesn't he?''

"For God's sake, Sorrel, yes, but no one likes to be fooled around with like that—'Go down to this house at Mustell, Major, and dog Seddall's footsteps. Changed my mind, Major. Come back again.' And anyway, soldiers aren't used to that. They're used to commanders who've made their minds up before they give orders."

Sorrel thought about this. "You said 'fooled around with'. Fooled around with like what, Mick?''

Gyseman put the butter back in the refrigerator. "I've just told you," he said.

"No," Sorrel said. "You haven't. You've told me what happened. But, *how* was he fooled around with, fooled around with like *what*?''

"Aha, you're on to something. Let's see—fooled around with like . . . like, like a pawn in another man's game?''

"Maybe. Yes, a pawn in another man's game. So maybe, staying for dinner, he's still a pawn in another man's game. Maybe he reacted too strongly, maybe he's acting out a scenario."

"That's a lot of maybe-ing, and Dudgeon's not an actor, and so why send a man who's so transparent? It doesn't work, Sorrel. I think he's just a guy who's out of his depth in this kind of stuff."

Sorrel, her chair tilted back and her feet still up on the table, looked at him along the length of her legs and said, not carelessly: "Unlike Mick Gyseman, who takes to it like a duck to water, and not one week in the business yet."

"Wow! What's that supposed to mean?"

The tone was exactly right: light, and only half-serious—taking the shift of target from Dudgeon on to himself only half-seriously—but the speed with which he turned amazed her. He was dressed in dark colours, black trousers and navy blue shirt and jersey, which under the bright flaxen hair and the deep look from the brown eyes made him tough and tricky all of a sudden, standing there, standing there with a razor sharp knife in his hand, so that it was all Sorrel could do not to start calculating avenues of escape from her position in that corner, defenceless in that tilted chair.

"It means that until I know better I'll ask myself where did you come from, Mick Gyseman, why now when you're past thirty, out of the blue?"

"It's all on paper, Sorrel. Harry's read it all."

"It's not personal to you Mick it's something Harry Seddall taught me. In this business you don't believe. You don't unbelieve but you don't believe. Why should you? You don't *have* to believe, so why do it, if it can be dangerous? So it's really sloppy, Mick, to write down Dudgeon as a guy who's out of his depth in our kind of stuff. Don't write him down as anything, just wait and see."

"Got it," he said, and moved his look off her, to one side, round the kitchen as a whole. He surveyed the pale blue Aga, the Dutch tiles that backed it, the old and solid elm table, the stone flagged floor, the cupboards and shelves and pots and pans and crockery.

"Well, it's a nice kitchen," he said, "but the mood's gone. What am I doing here, cooking fish?"

Dudgeon came back into the kitchen. Somewhere along the way he had shed the tea towel apron. He seemed baffled and at the same time resolute, as if he might well be out of his depth but was ready to swim strongly.

"They've gone," he said.

"Good, then," Sorrel said, wondering what was up with him.

"No," Dudgeon said. "I mean they've *gone*, I can't find them. Been up and down stairs, didn't you hear me calling for them? Quick shufti outside, no sign. Van's still there, but the chaps have vanished."

"Perhaps they're out and about, covering the grounds, no?" Sorrel asked him.

"Absolutely not. They wouldn't leave post without telling me, and their station was front door and hall, and one of them round the house *inside*, every so often."

"Do you mean," Gyseman said, "do you actually mean, that there's a chance your boys are not just out of sight and earshot, but that they've been—what?—dealt with?"

"That's what I mean," Dudgeon said.

8

"THIS IS ABSURD!" PRUVOT SAID. "IT MUST HAVE BEEN A trap."

"Shut up," the bad-tempered American said. "Wait it out."

"Ha, that comes well from you, you who have been so anxious to get going, as you call it."

"Well, we've got going. Give the boys time. They've only been gone twenty minutes."

"All the same, it is incredible. Two men sitting on a garden seat smoking and chattering—how can this not be a trap, a *ruse de guerre*? I should not have listened to you."

The American swore.

The man who lay fifteen feet from them, watching and listening, smiled maliciously into the dark. He saw the Frenchman's shape rise into the night as Pruvot peered out from the wood towards the house, tense and impatient.

"I should have ordered them to be killed," Pruvot said gloomily.

"Ah, for fuck's sake! With silenced handguns? A silenced handgun is not a reliable target weapon, Pruvot, and it's twenty feet from the edge of that gravel to where these guys are sitting. I don't know anyone who can count on a headshot with a silenced handgun in the dark, not at twenty feet. My way's better and my boys know what they're doing. A couple of country cops, that's all they have to deal with, just minding the place. We're the only people around here who know there might be something *worth* minding inside that house."

"Bouf!" Pruvot said. "You are shy of killing, my poor Wilson. You have too many principles, like your distinguished namesake."

"Hey, listen!" urged a voice from the edge of the wood, and the quarrelsome allies interrupted hostilities to attend to their outlying sentinel.

First one then the other, two men came out of the darkness over the meadow, made their number with the lookout and joined Pruvot and Wilson.

"How'd it go?" Wilson asked.

"Perfect," one of them said. "Ace, absolutely. The two of us started fighting, made a bit of noise—grunt, thud, ouch!—and they came pounding over to see what was going on. We zapped 'em, one each, stuck the needles in them and hid them in the bushes. Some kinda amateurs, there's no question of that."

"Find any ID?"

"Sure. Didn't stop to read it. There you go."

Wilson hunkered down and looked at what he'd been given with the help of a dimmed flashlight. "Well, shoot," he said cheerfully. "Just a couple of imitation security guards, Army detail on the Ministry of Defence door, something like that. Thanks, you guys. So who's got my little black box?"

"Here," the man who had reported said. "We left no litter, they made no noise. It was perfect, like I said."

"Great," Wilson said. "Right, Pruvot, let's move in."

"Okay," the Frenchman said. "Your crazy plan has worked, so that is perhaps a good signal for us."

"Omen," Wilson said. "A good omen."

"Wait a minute," Pruvot said. "What was the situation in the house?"

"No one outside, not now, not awake. These two we took will sleep till daylight. Inside, the woman and the two other men, all in the kitchen, cooking dinner, it looks like."

"That's pretty thoughtful of them," Wilson said. "Dinner, eh? Let's go get it. And, fellas—" he paused for effect. "No killing, no shooting even, unless we have to. We got more sleeping power left in my little black box, so let's use that to keep 'em quiet, right?"

"Right," Pruvot said. "Understood. No one will be killed, unless it becomes necessary. But *I*, my dear Wilson, I shall not be killed either."

There was the slightest pause, then Wilson said, with a little of the ebullience gone from his voice: "That's the idea, Pruvot. A nice clean operation. Neutralize the enemy, search the house and out again. No hassles. Ghosts in the night."

"We have talked enough," Pruvot said. "Let's get going!"

At these last words the lookout set off instantly across the meadow, with Pruvot striding after.

"Oh, boy!" Wilson said softly. "Come on, fellas."

He led his men out into the dark.

In a few moments the man who had been lying low in

the undergrowth came out of the wood, and began to move slantwise across the field, at a fast lope, as if he meant to pass the five men in the shelter of the night. With the moon behind cloud, and the rising wind to cover the slight sound of his passing, he had no fear of being detected by a party of men so engrossed in their own mutual unease, not to say antagonism. At the corner of the meadow he came to—of all things—a stile, which led to the orchard that neighboured the garden.

He ran round the end of the orchard keeping well clear of the apple trees to avoid treading on fallen twigs, till he came to the garden wall. Without pausing for a moment he hoisted himself to the top of the wall and lay there, with his head to the foot of the garden. He was only thirty feet from the gable end beyond which was the dining room, and he was in a straight line from the terrace which ran along the side of the house so that looking directly to his right he could just make out the door which led from the dining room on to the terrace. Behind him—on his starboard quarter so to speak—and fifty feet away, was the kitchen. Both rooms were lit. Being aligned so closely to the terrace-wall of the house he could see into none of the windows on that side, but he saw figures moving in the kitchen.

"Dinner for the American, Wilson," he said to himself, and thought: "We shall see about that." He decided, incongruously, that he would cook scrambled eggs for himself when he was safely back in the house in Gloucestershire, scrambled eggs with a whiff of garlic.

Then he saw the five men moving up the garden. He made a grimace—he should have heard them enter it: they were using more care, now, than they had on the edge of the wood.

As they came closer they changed from being an amor-

phous bunch of men, a thicker patch of darkness moving
in the night, into five individual figures. Just before they
reached the radiance cast by the lighted windows on to the
lawn, the five men stopped. Their dispositions must have
been already made, and this pause in their advance no
more than a brief muster before the attack, because in a
moment one man went off to the farther edge of the lawn
and slipped through the ungated opening that led from the
terrace to the front of the house.

As soon as he was gone, two more of the group came
swiftly to the end of the terrace where the man lay on top
of the wall, giving him a tense moment. Between him and
them, as they rounded the house, lay no more than the
width of the herbaceous border, nine or ten feet: had they
looked up, they must have seen him. He saw them clearly
enough—Wilson the American and one of his henchmen—
as they went by below him, obviously heading for the back
door that led to the kitchen.

Their plan of attack was plain. One man to watch the
front of the house, two to go in at the kitchen and two to
go in at the dining room. Pruvot, that meant, was one of
the two still on the lawn; and Pruvot, the man he wanted,
would move at any time now for that door into the dining
room.

He came down off the wall, and stole a glance over his
right shoulder even as he landed, to confirm his estimate
of the raiding party's intentions.

In the fraction of time that he did so, the gods smiled
on him.

By the light of the kitchen window he saw Wilson take
his stand at the back door, and the other man pass bent
double, below the level of the sill, to the far end of the
window.

And in the same moment, the kitchen light went out

and the dining room lights stayed on. He knew on the instant what that might mean: two men found to be missing, news brought to kitchen, lights off at once, light in dining room off immediately after.

He marked Pruvot and kept his eyes, at the same time, on the dark end of the garden. Whatever happened now, if that other set of lights went out, his vision would be better than that of his target. What would Wilson do? Unpredictable, so forget it. Predictable was, that Pruvot could not see from where he stood that the lights in the kitchen had gone out.

Night fell suddenly on to the garden, extinguishing those panels of light on the grass. He made straight for the two men there, the silenced Walther pistol in his hand, knew which was Pruvot as the Frenchman turned, bewildered by the vanishing of the light, but from some instinct or alarm turning when the man running at him was three yards away.

But Pruvot could not see him clearly, could not make out, with his eyes still adjusting to the darkness, whether he was friend or foe. He slashed at Pruvot's neck with the outside edge of his left hand, hoping like hell that he had not hit him too hard, and as he did so realized that Pruvot's companion had moved, had started for the house even as he began his rush.

Then everything happened at once. He heard glass break at the back of the house. So Wilson was going in anyway—the right decision, though it would not work now.

Round there a shotgun blasted, once, twice, and a shriek started and failed to finish.

He heard a car engine approach the front of the house, in a gleam of headlights saw the man between him and the house turned towards him, saw the flare of the pistol in the man's hand and himself squeezed the trigger of the silenced Walther. Nothing. Action jammed. Headlights settled on his opponent.

He let the Walther fall, plucked the knife from his boot and threw it.

It thudded into the man's chest and he clutched with both hands at the hilt sticking out of him with both hands and ran in a strange, unco-ordinated bounding motion for the corner of the garden, for the end of the terrace, towards the headlights of the newly arrived car, that seemed now to have stopped.

Lost the knife. Gather up the Walther and holster it.

Hoist Pruvot on to the shoulder. Dicey that, bloody lucky not to be wounded, fantastic. Tip the bugger over the wall into the orchard. Sounds from the house, voices, no more shooting. Trot for the stile, hear Pruvot's breath being whacked out of his throat, his lungs centre of gravity, bouncing on shoulder, *heavy* little Frenchman, aren't you? Can't keep this up. Heave him over the stile. So far so good.

Stand in the lee of the hawthorn hedge, May hedge, in flower, jolly nice that. What now? Hug the hedge, the edge of the meadow, ready to drop if there's pursuit, flashlights? No, cut straight across. In the balance of risk, of completing the mission, time is paramount. You *need* that Range Rover to get Pruvot away. Check two things: the key you took from the ignition still in pocket, Smith & Wesson snug in holster, take it out, spin the cylinder, no damage. You can trust a revolver. Put it back and get going.

Pruvot on the shoulder, but now we walk. Wind whooshing away, climbing to a gale, Force 8 anyway. Here comes the moon, bad that, but keep going. Survivors, if any, may be retreating this way, but they'll have to come round front to see who you are even in moonlight. Pursuit, if any, not likely to hit with a first shot, so keep walking, long and fast, get into the wood and then check it all out.

Shouldn't have lost the knife. Bad, that. Shouldn't have used *that* knife. Walk, long and fast, getting there. But that knife worked for you, it always has, it knew what you wanted.

You swore vengeance on that knife.

The man it killed, man it was killing when you came away, he had a minute's life in him, no more. And what can he tell? Nothing—a man, a shape, no more, came out of the night and killed him.

The wood, into the wood, here we are, right on the nose, entrance to the track. Scrambled eggs and garlic, definitely. Dump Pruvot, step over him, turn round, what do you see?

Nice moonlit meadow, trees thrashing in the wind up there, no sign of anyone. Could be two survivors, man who went off first to front of the house, and either Wilson or the one with him, unless that shotgun got both of them. So much for Wilson's dinner.

Adrenalin moderating. Kneel and listen, look. Noises of the wood, no other noise. Out on the meadow, nothing moving. Pull lengths of cord out of pocket, lash Pruvot's wrists, lash his ankles. One more lift, one more time, and quick and quiet down the track, here comes the tricky bit, the *last* tricky bit. No time to recce the vehicle, have to take the risk that Wilson or one of the others isn't there already, waiting in case another survivor is on the way to the evacuation point.

Bluff it out. Head low, half turned into Pruvot's torso, start to call out softly.

"Hey, Wilson. Wilson, you there? Wilson, did you make it? Pruvot's bought it. Goddam, what a mess, what a goddam mess!''

There she is, the little beauty. There's the man I killed first, knife didn't go thirsty tonight, did you my sweet? Easy, not out of the wood yet. Keep up the American voice.

"Wilson, are you there? I got Pruvot, Wilson." Open passenger door, dump Pruvot. Last call before departure. "Wilson? Wilson?" Round the front of the vehicle. Swear a bit. "Wilson? You there? Shit, what a goddam fucking mess!" Climb aboard, key out of pocket, into ignition, wrong key, head down out of sight, though it's as dark as Lord Hell's riding boots, right key, bingo! Headlights, tight turn, crash her through the bushes, that's a good car and go, go, go!

Hit the main road, left and away.

Not so fast, laddie! No need to hurry, not useful to hurry, clean getaway accomplished. Tension climbing up the backbone now, biffing you between the shoulders on its way out, let it go, yawn big, cant the seat back a bit, cool off, that's the boy.

Yawn, laugh, more like a snigger—who cares! Ah, that was rare, that was something all right! But I lost my wee knife—so it's I is it now, what happened to you? My good wee knife's gone then. Saved my life for me, didn't it? Saved your life, yeah. It will sleep well tonight, my wee knife, saved my life tonight and drank the blood of two others, killed two men tonight. Wee knife will look after itself.

Bad thing though, losing wee knife: left a trace, if they have a good tracker; but only if they have a good tracker. And it will be a long trail.

Watch out for police road blocks, not likely, they don't seem to be using the police, none round that house all week, Minister Burnt to Death in Car Crash all over the papers, so no road blocks likely—but keep the eyes peeled.

Prisoner moving a bit now, pretty secure but keep an eye there too, get the .38 off your belt, put it handy, under your thigh, clock him on the head with it if he gets too restless.

Clock him on the head if he starts talking, even. Just don't start talking to me, Pruvot, you little bastard, just don't talk, don't say one single bloody word, right?

Easy on that too, my son! Keep the hate for later, when it's time, this is not the time.

Think of the wee knife, won't forget the wee knife— Whack! into his chest and off he went bouncing around like a cockerel with its head cut off. Think of scrambled eggs. But my, that was rare.

This internal monologue was abruptly ended by the voice of the prisoner at his side, who now exerted himself to move from his position of being half on and half off the seat into a more comfortable posture. He did not find it easy.

"Bloody hell!" was his opening remark.

"You're with us again," his captor said. "Glad to have you aboard."

"What do you mean? Oh, yes. It is one of your nautical usages, and I am supposed to say thank you, but I don't. I'm definitely not happy to be here."

With a final effort, pushing his bound feet against the floor, he got himself more or less firmly planted on the seat. He looked through the windscreen into the tunnel of light that showed the road coming towards them at forty mph, and said: "I see you are a careful man as well as a violent one."

"There is a time for each. At this speed, handicapped as you are, I don't think you can do us any harm, do you?"

"Where are we going, to one of your safe houses, I think you call them?"

"My dear chap, I only have one house. Why, who do you think I am?"

"I don't know. Who are you?"

"I daresay that will emerge soon enough."

The Frenchman turned his head and studied him, and after a while nodded once and sighed, and faced to the front again.

"May I smoke?" he asked.

"No cigarettes, sorry."

"I have cigarettes. In the pocket of my coat, beside you. Also a, what is the word—?"

"A lighter. We shan't need that. I have one of my own."

He reached into the Frenchman's pocket, took out cigarettes and lighter, let down the window at his side and threw the lighter into the ditch. He fished out one of the cigarettes, crushed it in his fingers and felt nothing but fibre and paper, and threw the residue into the slipstream. He put the window up again and lit a cigarette with his own lighter and put it between Pruvot's lips.

"Thank you," the Frenchman said. "See—I did not bite you, eh?"

"Obliged. Now listen to me and tell me if you don't understand. Soon we shall come to a town called Woodstock, where I shall untie your hands and let you untie your feet, and we shall walk about half a kilometre to another car. As we walk, I shall hold your little finger in my left hand, and if you try anything—if you stumble, or just sit down on the road, anything at all—I'll break your finger."

"Is that all?" Pruvot asked sardonically.

"By no means. In my right hand, hidden inside this jacket I am wearing, I shall be holding a .38 Smith &

Wesson Special, and as a last resort I shall shoot you in arm or leg, and by last resort I mean that if in the instant after I break your finger you are still being difficult, then I shall fire. This pistol will shoot your foot off or tear your arm in half, and think of this—even then I shall still get you to the car and take you where we are going, and there will be no doctor there. When the shock wears off the pain will be appalling, and it will grow worse.''

Pruvot looked at him for a moment and then sat drawing on his cigarette. Eventually he said: ''You are behaving like a kidnapper, I think. You are,'' he looked for the word, ''an illegal, a bandit, an outlaw. Also, possibly, a lunatic. You are not Intelligence at all.''

''An outlaw is precisely what I am.'' The voice became solemn and introspective. ''It is indeed possible that I am in an unusual mental state.'' The voice lightened again, though with a strain of artificiality. ''As to lunatic, we shall see when the moon is full.''

''What! The moon will not be full for a long time.''

''We shall have all the time in the world. As much time as we need.''

At the extraordinary tone in which these words were uttered the Frenchman shivered, as if he felt suddenly cold. He spat the cigarette on to the floor to cover this reaction. He tried to extinguish it with his bound feet, but failed.

''No matter,'' the outlaw, perhaps lunatic, said. ''We'll soon be there.''

The Range Rover ran down the road by which he had walked out of Woodstock earlier in the day, and drew to a stop.

They reached the car park with all of Pruvot's fingers and limbs intact. It was dark and except for the Ford Sierra, deserted. At the rear of the Ford he released his hold on the finger and gave Pruvot the car keys, pointed to the boot, and said: "Open it!" Then he seized the finger again.

There was a fractional hesitation and he jerked at the Frenchman's finger. Something, bone or ligament, made a small but unpleasant sound and Pruvot's breath whistled in his mouth. He had made an involuntary snatch to free the injured finger, but the grip held. Now, however, it was painful.

"Open it!"

Pruvot found the right key at the second try and lifted the lid of the boot.

He had no sooner done so than his enemy let go of the damaged finger, stepped back, and kicked him with ruthless force in the testicles. He fell to the ground with a howl. The hands with which he was comforting his groin were pulled behind his back and tied once more at the wrists, the ankles next, and he was lifted with one easy movement and put into the boot of the car.

"The good days are over," his implacable opponent said, and the lid went down.

THE FORD RAN OUT OF WOODSTOCK ON THE OXFORD ROAD and soon turned west for Gloucestershire. The driver was calm and relaxed, no longer agitated with the excitements of the night, as he had been on the first lap of the journey. Now and then, however, he frowned, as if a question that troubled him recurred at intervals.

Suddenly he looked at the clock on the dashboard and laughed. He had just remembered that in six hours he was going riding with the brown-eyed girl.

He began to drive fast and well, with enjoyment, and sang the tune of *Tornami a dir* as he went.

9

HARRY SEDDALL WAS IN A RANK MOOD, EVEN BEFORE THE
man lolloped out of the garden into his headlights' beam
and came along the side of the car to scrabble at his window with bloody hands and slide with grievous slowness,
giving Seddall a long sight of his stricken countenance, to
the ground.

"The end of a perfect day," Seddall said.

He left the lights on, in the hope that anyone nasty out
there would be blinded, feel exposed, and shoot the lights
out before they shot him. He climbed awkwardly past the
bundle on the gravel, and stooped over the sad stabbed
blood-covered man dying down there. Messy knife-work,
almost missed the heart.

"Who did this to you?" he asked, and put his ear close
to the bubbling mouth. The man just breathed and bub-
bled: a deader for sure, and right at the exit.

Seddall pinched the man's ear sharply. "Who did this
to you?"

The man stopped bubbling, his eyes popped wide open, and he said: "Say-eeh-ah." After that he died. Say-eeh-ah. Wonderful.

Seddall went round the back of the car and ran like hell for the front door which was Thank-God-open and barged into the hall. The hall was dark. He noticed he had a pistol in his hand. Five strides to the drawing room, also dark. What goes on? Mysterious van outside; Sorrel's car; dead man; house in darkness.

His neck chilled. He knew, he *knew*, there was someone else in the cubic space round about him. Friend or foe? That's the worst of night action, you never know who's bloody friend and who's bloody foe. Neither does the other guy. Say "Don't shoot, it's me!" and if your voice doesn't fit you get lead in your teeth. Don't hang about, the situation is garbage, what the hell *is* going on in this house, find out fast.

Concentrate. His hand had touched—had it?—a light switch by the front door. Remember—was it a light switch? Good place to *have* a light switch. Give it a whirl. Got to get out of this anyway.

He walked down the hall, soft-footed as Agag on the carpet, and dropped his hat on the floor as he went. At the door felt for the light switch. Too high then, down again, over—found it! Open the door, outside, close door on arm, switch . . . down . . . and pull arm out, shut door and throw H. Seddall into angle of porch out of line of door.

Many moments pass, while Seddall dislikes line of light at foot of door lest it reveal him, hidden in corner though he is, to mysterious forces stabbing strangers out there in the dark. If an enemy within, hat meaningless; if a friend, very bashed hat, familiar object, who loves me loves my hat. Nothing happens, must be foe. Buggeration, what now.

"Harry?"

The voice was Sorrel's.

"Harry it is," he said, gave her time to recognize his voice, whipped through the door, slammed it shut, and locked it.

There she stood, all five foot seven of her, hat in one hand and a bloody great revolver in the other. So she had checked the hat out first; ever faithful, ever sure.

"What goes on?" he said. He sniffed the air. "You been shooting that thing?"

"You bet," she said. "I emptied it through the kitchen door when they bashed the windows in, then Dudgeon's shotgun got to them, both barrels, through the window. So I took the front. Gyseman took upstairs. Then you arrived. Three to four minutes, start to finish."

"I'll want a brief summary of that for my report," Seddall said.

"You shit, Harry," she said, then smiled, lop-sided.

"I am that," he said, and took the hat from her. "I'm glad it worked out. There's a corpse on the gravel; not shotgun, knife. What does that make the score?"

"At least two. Someone took the full load from one barrel anyway."

"Then I think it's over. Sorry you had a rough time, but this is all most interesting news. It means that very heavy people indeed think the late viscount may have left bits of dangerous paper or something behind him. We'll return to what we think of that later. How many people would you send to turn over a house like this?"

"Say, four or five; five or six."

"That should have done it for them, if you all hadn't been so quick off the mark. So since they've lost two, and lost the element of surprise, they should have high-tailed it for the tall timber by now. So, next question. Your little fire-fight must have made quite a racket. Do you expect agitated neighbours to call the police, or to come running round in their dressing gowns?''

Sorrel thought about this. "I really think not. Half a mile to the nearest house, and the enemy used silencers so the only serious noise was the shotgun. After dark a couple of barrels from a shotgun just means there's a poacher about.''

"I'll buy that." He plonked his hat on her head and said: "Now, Sorrel, dear heart, just who the fuck is this citizen who's so handy with a shotgun?''

She sat down on the stairs and gave him the quick sketch of that one. He thought the antique trilby looked good on her curly locks. When she had finished telling him the tale she tipped the hat back with her forefinger and looked up at him.

"Dear me," Harry said. "This is all desperately instructive. I think we'll have to do something a bit subtle about Major Dudgeon. There is much to do and much, more or less simultaneously to think about. So, fetch Master Gyseman and tell him to go with Dudgeon to scout about, see if the foe is gone. And, my compliments to Major Dudgeon and the same message, but be polite, a request, no more. I'll see him when he and Mick get back. I expect he'll do it—he'll want to hunt for his lost boyos, anyway. Oh, I'll take that hat back, I'm going outside again for a moment.''

Sorrel stood up. "Harry, I have a thought.''

"Well, what is it?'' He went towards the door, half sideways, listening.

"The man you found, knifed. I wonder who did it, that's all.''

"So?" He was still moving down the hall, impatient, impeded by her uncharacteristic hesitancy.

"Well, it can't have been Mick, he's been upstairs, and there's been no sound of . . . any other fighting from the back of the house, where Dudgeon is."

He stopped and turned. "Again, so what? Thieves fall out—he was done in by his own side." He watched her, a mocking smile held loosely on his mouth, like a father being unkind to a tongue-tied child.

"Damn it!" she said. "Stop that!" She was looking straight at him, her blue eyes very large and expressive, as if trying to tell him what her mouth would not.

Whatever that was, he felt it move and became suddenly alert, as if at a palpable touch on his skin. It reached him and far within, like the memory of a forgotten superstition, an answer stirred.

"What you're staggering towards telling me," he said, and his voice was so quiet that it seemed to still, even more, the silence, "is that the man we're after has been here."

"Yes," she said. Then she nodded. Then she said: "I think so."

He swung his head in a kind of rage. "Curse it!" he said. "Tell me!"

She said it all at once. "I was out in the garden at the very end of dusk, at nightfall. I felt something *move*, in the night." She looked not at him but askance. "That's all."

"Heard nothing? Saw nothing? Just felt something was out there?" There was no inflection on the words, neither doubt nor belief.

"That's right," she said sturdily, able—now that she had come out with it—to meet those sceptical but watchful eyes. "I saw nothing, but I *felt* something. Whatever it was, it happened, and to me it was real.'' So there, damn you.

"I believe you," he said, with wonderful ambiguity. "Now then, we must do things. You get Gyseman and Dudgeon off on their scouting expedition, and there is, on second thoughts, no need to be nice to Dudgeon. If he objects, tell him from me to bloody do what he's told." He went to the door. "I'll be back in two shakes of a lamb's tail."

With his hand on the light switch he spoke again. "That thing that happened to you in the garden. That's your very own personal built-in alarm system, and it never goes off by accident. It's a gift, lady, so trust it."

He put out the light and waited till his eyes were ready, then stepped out and closed the door softly behind him. He went to the front of the porch and stood just inside, taking the feel of the night.

The trees laboured in the wind, but the air was warm. He thought it would be a good night to be on holiday. The hollow moon was well clear of cloud and the floor of heaven nice and starry.

Oh, to be in England now that April's there.

Well, this was England, and April just past. Yet there were lines in that poem about May as well, must look them up. Now would be *quite* the best time, if no Browning in the late viscount's library, bound to be the Dictionary of Quotations.

Standing here like a would-be swimmer anticipating the first cold plunge. Come on, Seddall, you're the boss, up to you to test the temperature, and he ran across the gravel jinking blindly, intensely embarrassed though unseen (hopefully) in the dark.

The sad stabbed corpse was still there; gone, whoever he had been, to his long home. The knife was still there too, blood all over the bloody handle, stuck hard into the chest. The dead man's chest, the phrase occurred to him with dismal aptitude. Yo ho ho and all that, fifteen men on the dead man's chest. What price hearing Blind Pew's stick right now? Crouched there, handkerchief round the gory hilt of the knife, wrenching at the damn thing, pulling the bloody man's chest up and down, sickeningly reproducing artificial respiration. Not nice.

Knife slides out, *nastily* producing unnecessary sound.

The engine of the Alfa was still running manfully, the lights still shining into the garden. He turned off lights and engine and walked back across the gravel sweep to the house, enjoying the sweetness of the air and holding the knife away from his side.

Inside he ignored the voices, switched on the light in the hall, at the foot of the stairs, and climbed in search of a bathroom; washed his hands, wiped less blood than he had feared from the sleeves of his coat and sponged the cuffs of his jacket. Then he went off to find a clean shirt, for it was one thing to remove visible traces of blood from tweed and worsted until he could get them to the cleaners, it was another to remove the mortal stain from cream-coloured linen, and it had begun to occur to Harry Seddall that he might want to meet quite a few people in the hours to come, and that he might want to be seen, by some at least of them, without blood on his shirt cuff.

He left the knife soaking in the basin and made his way to the late viscount's bedroom, stripping off his shirt as he went. It did not occur to him to be squeamish about stealing, or borrowing, one of the dead man's shirts, but what he saw, when he opened the first of the two deep drawers that held them, gave him pause: an array of Turnbull & Asser's best, variously coloured and striped, for the young—conceivably, even, upwardly mobile—executive.

Not at all the thing, Seddall thought crossly, for a man of Blacklock's age, and not at all the thing for Seddall, now or at any other age.

He took, finally, a piece of magenta silk with white collar and cuffs, and pulled it over his head. A bit roomy, but clean and crisp, what? He caught sight of it in a pier-glass and his lip curled, but in the same moment he started thinking and wandered over to the bed and sat on the edge of it, staring at the carpet.

Ten minutes later he had it all worked out.

He went back to the bathroom, finding his own discarded shirt on the way, and let the bloody water out of the washbasin and turned the hot tap to run over the knife. There was rather a lot of blood in the sponge, so he rinsed it through and wiped down the knife, and then cleaned the basin thoroughly.

When he had done, and was sure there was no trace of blood left in the bathroom, he held the knife by the tip of the blade and hefted it in his hand. There was nothing unusual about it, wooden hilt, long thin blade, except that he knew people who used knives like this one. He looked more closely at the blade: there was a dog's face etched on the steel, with some letters below it; he could not make them out. The steelmaker's mark? Maybe.

He thought he could not be sure of rinsing all the blood out of the sponge, so he squeezed it as dry as he could and wrapped it in his shirt, picked coat and jacket off the chair he had flung them on, and went downstairs to find Sorrel.

She was in the drawing room, closing the last of the shutters, drawing the flowered curtains across. As she did this she gave a brisk little sigh and shook her shoulders to assure herself that some strain had gone from them. She looked round the room with a satisfied air, as if she had made it secure by shutting out the night, and saw him.

"Screening the cave against the dinosaurs, are you?" he asked ironically.

"Oh, shut up!" she said. "My, Harry! Don't you look pretty?"

He dumped his overcoat and the bundled-up shirt in the hall, and was holding his jacket by the nape a little away from him, so that the magenta silk was in full view.

He grinned sheepishly. "Yeah," he said. "Well. Where's the Scotch?"

"Beside you," Sorrel said, and he saw that bottles were set out on a walnut buffet against the wall. He hung the jacket over the back of a chair and took drinks up to the fireplace. Sorrel had stirred the fire. It was all very comfortable and civilized, he thought: a breathing space.

"Do you think I could get to like this shirt?" he asked her.

"You look sweet. Like an overgrown little boy in his pinny."

After that he felt unable to tuck the tails of the shirt out of sight, and sat down as he was. "So the troops are scouring the perimeter? Dudgeon went quietly, I take it."

Sorrel nodded. "He thought it was the right thing to do, and he's worried about his men, too."

"Stout fella, Dudgeon," Seddall said, sarcastic out of no more than habit.

Sorrel let that one go by. "He said you'd be interested in one of the firearms the enemy left behind."

"So where is it? Let's see it."

Sorrel stayed put, standing with an elbow on the mantelpiece, her eyes on the logs burning in the grate.

"It's in the kitchen," she said. "I don't want to go out there just yet. Do you mind?"

"I mind, but not very much. Are you in shock?"

"A bit, I think. It was a lot of violence in a hurry."
She swallowed whisky and added quickly: "And if you're
going to ask me if I like my violence long-drawn out,
don't bother."

Harry stretched his eyes and smiled a wide amazed
smile with worried edges to it. "Am I as crass as that, as
corny as that? I suppose I am sometimes."

"Only sometimes," Sorrel assured him.

"I'll get the weapon," he said. He watched her, the
wonderfully pretty face pulled with tension, the intelligent
blue eyes solemn in firelight: and he looked at the bright
curls and the fine body in the burgundy running outfit, or
whatever it was. "You don't have to stay with this lark,
Sorrel. You don't *owe* anybody."

She had felt the scrutiny, and a flush that was from more
than proximity to the fire climbed up her face.

"In case I get hurt, get myself shot or something?"

"It would be a waste," he said, "but not that so much.
I don't want you to get damaged, inside."

"Like you, for example." It was a statement, not a
question.

"For example," he said in a voice suddenly cold, and
stood up and went out of the room leaving the words behind him like a gloom.

Sorrel sat on the hearth rug and looked into the flames,
carrying on the conversation without him, so that when he
came back into the room she spoke as if he had not left,
as if he knew what had taken place between them in his
absence, and as if she was facing him instead of the fire.

"Loyalty embarrasses you, doesn't it?" she asked him,
and nodded as if she were making the answer herself.

"What! What do you mean?" He stopped short, behind
her, and though the bad temper in which he left the room

had been alleviated at the first sight of the weapon he now brought with him, he was exasperated at this return to the consideration of his personal state.

"You're loyal," she said. "What are you loyal to—Queen and country?"

"Damn it, Sorrel," he said, "leave me alone!"

She looked up as he came into her view. "You're loyal to something. I know that."

He was intensely embarrassed. She thought that if he got any more embarrassed he would match that magenta silk that ballooned round him. The strange-looking weapon he had brought in with him hung forgotten at the length of his right arm and he tossed a small object impatiently up and down in his left hand.

The object fell beside her and as he stooped to pick it up she closed her fist round it. "Come on, Harry! Be brave. Forget about bad form or whatever it is that resents the question."

He bent his knees to face her, squatting on his toes. "You are an absolute harpie, Sorrel. We've got things to do and here you are rabbiting on about why we do them."

She smiled, despite herself, at this irresistibly visual mixing of metaphors. Seddall had heard it too, and smiled sourly in return. She thought that for a middle-aged man with a bit of a paunch who smelled of French tobacco he was undoubtedly attractive.

He sat down on the rug, easing himself back along it until the armchair he sat in before now made him a backrest. "Something, then. You're right. I'm loyal to something, but I don't know what it is and maybe don't care, because whatever it is I don't think it's around any longer. Now let up on me, would you be so kind?"

Sorrel nodded again, as if she had his answers all mapped out in advance and all he was doing was speaking to her script. "That's right," she said, "so I'll quit some-time, but I won't quit you yet."

"Uh-huh," Seddall said shamelessly. "Fine. Now we can get down to business. Do you know what this is?" He flourished the gun in the air. "Do you know what that thing in your hand is?"

Sorrel opened her hand and looked at what she held. "It's a triangular plastic object like a—cartridge?"

"Got it in one. A triangular cartridge. And this," he tossed it on to the hearth rug, "is the pistol that goes with it."

She peered at the stubby little pistol. "Is it a revolver or an automatic?"

"Precisely," he said. "In fact it's a bit of both. No slide, no reciprocating parts, a fifteen-shot pistol with a revolving chamber that ejects the fired cartridge *and*, if you're in love with such things, you can take the barrel off and insert the basic mechanism into a rifle assembly. That is a Dardick pistol."

"Extraordinary," Sorrel said. "All the same, why are you looking so particularly pleased? Have you always wanted one of these and been too shy to ask, or what?"

Seddall, as a sign that all his decisions had been made, and he was about to act on them, set himself to building up the fire. "What I'm pleased about," he said as he raked at the ash with the heavy poker, "is that the kind of guy who would use this weapon, which was a novelty in America over twenty years ago, is an old-hat CIA man. Before he died the one thing the corpse out on the drive said to me was 'Say-eeh-ah,' which it took me quarter of an hour to interpret."

He put just the right chunk of elm in just the right place. "He was speaking French, then," Sorrel said. "The initials CIA in French."

Harry frowned, and found that while the piece of elm was well enough placed on its own, he had to shoogle it around to accommodate another piece: compromise was death to perfection. "Quick of you," he said, "but you had a clue; I had mentioned the CIA already."

"Absolutely," Sorrel said. "Go on."

"So we can assume confidently enough to risk acting on it that it was a CIA team that you fought off."

"Hold your horses," Sorrel said. "What does that mean—'risk acting on it'?"

"A gamble, no more." He stood up and tucked, at last, the tails of the exotic shirt into his trousers. "I admit it, a gamble. But the odds are better than you know. Let me tell you all the news I heard from Mendham last night."

"You told me on the phone this morning that all you did was play trains."

"I said we played trains. I didn't say that was all we did."

Fresh whisky in his glass and a cigarette in his free hand, he walked about the room while he recapitulated Mendham's suspicions about Arkley, and his own views about Mendham's ambition.

When he had finished: "I seem to be missing something," Sorrel said.

"So tell me what you're missing."

"That's Arkley you've been talking about."

Seddall ingested some whisky and inhaled some smoke. "I noticed that for myself," he said rudely.

"We're dealing with Lord Blacklock, and why he got killed."

"This too I know."

"Well, Harry, all you know about Arkley is that he may have been running with the CIA and keeping it private from Mendham—and why shouldn't he, as you told Mendham yourself. All you know about tonight's little do is that there *may* be CIA involvement, and your evidence for that is light. And out of this you make a bridge between Arkley and Blacklock. That's not a bridge, Harry, that's one hell of a leap. If you plan to act on that kind of basis you could fall flat on your face.''

''It's much worse than that,'' he said happily. ''It's a leap in the dark. We could break all our ankles.''

Sorrel stood up. ''Well, they're not broken yet,'' she said. ''How sure are you?''

''Oh, pretty sure. By the pricking of my thumbs, all that kind of thing. As sure as you were that our latter-day Grendel was out there in the dark, just biding his time to tear off more heads.''

Sorrel's eyes quickened. ''Where does he fit in?''

Harry smiled, with a kind of speculative confidence. ''I don't think he does. What he does is not fit in. I think he helped you out, killed that man I found dying. If so, I've got the knife he killed him with.''

''With all this stuff about the CIA, I'd almost forgotten about him.''

''Well, don't,'' he said seriously. ''That man, whoever he may be, is the end and object of all our desire.''

Gyseman came into the room from the hall. ''Are you receiving?'' he enquired.

Seddall just looked at him. ''Yes,'' Sorrel said.

Gyseman threw the door wide to admit Major Dudgeon, and Seddall went at once towards him. ''Dudgeon, good to meet you. Have you found your men?'' He put this question with a remarkable blend of solicitudes, one expressing concern for the welfare of the missing men, and the other for the misfortune of an officer who was so careless as to have mislaid them in the first place.

Dudgeon handled this without subtlety. ''Yes,'' he said.

Seddall waited, until he was forced to ask: "Well, how are they?"

"Fast asleep." Dudgeon said. "Hit on the head and then drugged. No serious injury."

"What's the picture outside?"

"Coast's clear," Dudgeon said. "I've no doubt of it. They hit us and they ran. Cut their losses, abandoned the op. Whoever they were," he added.

Seddall waved an arm. "Scotch, Dudgeon? Mick, fill me in on details."

"Corpse outside the kitchen, shot to rags by the major's shotgun. Corpse at the corner of the house, stabbed to death, and not by any of us." He paused. "And another corpse on the far side of the wood to the north, little way up the track from the main road, road to Woodstock. Also stabbed, and not by any of us. Vehicle tracks in the mud there, I don't know how recent."

"No sign of agitated neighbours roused by the racket?"

"Not a thing. Peaceful night out there, lovely, actually."

"Excellent," Seddall said. "Three bodies. That should do it.

"Do what?" Gyseman asked.

"Time enough," Seddall said. "Wait and see." He turned to Dudgeon again. "You're my only problem, you and your unconscious men. I want us out of this house, house cleaned up, no sign of our presence here, within the hour. We leave the bodies. There was a shoot-out here but nothing to do with us. We had not yet arrived. I changed my mind, we had other fish to fry, and we will not arrive until tomorrow. But you, Dudgeon, you did arrive, and unless your story will be that you were overpowered along with your men, the scheme I've been hatching is a non-starter."

"I can't think why that should be my story," Dudgeon said. "From my point of view it's bad enough having my men nobbled like that without throwing me into the pot as well."

"Equally," Seddall said, "from your point of view it is not good that you killed a man with a shotgun, and if we're telling the plain unvarnished truth that's part of it. Why the shotgun?"

"That is a very good point indeed," he said. "We're not licensed to carry firearms everywhere we go. When I got my orders—you'd better look at them." He took out the envelope that he had offered earlier to Sorrel, and passed it to Seddall.

Seddall took the folded sheet of paper out of the envelope, opened and read it, and looked intently at Dudgeon. "What on earth did you do, when you were given this?"

"Phoned my CO on the spot, right? He said do it, but go unarmed, take the whole thing very easily, and he'd try and get us back first thing in the morning. Not our beat, he said."

"Where did you get the shotgun?"

"Blacklock's gun cupboard in the study. First thing I did when we cottoned that something was up. Nice gun."

"It puts you in a fix, though, I mean you don't even know who you shot with it, do you?"

"I don't much care, either. All I know is that nine mil started coming through the window like there was no tomorrow, and I didn't take to it. No I don't know who I shot, and yes, I am in a fix. I simply joined your team, didn't I?"

They looked at each other, and between Seddall's cat-coloured eyes and Dudgeon's, grey as the winter sea, an understanding passed.

"I think perhaps we can make it that you never shot

anybody," Seddall said. "I would, though, value a quid pro quo."

"What form would it take?" Dudgeon asked. A married man, Sorrel thought, in the same instant that she realized his Army career was at risk from pulling those triggers on the shotgun. Yet he was facing Seddall as cool as ice across an invisible bargaining table.

"We shall work it out. If you are willing," Seddall said, "and say I can get clearance for you overnight, the best thing would be to have you seconded to me for a space. I can get you orders over a better signature than that—oh, yes I can can," as Dudgeon looked wary, "—and I can clean the slate of tonight's business too. But the phone here is cut, of course, and I have to make some rapid phone calls. So you'd have to take it on trust and come with me now until I can give you a convincing voice to listen to—I imagine you'd like to hear from someone higher up the chain of command, after the mess this civilian stuff," he flapped the paper in his hand, "has got you into."

"That would be best," Dudgeon said cautiously, and reached out a hand to take the paper back from Harry and stow it away in a pocket. "Where do I hear a convincing voice?"

"I'll gate-crash the Special Branch office in Oxford, do my phoning there. I'll want to keep your sleeping beauties incommunicado, too, and that's as good a place as any. Will you mind if I have them posted somewhere out of sight for a few weeks, Baffin Bay, for instance, or embassy duty at Ulan Bator?"

"Not a great deal, no." Dudgeon was thinking hard, but would not be hurried. "No, I shan't mind, if you believe you have that kind of pull. Very well, I'll come to Oxford, and we'll take it from there."

Seddall said: "Good, first-rate. I'll have your boys flown out of RAF Lavenham tomorrow, and once they're away they can gossip till the cows come home."

"You will, will you?" Dudgeon asked. "Look, I've said I'll come to Oxford, but I shan't commit to you until I've satisfied myself at first hand that you can come good on these rather high-powered assurances. The fact is, Colonel Seddall, I'm not naturally an irregular kind of soldier. I like it when everything is done through channels, and I'm not that keen on your kind of operation. I'm not in a panic at the thought of being court-martialled or even going to jail for manslaughter, so don't think you've got me over a barrel. I'd sooner come up smelling of roses than dung, and if you can fix that for me I might go along. That's all."

"I am much subdued," Seddall said, "but if that's the best I can get, I'll take it. So let's move. Mick, will you help, ah, Alistair load his contingent into the van; I'll go in the van too, I think. You two can bring the cars into Oxford when you're finished clearing up all the domestic mess you've made here. We shall RV at the Randolph, and we'll sleep there tonight if they can take us."

Even the blasé Gyseman had been silenced by the meeting of minds between the phlegmatic Dudgeon and the wily Seddall, and he left the room without a word.

"Alistair," Seddall said, trying hard to get used to the Christian name of a man who was a surname-person if ever he saw one, "better steal that shotgun for the time being, it will be all over fingerprints."

Dudgeon nodded, and departed.

"Sorrel," Harry said, "you must be absolutely sure that you and Mick remove all signs of your being here. Blood and bullet-holes don't matter but anything you brought in must go out again. Anything any of us brought in must go out again.''

''Understood.''

He looped his tie round his neck and struggled into his jacket, and was about to follow after the others when he came back, rubbing his chin, making a considerable rasping noise.

''I'll tell you what, Sorrel,'' he said. ''That chap Dudgeon's not devious at all, is he, not the least little bit? Leaves a man no room for manoeuvre.''

''That'll be the day, Harry,'' she said, straight-faced.

''It will, won't it,'' he said, and went on his way.

10

"Brrr-brrr," said the earpiece, "brrr-brrr, brrr-Mendham, it said.

"Hallo, John," Seddall said. "Is that phone safe?"

"Who is this?"

"John, after all these years! We used to play trains together."

The earpiece was silent. "Got you," it said.

"Your phone, is it secure?"

"Who knows a thing like that, for God's sake!"

"Go somewhere else, and call this number." He read off the figures.

Silence again. "Why should I do that?"

Harry put the receiver in front of his face and grinned at it. What Mendham was saying was: I can assume there is to be an advantage for you in this; is there to be an advantage for me?

He thought he could get to like doing business with Mendham.

"John," he said "Listen.

> 'He either fears his fate too much
> Or his deserts are small,
> That will not put it to the touch,
> To win or lose it all.' "

Mendham's voice said: "Who."

"What do you mean, who?"

" '*Who* will not put it to the touch,' " Mendham said. "You got the line wrong."

"Are you sure?"

"Absolutely. But I perceive your meaning. I expect you think Sir Walter Raleigh wrote that."

"He didn't?"

"No," Mendham said with satisfaction, "it wasn't Raleigh. Very well, I'll call you back."

Harry laid the receiver on its rest and sat in the quiet, looking round him at the office he had borrowed. It was the top of the hour and the bells of Oxford colleges rang across the Meadows. The sound came in at the open window, ancient and clear, suggesting falsely that its resonances issued from metal forged in a purer time. Some of the towers were medieval; how old were the bells? However old they were, the age in which they were made had been no less wicked than his own. Men as tricky and cynical as he had dealt with, men as knowing and ambitious as Mendham, even then.

The bells finished. The office they had given him was neat and spare, the floor bare, so that it resonated when you walked on it like the bells; a desk, three chairs, and a considerable rank of filing cabinets. The walls were maps, six inches to the mile, for the close view of the Inspector's hunting-ground—they had told him it was the

Inspector's office, laying a capital letter on the man's rank, as if he bore with it some special gravity, as you might say the Pope, or the General—then for the larger view the Ordnance Survey sheets at the scale of 1:50,000, then a map of the British Isles and one of Europe.

You could suppose that the Inspector was a man who saw perspectives within perspectives, that he saw a place for himself within a large scheme of things; or simply that he had wanted something on the walls and thought pictures would be out of place for an officer of the Special Branch, and that you could deduce nothing about him at all from the sparseness, say rather the absence, of any personal trace in the appearance of his office.

On the desk the black telephone rang.

It was Mendham. "Where are you, Harry?"

"In Oxford, Special Branch office."

"How very respectable, for you."

"Isn't it? Now, hear this John, and see how you like it. Your friends at Grosvenor Square—"

"You mean the Cousins."

"I don't talk your MI6 dialect, John. I mean the CIA, and what I have to tell you is that they've made a mess at Mustell, at Blacklock's house."

"So. What kind of mess?"

"The kind of mess that means there are three bodies lying about the place, one of theirs, one French, both close to the house, and one other on the track that cuts through the belt of woodland due north of the house."

"The third one, what distance from the house?"

"About a mile."

Mendham digested this news, and no doubt began at once to flavour the aftertaste of its implications, how he could make use of it. "And what do you propose we do about this?" he asked in the inflexionless voice of the trained manipulator of events running in top gear at high speed, with hands as light and strong as a pianist's on the power steering.

"I simply make you a present of it," Harry said, and leered affectionately at the shape of his own head reflected in the darkness of the window.

"That's most kind of you, Harry, and most hard to believe."

"Your friend," Harry said with extra meaning upon the noun, "who has been shooting grouse in Yorkshire with what you call the Cousins, and yachting with their relations in Italy, could at least be startled by this, startled enough to make some giveaway movement; and he might even be scared into breaking cover altogether, *if* we handle it right."

"Why do you connect my friend with a CIA mess at Mustell? Why do you say it *is* a CIA mess? Why do you connect the friend with Blacklock's death?"

Mendham was hooked, but he was not coming quietly to the river bank, he was swimming for the deep water at the neck of the pool, keeping room to manoeuvre, to dive, to jump, to break loose if he had to; if he could.

Harry lowered the point of the rod, and gave him some line.

"I say CIA, John, because before he died and with a bloody great knife sticking in his heart, one of the corpses breathed in my ear the sounds 'Say-eeh-ah'."

"CIA in French," Mendham said. "One of the frogs, then."

"Yeah," Seddall drawled, "one of the frogs, you would say. You civil servants are so damned insular, John."

"Does it offend you?" Mendham was truly interested to know.

"It offends me," Harry said. "It is an unwisdom but more than that, it just offends me."

"I'm not sure it's an unwisdom, you know. In our business, complex and devious as it is, it is perhaps just as well to employ forms of speech that remind us who our enemies are, because in our business our enemies are at the very least everyone who is not British, for a start. I mean we all spy on each other, after all."

"Goddam," Harry said. "I do believe that if you were minuting this conversation you'd make a note that H. Seddall was pro-French."

"Possibly pro-French," Mendham said easily. "Your problem is that you're a soldier, Harry, and soldiers are an international brotherhood, the professional ones."

"Put that where the sun don't shine," Seddall said rudely. "Let's get on. I also say they're CIA because one of them used a Dardick pistol."

"A Dardick pistol?"

"Sure. It's a gadgetty kind of firearm that came out when Dulles was still at Langley, and it tells me I'm thinking about an old-hat CIA man, same generation as your friend," and he laid the special emphasis on the word again.

"My friend," Mendham said. "We've established, I think, whom you mean by my friend."

"I like your whoms, John. Same generation as your friend and, notice, same generation as the slaughtered viscount, Minister of State for War."

"I begin to hear you rather clearly," Mendham said. "Do not stop.

"Well, you see, I put a CIA man of your friend's generation with your friend, since you have told me your friend is up to some high jinks all on his own, all private and mysterious, with the CIA. One does not say one draws the absolute conclusion, you understand me, but one observes the possibility of the link, don't you know?''

"Goodness," Mendham said. "Does one not feel one is jumping to conclusions, never mind drawing them, absolutely or otherwise? This is the well-known Seddall intuition at work, I take it."

Harry was instantly suspicious. Mendham was about to pull something out of the hat. "What are you going to tell me now, John?''

If cats that had just licked the cream spoke on telephones, they would sound like Mendham sounded now. "Ark—'' dear me, my *friend* had a little migraine this week, after Blacklock died.''

"Why the hell didn't you tell me?''

"Took the day off on Tuesday; he never came into the office,'' Mendham went on. "And I didn't tell you, if you haven't worked it out already, because at that time I knew nothing about dying Frenchmen at Mustell or quaint gadgetty pistols either. What is more, our friend often has migraines.''

"Oh," said Seddall. "Then you don't find this one instructive, is that right?''

Mendham did one of his pauses. Harry wondered where he was phoning from. He did not have the impatience of someone standing in a telephone booth. "I find it possibly corroborative of your reckless intuition, Harry. I could still ignore what you're telling me, and my conscience would be clear. And I would be safe. I would have taken no steps, you understand. You are shortly going to ask me to do something I would not normally do, something unwise, perhaps even risky. For me. I am therefore listening to both of us, as closely as I can, and I am employing all my sensory apparatus and bringing to bear such intellectual capacity and whatever elements of tactical apprehension I may be fortunate enough to have at my disposal, to assist me to meet your proposition, when it shall have been put to me at last, with such sophistication of judgement as I can assemble."

"By the living God, Mendham, you must be sitting comfortably—all these syllables and subjunctives. Where are you?"

"Friend's house. They're away. Jane feeds the cats. We have the key. That brief enough?"

"Just about. Time presses though, just a little bit."

"Oh, I was sure it would, Harry. I think behind the persiflage, you know that. Tell me the rest of it."

"Your friend, or our friend," Harry said. "I've had the same kind of thoughts about the late Viscount Blacklock that you recited to me in your playroom about our friend. Blacklock was getting on, starting to sound like yesterday's man, unlikely, no, definitely *not* going to reach the top. Feeling his power, though, such as it was in that job, and feeling it was more than it actually was; but dissatisfied and feeling at the same time that he was in his prime. You said your friend was up to something, and I told you, maybe it was a coup, maybe he was going to bring off a coup, admit modestly to being a mastermind and get shifted up rather than sideways."

"What else?"

Harry felt heat come into his face. Shit, he'd lost him. "Nothing else," he said. "That's the lot."

"Well then," Mendham said briskly. "This is not even poker. This is roulette. An intuition, a couple of bits of circumstantial, and now another intuition. That's what you want me to gamble on."

He stopped.

"That's right," Harry said. Never put a losing case, he told himself. Let the other man come towards it.

"It would depend, then," Mendham said, still brisk, "on what you are asking me to stake."

"That's right," Harry said.

"Very well," Mendham said. "Tell me."

"I don't think it's a big stake," Harry said. "I want you to call the CIA at the embassy or wherever you have a number for that you like for this, and tell them they have made a mess at Mustell, that it is still early in the night, that the police do not know about it, that the police would not like a three-corpse mess one tiny little bit, and that your department are giving them the chance to clear this mess up, because although you are very angry about this at Six, and will want to know from them what the hell they think they're playing at, any noise about it even in Whitehall, never mind the media, would raise very nasty questions about the state of relations beween the security services of Britain and the United States, which would make your lot look bad, as well as presenting once again the spectre of America assuming that the fact of its having USAF and naval and Cruise missile facilities in this country entitles it to extend its role in the common defence function of NATO into a security role."

Harry could almost hear Mendham running this rapid speech through his mind. He found he had the earpiece pushed hard against his ear, and he held it away a little. Not cool, Seddall, he told himself: not cool at all.

Mendham spoke. "The actual argument you give me to attack them with is not bad," he said, and then he paused. "I think," he went on, "they would accept it, and that they might act on it. That would be because they trusted me. I must assume that in some way you are going to disturb that trust?

"Disturb is right," Harry said, and grinned into the unresponsive office. He felt the fish coming to the bank; that he was going to land it.

"I would not want to know how," Mendham said, carefully returning to the conditional case. "I want to know what it gains for my department."

"Like I said, John, what it gains for you and the department, for *both* of you, John, is the chance that my bits of intuition and circumstantial evidence actually mean something, which would mean that your suspicions about your friend are at least partly right, and that therefore your friend might, as the Nixonese used to say, make a misstep in the ensuing fracas. And if you are seen as the man who has exposed our friend—"

"Yes, yes," Mendham interrupted. "Unless I'm wrong about our friend, on the face of it I quite see that it would do me no harm. It all depends on what you're going to do at your end. I don't want to know what it is. I *can't* know, but I would at least like your assurance that you're not going to drop me in it." Mendham waited. "For what that's worth," he added.

"Can we look at it this way?" Harry said. "I won't drop you into anything you can't handle."

"Yes," Mendham said slowly. "There is some credibility in the way you have phrased that."

Then he said it: "I wonder who's the best man to call. I rather think . . . Harry, on your word, there will be no gunplay, you're not going to be killing any of these people?"

To his own surprise, Seddall felt quite shocked. What sort of reputation did he have with these desk-bound people at Six? Billy the Kid? Genghis Khan? "Oh, I don't plan to kill anyone else tonight, John, I shan't have time. Listen, Mendham, and this is important. Neither I nor any of my people have been to Mustell today, and that is a lie which you must sustain if the question is raised, or at least until I concede it. What follows is not a lie: none of us, me or my people, will be there or anywhere closer to there than Oxford, when and if the CIA clearing party turns up. I shall put it out of my hands, that part of it.''

"Look here, Harry, not *Five*?''

"Bloody hell no, not Five.''

"I want to think for one full minute," Mendham said. "Will you hold?''

Seddall sat and waited, laid the receiver on the bare desk top, rubbed his face roughly with both hands, sat up and lit a Gauloise. If Mendham made up his mind to it, there was no doubt that, being in himself so careful and career conscious, so *sound*, and known for it, he was the perfect man at Six to play the story back to the Americans. The phone crackled, and Harry picked it up.

"I'll do it," Mendham said. "You want it done now?''

"Please. Will you do it from there?''

"Yes.''

"Will you call me back when it's done?''

"Yes.''

"Thanks,'' Seddall said.

"Yes," Mendham said, his voice flat.

"I appreciate this, John, very much. It will work out, you know.''

"That's what I don't know, and neither do you, but we shall see. 'Bye.''

What is it we do nowadays that Machiavelli didn't do? Why is it, Seddall asked himself, that Mendham has made me feel guilty? Because I am not Renaissance man, not Italian Renaissance man; because when it comes to state-

craft, if that's what this negotiation with Mendham has
been, I do not deal only with Facts, and the relation between Things. I deal with people. I think of John Mendham's right to his career, I think of his, wife, Jane and the
trains in the attic of their home, and I persuade him to
throw his career on what he calls a roulette table, and he
and I know that if it is not a lucky throw he'll be cleaned
out, because the croupier will turn into Arkley and Arkley
will do him down as only an old hand at this game can,
and he'll be out and unemployable this time next week.

I know all that and I do it anyway, and whether I'm
having qualms about it or only pretending to have qualms,
I'm a bloody hypocrite.

The door opened and a man came into the room, closed
the door behind him and stood there looking at him.

"Colonel Seddall," the man said in a hard and quiet
voice. The newcomer was a tall thin man with a lean face
and hair so short it was only one remove from bristle.
He had pale blue eyes that not only looked, but searched
what they fell on and calculated while they did it. He was
that terrifying thing, a single-minded security policeman.

"What the hell," Harry said. "If it isn't Sergeant Gatenby."

"Inspector," the man said.

He moved quickly and sat in the more comfortable of
the chairs across from the desk, the movements as neat
and athletic as if he were a gymnast performing a routine
before the judges.

"Congratulations, Inspector. They told me you were off
duty."

"Off duty," Gatenby repeated the phrase as if it were
alien. "I went out to eat. They called me there and told
me you were here."

"There was no need for you . . ." Harry waved a hand, deprecating the news that he had put Gatenby to such a courtesy as interrupting his dinner.

"Every need," Gatenby said. He reached out a hand and laid it on the telephone. "Warm," he said. "You've been busy." The pale eyes drifted over Seddall. "I'd like to see your ID, Colonel, if you please."

"Good Lord, why?" Harry said. "You know me perfectly well."

"If you please, Colonel."

There was plenty that was dynamic in this Gatenby. No one likes to find another man seated behind his own desk: it usurps control. Gatenby while seeming to ignore that element of the situation completely, had plainly taken it in at a glance, sat himself down and adjusted the balance of power by demanding Harry's security identification.

Harry passed it across the desk, and Gatenby barely looked at it before passing it back again. "The trouble with that, Colonel Seddall, is that it doesn't give you a laissez-passer to any Special Branch office you care to walk into, or any police office for that matter. You have two soldiers stashed in civil police cells downstairs without a charge against them and a police doctor checking them over, and a major from the Ministry of Defence who says nothing but refers me to you. What's your authority for that?"

"Downing Street," Harry said. "Phone the Private Office at No. 10."

Gatenby left the chair and the room in a faultless flow of agile movement. Harry's gaze travelled slowly from the empty chair to the closed door as if Gatenby's essential self had been left behind by the speed of his physical departure, and could be seen following after like a delayed shadow.

This Inspector Gatenby, recently promoted and still in his twenties, was a man to be reckoned with. Totally impersonal and intensely confident, it was even possible that he could, by hewing to his manifestly clear but precise vision of duty and ambition, rock the subtle balance of the scheme whose first phase John Mendham had already put in motion.

Gatenby was back and in his chair again, staring at his black shoes to be sure no dust from the police station corridors had flawed their highly-polished shine. "You are working," he told his shoes, "to an ad hoc committee of three chaired by the Prime Minster for whom the Permanent Secretary deputizes and you have the fullest authority at the highest level of security." He turned his eyes to Harry, and there was a strong gleam in them, not of resentment or any other personal response at being outfaced by another man's power, but of recognition that in Harry's arrival and need of cooperation might lie opportunity for Gatenby to show his mettle. "Therefore," Inspector Gatenby said, "what can I do for you?"

The telephone on the desk rang, as if in answer. Seddall put out his hand and took it.

"It is done," Mendham said. "They will clear up the mess tonight."

"Ah!" Harry said. "Many thanks."

"I will hear from you?" Mendham asked.

"It is one of those things," Harry said, "where you will hear before you hear from me."

"Ah," Mendham said in his turn, and closed the call.

Seddall felt good. He stretched the tension out of his shoulders, stood up and crossed the room to the open window, where he leaned out and breathed in the damp river air coming across Christ Church Meadows.

He came back into the room.

"What you can do for me," he said to Gatenby, "is get Superintendent Kenna on that phone, faster than light."

Gatenby gathered the instrument to him and put in the call. The gleam in his ambitious eye was as if the sun had set in the heart of an iceberg.

11

THE GIRL SAW INTO THE EYES OF THE MAN ABOVE HER and as he moved within her felt at what she saw there the outrage of fear. With the fury driving into her and the exaltation rising through her and the outrage and the fear, she groaned low in her throat and shouted what sounded like a word and then simply shouted, out of her head, tossing and rolling in despair to have and to escape, shouted and shouted until she whimpered and gasped and spoke—"No, no, no"—and when he came at her still, sobbed and growled and again shouted, and gripped him with all her being, striving with him and against him while he drove and drove at her until she lay inert, everywhere within, and whimpered and slobbered while he went on and on, destroying and ravaging what he had mastered, as if to kill and kill her again and again and again.

* * *

TWO FLOORS BELOW THEM IN THE BLACKNESS OF THE CEL-
lar the Frenchman, trussed wrists to ankles, bound all together like a fowl and with plaster sealing his mouth, lying
on his back trying to press his toes against the wall to ease
the cramp, suffered the torture of the damned and heard
the girl shouting out in terror or ecstasy, he could not tell
which: but he knew what caused it.

Pruvot was a tough and vicious man, who had learned
torture in Algiers and practised it, for the fatherland, in
France, but already the inflexible and seemingly dispassion-
ate cruelty of this hellhound devouring the woman upstairs,
had brought, first the Frenchman's spirit, and now his mind,
to doubt whether he had the resolution to withstand him.

The man's way of exerting his will on his victim had
none of the sophistication of the modern torturer, he used
no equipment and he had no *style*. Last night he had
hoisted Pruvot from the trunk of the car, carried him into
this house and thrown him down the stairs. He had tied
him up into this crippled shape, clamped the sticking plaster over his mouth, and left him in the dark without a word
spoken.

This morning—presumably it was this morning—he had
come downstairs, placed something in a corner and had
said only: "Breakfast." Then he had kicked Pruvot with
the force of gigantic rage though nothing showed on the
face, kicked him in the testicles (which made that the second time in a few hours) and once in the stomach, so that
when the shock was over and the pain steadied Pruvot had
begun to fear for his spleen. Then the man had gone and
left him again in the dark, or, as he discovered when he
had stopped gobbling the stuff that had risen to his throat,
and had settled to swallowing in an organized manner so
that he should not choke to death, in the almost dark.

For in the corner where the object had been placed,

shone also a torch with a fading battery. It then became essential for Pruvot to identify the object before the torch failed altogether, even though he knew that by doing so he was fulfilling the will of his captor. It took much pain and effort to cross the floor and a great deal of ingenuity in invented technique, on which he was congratulating himself until he understood that this too—this pathetic victory—was merely the achievement of a task set for him. He did not allow himself to accept, at this point, that the tears which came to his eyes were other than the involuntary expression of physical anguish caused by the difficulties of movement.

When, at length, he reached the corner, he found that the object was in fact five similar little packages stacked one on top of the other. The topmost package had printed on it: "£1000." So, as he made himself learn by lying on his side and with careful motions of the head (husbanding himself against unnecessary pain) knocking the stack into a heap, did each of the other packets.

Five thousand pounds, then, and two ferocious kicks, were his breakfast. A man could stomach, he thought—contriving to be humorous even in this extremity—only so many meals like this one.

It was not long till the torch went out, and blackness closed round him again.

THE MAN BESIDE HER SLEPT LIKE A CHILD, NOT LIKE A baby but like a schoolboy: rather, for to seek out such a distinction was absurd, he looked like a schoolboy as he slept. He lay on his front with his face towards her, an exhausted sleep disturbed by dreams, and the intelligent schoolboy's face altered now and then back to its manhood, the mouth pinched and the brow started and furrowed again into the lines that were always there: after all, only the memory of a schoolboy in that face.

She looked down his long back, which she thought beautiful. She wanted to run her hand over it, but would not, in case he woke up and started to make love on her again. On her, not with her; and she had had enough. She felt savaged and violated—not raped, for she had been willing, and even when she had wanted him to stop she had also wanted him to go on; even when she was finished and he went on raking her, pounding at her with a relentless fury that was to her an incomprehensible pain from which she responded now and then with uncontrollable spasms when there should have been none left in her, none left at all.

She had stared into his dark eyes, blue and dark as lakes of unthinkable depth, and from astonishment and horror she had then grown calm and watched him, watched his eyes on hers. She had passed to the other side of panic into a state part dreamlike, wondering what he was that could compel this on her; part fear, for she felt herself in the calm at the centre of a storm and that the fury being unleashed on her body was a fury that would never abate, but would ascend until it reached a pitch she could not bear—though she could hardly bear this; how could she bear this?—and she would be killed by it.

The last she remembered was tears coming suddenly to her eyes and weeping with the sorrow and loss he had wrung from her, or laid into her—well both then. She had lifted her hand to stroke his face but could not, even for sorrow shared, hating it at last, that implacable striving mask with its unseeing eyes upon her.

She thought I am beautiful, I am myself, he should not do this any more, not any more, and that was where she had left herself, under that working, inveterate, savage body, left him by himself to tear alone at her beaten body and her wounded self.

So she must have fainted.

THE MORNING SUN REACHED THE WINDOW AND WAS WELcome, for the sweat drying on her skin had chilled her. She looked at the sunlight on her body, on her breasts. There would be bruises there tonight, bruises all over, for he had hurt her with his hands as well. She felt on her lips something between a sneer and a smile. It was not making love, not copulating, it was an ordeal by fucking. Not a thing you would want to go through again.

She shifted her eyes from her body to his. It was all sinew and muscle, at least she had scratched his lovely long back for him. That schoolboy face, that touchingly schoolboy face he had when he slept.

She was watching it when the alarm on his wristwatch went off. His eyes opened, wide awake at once, seeing instantly what was in front of him and knowing where he was, as wary as a fox. Then his face relaxed to half sleep again, recalling its very young look, so that the smile was the best she had seen on him.

"Would you like," he asked her, "a second breakfast?"

"Strong coffee I could handle," she said, and added firmly, "I'll come down for it."

"So I should hope," he said. "We'll have it in the garden. Lord, it's going to be a particularly fine day!"

He knelt on the bed and smiled at her. "Do you want another shower?" he said.

"I'm going to lie in the bath till lunchtime when I get home," she said.

"Lazy creature," and he walked over to the window

and looked out at the day. "That's a good horse of yours," he said. "A good ride."

"A *great* ride," she said, and when he went into the bathroom to shower himself, she spoke again, this time to herself. "Joanna darling," she said. "Does he even *remember*?"

She got out of bed and dressed. Christ! She could hardly *walk*! It was a good thing they'd had to stable the horses and rub them down before they drove up here. She wouldn't put her leg across a saddle today for all the tea in China. He was gentle with the horse too, clever with the horse. Why not with me, damn him!

While she was making coffee in the kitchen she thought of the kind of man she would like to marry, and designed him different from this man in almost every particular. Once, while she was doing this, she laughed a little.

At the first ring of the telephone he came bounding downstairs with a towel round his waist, and as she passed him with the coffee on a tray, going out to the garden, she heard him speak to his caller.

"Things are on the move," was all he said, and then he replaced the receiver.

AFTER SHE HAD GONE HE LAY IN THE SUN AND SLEPT, woke in the afternoon and made the rest of the day a holiday; made himself a late lunch, cleaned the Walther and the Smith & Wesson, and went for a walk on the hills above the house. Now and then he stopped to sit on the grass and scan the country around him with binoculars. Once he lay on his back for a space and watched the skylarks rise and fall, and coming home again towards evening he sat on a stone wall, while the swallows swooped

and turned overhead, snatching their food out of the sky,
until the cool in the air told him it was time to move.

He went back to the house and down to the cellar.

PRUVOT THOUGHT THAT IF HE DID NOT DIE OF WHAT HAD
been done to him today, he would die of what would be
done tomorrow. This time there had been no torch with a
failing battery. The man had entered with the five packets
in his hand, knelt beside Pruvot to let him see he was
leaving another five thousand pounds with him, and laid
the money in the corner. Then he turned Pruvot over with
his foot and kicked him as he had done earlier, but twice
this time in the crotch, and twice in the belly. A rib had
cracked.

This time the man had said nothing at all; he had not
announced dinner as he had announced breakfast.

As the man left Pruvot with the agony tearing through
him, and the door closed returning him to his darkness,
the Frenchman screamed silently behind the tape binding
his mouth: "You have not even told me what you want!"

The key turned in the lock, leaving him with nothing
but pain, thirst, hunger and ten thousand pounds for company.

UPSTAIRS, THE MAN GRILLED HIMSELF A STEAK AND AFTER
he had eaten went outside to smoke a pipe in the garden.
He saw the girl passing among the horses in the meadow,
fondling each one as was demanded, blowing into their
nostrils and giving them something out of her pocket. She
crossed the meadow and came on up the hill, her shadow
long and clear across the grass, for the sun was going
down in glory.

He watched her come along the lane swishing her riding crop in the meadowsweet and wild garlic that grew beside the hedge. She came straight up to him and smiled. "Hallo," he said. "Best day of the year."

They stood in the still evening, with roses and wallflower and lilac wafting in the air about them. Even the jackdaws in the elms were silent. She looked at him a long moment.

"Take the pipe out of your mouth," she said. "Close your eyes and put your hands behind your back."

Smiling a little, he did so.

She studied him a moment more, watching the smile fade from his mouth while a droop came on to the corner of her own, then she smashed the riding crop across his face.

He made a quick involuntary movement with his whole body and then checked it, and looked down at her, blood on the corner of his mouth and a bright red mark on his cheek.

He did not move. She slashed his face with the crop again, and he stood like a tree. She did this once more, and let the crop fall on to the lawn.

She put a hand behind his neck and kissed the marks she had put on his face, and licked the blood, not with tenderness, but like a cat licking human skin for salt: caressing not him, but the wounds she had dealt him.

Then she stepped back and scanned his battered face until she met his eyes. "Fuck me," she said. "Fuck me again."

PRUVOT IN HIS CELLAR, NOW THAT THE ORIGINAL SHOCK of confronting his situation was past, had found the resilience during those periods when the pain of his afflictions (which came and went like the tide) was at its lowest ebb, to reflect with some objectivity on his predicament. When the same wild shrieks that he had heard in the morning, therefore, came belling down from the top of the house and broke into his attempt to make sense of what was being done to him, he was irritated into the sarcasm of asking himself whether the madman upstairs was celebrating life upon the body of the same girl as before, or whether he had buried her and found a new victim for his bed.

Not that Pruvot's thinking had taken him very far; or rather, insofar as it had taken him anywhere, his arrival left him as baffled as he was when he started. For he had observed a curious aspect of his confinement: his jailer had not sought to create the false friendship which can be set up between an interrogator and the one interrogated, since in fact there had been no interrogation at all. Pruvot assumed that there would be an interrogation, otherwise he could see no logic in the carrot and the stick with which he was presented, instead of meals, at mealtimes: the carrot being the growing pile of thousands of pounds sterling, and the stick the destructive kicks which were apparently to increase by some mathematical progression, and which, if they were not stopped sooner rather than later, would kill him before he had a chance to open his mouth.

In which case he would be dead in his corner, and the accumulated thousands of pounds (and tens of thousands of francs), representing whatever capital value he had survived to attain, would lie beside him in mockery.

It was in the open-ended nature of this question, of how many thousands he would be worth before he succumbed, that he perceived the perverted ingenuity of his jailer, because it had raised other questions to which Pruvot now wished, with an intensity that had grown to a fixation, to know the answer.

The obsession which, despite himself, had become fixed in his mind—despite himself, because part of him knew it meant he had surrendered to the isolation of pain, violence, darkness and banknotes which was the cellar—was the trivial one of whether the fact that the banknotes had doubled in value between breakfast and dinner (which is how he thought of the visitations of his jailer) indicated that they would double again at the next day's breakfast. It was a question of arithmetical progression, and it might simply be that five thousand pounds having been added at the second visitation to the five thousand pounds of the first, then five thousand was the sum that would be added in increments at each "meal."

On the other hand, since the second £5000 had doubled the first, it might be that the amount was to be doubled each time, so at breakfast tomorrow he would be worth £20,000, by tomorrow night £40,000, and by the time he had received both meals the day after, he would be worth £160,000 which was to say he would be worth over a million francs.

To Pruvot a million francs was a prince's ransom. He had been thrown out of the French counter-espionage agency when it was purged of its more extreme reactionaries, which is to say that the SDECE closed its doors one Friday and opened on Monday under the new label DST. Since then he had worked on short-term contracts for any outfit that would use him. He found this humiliating and the financial return wretchedly inadequate.

Yet he was interested to find that though the idea of a million francs gave him furiously to think, the focus of his obsession was not a desire to share the cellar—and his future, if he had one—with a million francs, but the abstract desire to know in what form of arithmetical progression the amount of money was to be increased: Pruvot was becoming a philosopher.

He saw a grotesque irony in this. As an interrogator, after all, he had been obsessed in a wonderfully corrupt sense with the quest for pure knowledge, and now when he was himself cast in the role of victim, the same need for pure knowledge outweighed even so formidable a sum as a million francs. All he wished to know on earth was whether at the next visitation another £5000 would be added to the £10,000 already beside him, or whether the £10,000 would itself be doubled.

Another burst of shouting from the sexually deranged woman upstairs reached the cellar, which by a natural association of ideas reminded Pruvot that in learning at the next visitation, the next "meal," how the thousands of pounds were to multiply, he would at the same time learn at what rate the violence done to him was to escalate. In this question, however, he had no academic interest. He brought to it not the enquiring instinct of the natural philosopher, but the fatalistic acceptance of the stoic.

He wondered about the regime to which he was being subjected—the kicks, the money, the hunger, the silence imposed on him and practised by his jailer, the hours of darkness where he lay cramped and immobile in his pain. He thought it was the man's own cunning that had devised it. A strange aspect of it was that although Pruvot was not being cozened with the false kindness of the professional interrogator, was being offered no cigarettes, no food or drink, no bouts of concerned expressions of interest in himself, no companionability of any sort at all, he had all the same developed what was generally held to be the desired dependence on his jailer.

This was simply because Pruvot was being exposed to

a new version of the blind auction. Instead of there being more than one bidder, each ignorant of how much the other was bidding, there was here only one bidder, but the object to be bought remained undisclosed. The Frenchman's lips were sealed, not by himself as an act of will to withhold desired information, but by sticking plaster; and he had no way of knowing what the other man wanted of him, because the arbitrary rule of silence meant that there had been no questions.

Pruvot's dependence, therefore, was absolute and uncomplicated. He was obsessed with the growth of the money supply, he desired to know what was wanted of him, and he was eager to share in the act of human communication with the sex-mad psychopath humping the noisy girl up there in the house. If this was not dependence, Pruvot thought grimly, he would like someone to tell him what it was.

Pruvot lay in his agonizing bundle and stared these thoughts into the darkness.

HE STOOD UNDER THE MOON AND WAITED, LEANING ON the gate, while the pipe he had been smoking when she left cooled in his hand. He had planned to wait till tomorrow, but now he decided to try tonight. He had a feeling it was the time for it. When he saw the headlights of the girl's car sweep across the house down in the valley he went into the cottage and locked the door.

On a tray he put Perrier water, milk, a pot of coffee, a bowl of lettuce with oil and vinegar over it, and took these down to the cellar. He switched the light on at the foot of the stairs and left the cellar door open when he went in to let his prisoner see what he had brought.

He seized Pruvot's head in one hand and with the other

ripped the plaster from his mouth. Then he took a knife from his pocket and cut the ropes away from him. He helped him drink some water, and then at last he spoke.

"I'm going to ask you questions. Will you answer them?"

Pruvot said, "Yes."

"Can you eat?"

"I hope so. I shall try."

"I'll make you an omelette."

He stood for a moment at the door and watched the Frenchman deal with the pain that came to him as he made the first tentative moves to ease out of the knot into which he had been bound.

Then he made a joke. Pruvot was amazed, and allowed himself to laugh at it. "Don't go away," his jailer said.

In the kitchen he stirred three eggs together while the butter in the heavy iron pan melted, and when it began to turn brown he dropped the eggs into the pan and mingled the eggs and butter with a fork. He put the omelette on a warm plate and went back to the cellar.

Pruvot was lying on his back groaning as the blood resumed its interrupted circulation. The man helped him sit up against the wall and asked him if he was ready to eat.

"Coffee first," Pruvot said.

He sipped at the coffee and shuddered as it went down, and then he was ready for the omelette. After the first mouthful he nodded and then a pleasant idea came to him. "Will there be cigarettes?" he asked.

The man took a pack from his pocket and laid them beside him, on the tray. The Frenchman ate most of the omelette, a little of the salad, experimented with the milk and settled for coffee.

When the man had lit a cigarette for him, he said: "Ask your questions."

LATER THAT NIGHT THE MAN WENT TO THE TELEPHONE. When the phone at the other end was answered he said only: "I leave first thing."

Then he went up to bed.

TWENTY-FOUR HOURS LATER, FROM A NICE LITTLE CUTTER lying-to in the middle of the English Channel with her mainsail flapping loose, he sent Pruvot for a swim in the moonlit sea. Pruvot had an iron weight, such as coal merchants once used, tied to his ankles, and there was no money in his pockets, but he did not complain at this disillusioning turn of events because earlier in the voyage a bullet had blown out his heart.

Freed of its unlucky burden, the cutter hauled off before a fresh breeze and sailed briskly for the coast of France.

12

THE ROOM THEY MET IN WAS A BOWER OF COLOUR AND refracted light, a huge chamber as big as a ballroom with serving tables against the walls covered with porcelain and glass and silver, all of them scintillating under the sparkle of three glorious chandeliers; and everywhere flowers, flowers making arbours, flowers in islands, flowers in serried ranks, their chromatic beauty radiant in the glitter of a myriad exhilarated prisms.

"You would not think," Miss Palmer of the Cabinet Office said to Harry Seddall, "that the building was overrun with rats."

"I had no notion of it," Seddall replied.

"Quite true," Miss Palmer said briskly. "Though why the Foreign Office, rather than any other building in Whitehall, I can't imagine. Do you suppose it is symbolic, Sir Edward?"

Sir Edward Pinkney, on her right, correctly receiving this as a jibe expressing Downing Street's contempt for the

Foreign Service, responded with the encultured phlegm of
the diplomatist. "Can't see it myself, Miss Palmer. Time
enough to worry if they all leave. Sinking ships, don't they
say?"

At this rate, Seddall thought dourly, they'd be married
before the year was out. That was an extremely considering glance she threw at the man. Pinkney and Palmer were
two intelligent, capable and well-looking bureaucrats in
youthful middle age. Seddall let their silence run. However civilized their manners, however elegant the environment of this meeting, when it was done their judgements
of it would in effect be votes for or against him, and he
was too perverse to make himself socially agreeable on
that account.

Sorrel came down the room in a green silk dress, just
the thing for going on to dinner on a Sunday, making
pleasant conversation with Willocks-Moyle, Sir John of
that name, Lieutenant–General and Knight of the Bath,
chairman of this attenuated version of the Joint Intelligence Committee, tweedy and up from the country for this
hastily summoned conclave.

"My word, Pinkney!" the General said. "How very
pretty you have this room! Who's it for?"

"The French," Pinkney said. "Afternoon, General."

"Quite so," the General said, as apprehending what
was the best thing when entertaining the French. "Miss
Palmer. Colonel. Where will you sit, Miss Blake?"
Knowing perfectly well where she would sit, but suggesting that if this were his own table, she would be at his
right hand.

Sorrel sat beside Harry, and Willocks-Moyle had no
sooner put himself at the top of the table, opposite Miss
Palmer, when as if at a prearranged signal MI5, MI6, and
the Special Branch came into the room and disposed them-

selves: Banks and Considine for Five, and Arkley and
Mendham for Six ranged themselves along the opposite
side of the table from Seddall, Arkley next to the chairman, and Kenna and Gatenby (geographically at least) took
Seddall's side.

The space at the chairman's right was vacant, and he
said: "We are all here, bar the Home Office. The Home
Office is sending I believe?"

"I am here, Sir John," said a voice from behind the
flowers in a neighbouring window, and a grey-haired
woman with a face of strong intellectual force wearing,
however, an absent and thoughtful appearance, emerged
and sat confidently beside the general.

"Mrs Heron," he said, "good afternoon to you. I hope
no one else is hidden from us so successfully."

"No one, I can assure you," Mrs Heron said. "I have
looked."

"Then we are secure," Sir John said. "All the doors
are double doors, and sentinels are posted."

The word "sentinels" reminded Harry that the last time
he had seen Arkley, he had occurred to him as a *condottiere* in Renaissance Italy. Today, with a glow of passion
tempering his cheeks, which gave Seddall a strong and
discouraging sense that he was looking at a consciousness
of imminent triumph biding its time, the image of Arkley
as *condottiere* was swollen to the very Sforza of Milan
reaching for power.

The Sforza stroked his black and white moustache with
the top of his gold propelling pencil, laid the pencil on the
bare table in front of him where it sat on its repeated self
on the polished black oak, and gazed into the great room,
and waited. He had not once turned towards Seddall.

From Mendham, however, he now found there came a

bland and expressionless stare, collusive only insofar as it told him: Beware, you're on your own, laddie.

"I thought it as well to meet here," said Sir Edward in response to some sign from the chair, "since for one thing the room is all tarted up for tomorrow's luncheon, and for another it saves us from waking the interest of duty officers other than whom there are very few people about, saving always the Irish Desk, poor devils; since we could use the kitchen stairs, so to speak."

"Most thoughtful," the abstracted Mrs Heron surprisingly said. "If we cannot be in our gardens on a Sunday, it is as well to be among flowers."

Pinkney bowed slantwise up the table. "For my part at this meeting, it is to assert with the greatest possible emphasis, with absolute definiteness, indeed, that nothing must be allowed, nothing must be done, which would risk marring the record of progress being made at the East–West talks now taking place at Vienna, Geneva, Stockholm and Cuneo, known to the media as the Four–Cities talks. When Colonel Seddall advised the Prime Minister's office that in his judgement the barbarous killing of Lord Blacklock suggested the possibility of there being profound political implications involving matters of State secrecy, since in his view the exotic style of the killing, combined with the fact of its having been carried out with professional expertise of a high order, precluded its having been executed by a mere robber or a deranged mind, the Prime Minister accepted this judgement—with which, therefore, it would be impractical to quarrel—and appointed an ad hoc committee of three, of which number Miss Palmer is one, and to this committee Colonel Seddall reports and makes his recommendations. An early recommendation, for example, was that the killing be disguised as a motorcar accident, and this was accepted and was carried out by Colonel Seddall. I shall stop there, Sir John, if it seems good to you, and I shall have a comment to make later.''

"It seems good, thank you," Sir John said. "Do we have question or remark on what Pinkney has told us?"

The gold pencil spun on the table. "Surely," Arkley said, "the Prime Minister must have had more to go on than the hypothesis that Blacklock's death was not a mere criminal murder. Did Colonel Seddall suggest some alternative? Otherwise I do not see where State secrecy comes into it?"

"Hallo, Arkley," Harry said, "For one thing I suggested vendetta, which implies more killings to come."

"To be pedantic," Arkley said, "that is not so. It might have been the last killing in a vendetta."

"It sounds pedantic, but it ain't," Harry said. "Vendettas have a beginning and middle, but very often they have no end, not to signify. They run from generation unto generation."

"Ridiculous, surely?" Arkley came back. "That is to talk of savage hill tribes. We are talking about Viscount Blacklock, a Minister of the Government."

"Afghans," Willocks-Moyle said. "Kurds. Circassians."

"What about America?" said George Banks of M15. "The Hatfields and the McCoys. Tennessee wasn't it? Hill tribes of a sort.

"That was nothing," said the flower-loving Mrs Heron, "to the Graham–Tewkesbury feud in Pleasant Valley, Arizona, where the feud was so ferocious that whole families were ambushed and shot, and in one incident a small child was eaten by the farm pigs, a truce to allow the body to be retrieved having been denied. We must conclude from this that feud, or vendetta, releases a deep and primitive force within human nature, such as would cut off a victim's head and set it on the dining room table. I understand Colonel Seddall's view of that perfectly well.''

Arkley tucked the gold pencil away in his pocket as if the sight of it was a treat they no longer deserved. ''None of this,'' he said, ''explains to me why Blacklock's death raises a question of State secrets.''

Harry said: ''The head was left on the table as a message. Not to family, Blacklock had no family. Therefore, to people Blacklock was engaged with. To Government maybe, even people like us.''

''What message?''

''I've got Blacklock. I'll get the rest of you!''

''That is a very melodramatic interpretation,'' Arkley said with scorn.

''Of a surpassingly melodramatic act, however,'' Mrs Heron said.

Pinkney interposed. ''The suggestion would be, that Blacklock and some other people had combined to do something for which the killer sought vengeance.''

''Yes,'' Harry said.

''And the Prime Minister accepted this?''

''The Prime Minister certainly accepted it as a possibility,'' Miss Palmer answered.

Arkley came in again. ''I still do not see why it was required to keep the killing, even the manner of it, secret.''

''For this reason,'' General Willocks-Moyle said. ''That there was nothing done by Lord Blacklock in his time in Government which was found to be, in the remotest degree, capable of attracting violence upon him. He had never had Ministerial responsibility for Northern Ireland, for example to draw the anger of the IRA; or in the Foreign Office, to inspire blame for God knows what act from foreign terrorists, and even at that, terrorists have no record of putting any resentments they might have against British foreign policy into effect on the persons of our Foreign Office Ministers at home—ambassadors, unhappily, yes. But as I say, Blacklock was never a Foreign Office Minister in any case. So far as we look at his murder from the point of view of his official life, it is unaccountable. Colonel Seddall was therefore compelled to the conclusion that Blacklock might have been in dealings with people outside the known occasions of his responsibilities at the Defence Ministry, and that this led to his death.''

Arkley, looking less like a *condottiere* and more like a headmaster, appeared astounded. "Are you suggesting— is that to suggest . . . ?''

"Hanky-panky," Seddall said. "Jiggery-pokery, yes. Dirty work at the crossroads. By Blacklock.''

Arkley settled his shirt cuffs on the table and looked at them, nice and white against the polished black wood. "And it was thought fit to keep the Intelligence services out of it?''

"It was thought," Miss Palmer said tartly, "that Colonel Seddall was best qualified to deal with it.''

"Once Seddall was assigned," Willocks-Moyle said, "the need-to-know principle operated against including the Intelligence services.''

"The colonel is unorthodox," said Mrs Heron, "but he has a good track record. He may be compared in that to Zola Budd, running barefoot as she does. On the point of security, he employs an extremely small staff, whereas there is still some reorganization going on in the Intelligence services; weeding-out still to be done, I believe.'' She uttered this last phrase with particular satisfaction, as if it connoted for her the physical pleasures of wielding the hoe.

Ungratefully and—he was aware of it—chauvinistically, Seddall wondered gloomily how useful it was to have this woman of highly independent style rooting for him, in a gathering dominated, numerically at least, by men. What the hell though, she was his kind, wasn't she?

"I am in accord with what Mrs Heron says," went on Willocks-Moyle, "and on Colonel Seddall's preference for the unorthodox route, I'll ask Superintendent Kenna of Special Branch to describe the collision between the Branch and the CIA which has brought us to meet here today."

"The collision was intended by Colonel Seddall," Kenna said. "I can't say he set me up because I knew what I was getting into, and he had warrant from Downing Street. Once he told me the CIA had been in a shoot-out at Mustell and were still clearing up the mess I had no option. I met Inspector Gatenby here, who's stationed at Oxford, on the Oxford ring road and we got out to Mustell just too late, met a car and a van coming towards us as we approached Mustell. We'd not caught them in a criminal act so I had a problem, and I had another problem, they had CD plates up.

"Well, I turned and followed to see where they were bound and do my thinking as I went, and I sent Inspector Gatenby round to the cart track north of the house to see what was happening there. Two bodies at the house, Colonel Seddall had said, and another up the cart track. I took one of the inspector's men into my car for local knowledge. We followed the van and the car to the Banbury road, that runs north out of Oxford. They pull into a lay-by and we drive past and turn up a side road and I climb up the bank and I can see 'em, just.

"It looks as if they're just sitting there, waiting. After a bit another vehicle approaches them from behind and flashes its lights, slows down to let them fall in behind, and off they go again. I get back in the car and when we're out on the main road I see Gatenby's car in front of me. They know they're being followed of course but either they don't feel the need to do anything about it or they can't think what to do. The copper beside me suddenly says: 'Christ, Super, they're going to the US base at Upper Heyford, it's not a mile away.'

"That gave me to think, I can tell you. If they did have the bodies in those vehicles they were going to take 'em into the base and fly 'em out. I had no time to find out what Authority would have wanted me to do but in any case, as a policeman, I had only one duty. The road was running along the wire of the base and I put the car up past them and blocked them off just as they were ready to turn in at the gate."

Kenna paused and wiped his hand over his face and rubbed his scalp. The big red face looked down the table at Seddall, and Kenna shook his tousled hair. "Harry," he said, "the things you get me into!"

Seddall smiled a rueful smile. "It's because you always come out of them so well, Gerald," he said. "Don't stop. You have the gift of telling."

"Do I so? Here's the rest of it. They were expected, all right. Half a platoon ran out the gate with a major in command, carbines all over the place and the major with his hand on his pistol butt. Move the car, he says. I tell him who I am and that I will not. I tell him that if these soldiers are threatening me and my men they must immediately cease and desist—I actually used those words, so help me. Or you will see, says I. Get your men back into that base. He refuses. Gatenby, I say, come here! Draw your firearm, I say to Gatenby, I am going to look inside those vehicles, and I leave Gatenby with a uniformed officer beside him and I go to the first vehicle. They're sitting tight with the doors locked, looking straight ahead, saying nothing, two men in the front and nothing in the back.''

Kenna became aware that he was holding his audience spellbound. He opened his arms in a disparaging gesture and said: ''Och, well,'' and continued. '' 'I must ask you to come out of that car,' I shout at them through the glass. I shout twice and they just sit there staring straight ahead. I go to the constable standing at the back of the car and tell him to draw his truncheon and go straight up to the driver's window and break it in without warning, one blow, and by God he does it. I hear Gatenby call out 'Stand back!' and see the half-platoon standing like puppets stopped in the middle of a move and the major on the ground with Gatenby's thirty-eight at the crown of his head.''

''The man in the car says diplomatic immunity. *Diplomatic*, I say, *this*? And I unlock the door and tell the constable to pull him out. At this the fellow comes out of the car and bugger me if the other one does not have a silenced pistol in his fist aimed at me, so I throw the first fellow on top of him and there's a little soft sound and the fellow on top says 'Fuck you, Jerry!' and there's the bullet come through his shoulder and missed me, thank God, so I take the car keys and open the boot and there's a body-bag with a corpse in it. Now I have a leg to stand on and I thank Providence on my knees, if you take my meaning, and I even thank Harry Seddall too, which is hard to believe.''

''I appreciate that,'' Harry said earnestly. ''I never give you a bum steer, Gerald, but I appreciate that.''

''No problem,'' said Kenna with a grim voice. ''The constable and I confiscated two silenced pistols out of that

car and left the gunman to console his friend, who was
First Secretary at the US Embassy, Sir Edward.''

"Dear God, I know," Pinkney said. "Hopeless way to
behave. The Americans I mean. For yourself, Superintendent, I am lost in admiration.''

"Thank you. I go over to Gatenby and the major and I
kneel down and I speak to him in American, to drive the
message home, and you'll have to excuse the language. I
tell him Major, your CIA pals have been committing ho-
micide in my bailiwick and they have fucked up, I have
found one body in those vehicles and I'm about to find
two more. I may or may not arrest them tonight because
I can find them any time I want, but so far as they have
diplomatic immunity it will not be enforced by the US
Army or Air Force or whatever the hell you are. What I
shall do is arrest the bodies, because they do not have
immunity, and if you try to stop me, Major, if you do not
simply fade quietly into the night with your men then your
commission is dust, and you better believe it, what are
you going to do, Major?

"He says he is going to withdraw his men, and that's
that. We find two bodies in the van, we load up all the
corpses, we impound the identifications of the six men in
the vehicles, and we leave. I've never been so angry in my
life.''

Into the respectful silence, Sorrel said: "Well I think
that's stunning, Mr Kenna. I think you and Mr Gatenby
performed miracles.''

Kenna stared at her amazed, as if to say he had just
hammered a nail into the coffin of the Seddall team, and
did she not realize this. Harry thought there were times
when even the best girls ought to keep their mouths shut.

Sure enough, Arkley took his cue. "I'm sure Mr Kenna
will welcome Miss Blake's encomium, and it is indeed

well deserved, but questions arise. For one—how did Seddall know in the first place that the CIA had been involved in a shooting at Mustell?''

"What does it matter, Arkley?" Harry asked him. "The gunfight took place, and they tried to make off with the bodies.''

"We will not go into questions of that kind," Willocks-Moyle said dogmatically. "It's not what we're here for. I think Sir Edward may now want to make the comment he reserved earlier.''

"If I may," Pinkney said, and gave Seddall a not unpleasant smile to prepare him for the bad news "It is vitally important at this time for there to be no *frisson* of disagreement between the British and American governments, in view of the close unity between our two governments in the Four–Cities talks between the western democracies and the Warsaw Pact countries, and yet here we are faced with a situation, provoked deliberately by Colonel Seddall, which for one thing calls in question the sensitive matter of the conduct of the Americans in their occupation of military bases on British soil, and for another makes it unavoidable that we make some protest to the American ambassador about the behaviour, in this incident, not only of the CIA in their operations in this country, but also of the ambassador's own staff. The Foreign Secretary, to whom I spoke this morning, takes the gravest view, certainly of what the Americans have done but, in addition, of Colonel Seddall's having manipulated the open confrontation just described to us by Mr Kenna. He will by now have presented this view to the Prime Minister.''

Pinkney looked enquiringly at Miss Palmer.

"He has done so," Miss Palmer said.

"The Foreign Secretary," Pinkney resumed, "will also

have indicated to the Prime Minister that if the difficulties now raised between the British and American governments are exacerbated further as a result of Colonel Seddall's researches into Lord Blacklock's death, or his pursuing the line of CIA involvement in the circumstances that led to Lord Blacklock's death, or his exposing—and in the Foreign Secretary's view that would be worst of all—CIA involvement in these circumstances, then the result could be catastrophic and would far outweigh whatever benefit might be seen to accrue from such exposure. That is the extent of my comment.''

Weighty stuff, Harry said to himself. I'll not be coming out of this one with a whole skin. Pinkney's little speech won a longer and more respectful silence even than Kenna's story had.

It was Willocks-Moyle who ended it. ''The Foreign Secretary's view is strongly held, as Sir Edward has made plain to us. Whether it is to be paramount we shall not know until we hear from the Prime Minister, who is at Chequers. We expect to hear shortly, Miss Palmer?''

''We do,'' Miss Palmer said. ''No later than seven o'clock.

''Whatever the outcome,'' the general went on, ''it has been already decided to form a liaison committee from among those present so that there will be no further hitches in communication among the several services who may be concerned. But that can wait. We will have a recess now, I think, until we hear from Chequers.''

To Sorrel, Harry said: ''We're going to go down. I want you to go to my house. Give yourself a drink, and when I get there we'll go for dinner.''

''I won't run,'' Sorrel said.

''Listen, Sorrel. It's easier for one to make the heavy exit than for two to do it. Here's the key.''

The blue eyes looked at him hard. They were held a little wide. "I'll just say goodbye to Sir John, then," she said marvellously, as if this were a social event.

Harry watched her go, and as he lit a cigarette he saw Gatenby was watching her too. She's made a friend there, he thought, with that spontaneous tribute to him and Kenna.

He went over to Kenna, who was standing at one of the fireplaces talking to Mrs Heron.

". . . garlic among the roses," she was saying. "It works, you'll see. Colonel Seddall," as she turned to greet him, "if it was to be put to a vote, you'd have mine, but it never is, in Whitehall."

"You're very kind," Harry said.

"Not at all. I'm a practical person in such matters. I think the Foreign Secretary owed a good part of the view which Sir Edward has just recited to us to his fastidious nature. He finds the whole affair uncouth, and finds his arguments retrospectively to suit. I daresay he's quite unaware of it."

Gerald Kenna opened his large face in a wary, half-amiable, half-hostile, grin. "I doubt if you'd have my vote, Harry. If I'd known what I was getting into I'd have . . . I don't know what I'd have done."

"Just the same, probably," Mrs Heron said, "but perhaps, not so well as you did."

"What does that mean?" Kenna asked her.

"That if you make a habit of trying always to foresee eventualities upon which you may have to act, your character will become less disposed to act with automatic confidence in sudden exigencies."

"Mrs Heron," Seddall said. "I think we should have luncheon one of these days."

"So do I," she said. "I like lunching with the black

sheep, and you're about to become one, as I'm sure you know."

Seddall laughed, a rare thing with him. "Yeah, I know."

Miss Palmer came up to him and said: "Colonel Seddall, the Prime Minister's wish is that you withdraw from the Blacklock operation. If you want to see him he can make time tomorrow afternoon at four. I have told the general and we are about to resume."

"Thanks for telling me," he said to her.

There was no expression on her face. "Not at all," she said. "It is only proper for you to be told in this way, rather than in meeting."

The world was full of direct women, these days.

"The Prime Minister has decided to take Colonel Seddall off the Blacklock operation," Willocks-Moyle told the reassembled company. "Best not to beat about the bush, you'll agree, Colonel Seddall. You will want to make a final report to the ad hoc committee, and after that the committee will pass relevant information to your successors in the operation."

Harry, facing up the table to receive the general's pronouncement, found himself sharing a look with Gerald Kenna. At the word "relevant" Kenna's heavy eyebrows lifted and at the plural of the word "successors" he bent his head low and looked at the blank table top.

Sounds like a nicely disseminated combined op, that's what Kenna's thinking too. A nice disorganized shambles receiving only so much of what he had told the committee. A nice, limping, going-slow, bunch of obliging careermakers with a sophisticated understanding of how not to do what was not wanted. This is bitter stuff, Seddall, don't be so bloody self-indulgent. He looked over at Pinkney, and received the same not unpleasant smile as before.

He looked at Mendham, who was sitting with the back

of his hand to his mouth and his spectacles dangling loosely from his fingers, and who met him with a cool and contemplative gaze which acknowledged, imperceptibly to others, that bargains had been kept: not a cut-off.

And he looked at Arkley, who did not look at him.

"If there is urgency," he said to the general, "I'll have my report ready tomorrow. If not, Tuesday."

The general regarded bleakly the insolence in the suggestion that urgency might now have left the official approach to the Blacklock affair. "If there is a serious question there, it is for Miss Palmer."

"Tomorrow will do very well, Colonel," Miss Palmer said. If ever there was a woman not to be drawn, it was Miss Palmer.

A short, careful hiatus followed, created by those who had an opinion about the Prime Minister's decision, one way or the other, refraining from displaying it.

Except for Mrs Heron, who said at last: "The liaison committee you spoke of, General. Shall I be required to participate?"

"No, Mrs Heron, you will not." The briefest pause. "Neither shall I."

"Then the operation is being down-graded?"

The general's smile was full of charm. "I don't think we have enough information to say that. I think it not yet decided."

Mrs Heron persisted. "I think it should not be down-graded, and if we were minuting I should want it noted as my advice." Who the hell was this woman? Was she taking risks, or was her standing that high?

The general smiled again, but spoke with a cautionary note. "Then I daresay Miss Palmer will take note of what you say."

"I concur with Mrs Heron," Kenna said surprisingly.

"I have no written agenda for this meeting," the general said, "but if I had none of this would be on it. Let us pass on."

Harry was watching Arkley. The man was profound with triumph, glittering inside himself, as if he was watching an army he had conquered march out of the city he had won.

"I'd like not to wait for Seddall's reports," he said, "to know the answer to this: why did he instigate this impolitic collision between CIA and Special Branch?"

And he faced down the table at last to see Seddall answer.

"To start a hare, Arkley."

There was the slightest diminution of the glitter, far within.

"And did you? Start a hare, I mean?"

"Oh, yes," Harry said. "I rather think I did."

He stood up from the table and went to fetch his overcoat from where it lay on a chesterfield against the wall. As he bent to pick it up his head went into a perfume of flowers. He stayed there for a moment, a lift of the heart, before he took the coat and returned to them.

"Mind you, Arkley," he said as he shrugged his way into the sleeves, "a hare jinking away from you is not an easy shot. But that's up to you chaps now."

He looked at MI5, as at two fossils that had neglected to die before being fixed forever. "Considine," he said. "Banks. Never saw you down there."

Banks stared and nodded. Considine enlarged his eyes.

"Good day to you, Sir John," Harry said to the general. "Mrs Heron."

He walked off down the long room, among porcelain and glass, silver and flowers, feeling strangely successful.

13

Seddall and Mendham met for an early pub lunch
at the top of Gloucester Avenue in Camden Town. It was
just after noon and they had the place to themselves, and
the area in front of the fireplace, which was furnished with
three sofas, entirely to themselves.

"This is the life," Harry said.

"You don't seem as cross as I would have expected,"
Mendham said.

"I'm not cross at all. I'm on leave."

"Ha ha," Mendham said.

"Sorrel asked me if I was going to resign," Harry said.

"What did you tell her?"

"Not my style. 'My commission is at Your Royal Highness's disposal, that sort of thing. Anyway, John, I'm winning, or at any rate I'm going to win. You're going to win
too, old son, unless I find out you're in it with Arkley up
to the neck."

"I'll get some beer," Mendham said, and went off to

the bar to think. When he came back with the beer, he said: "You're going on with it, I gather."

"Bloody right I'm going on with it. What'd you think?"

"What about resources, back-up—what about money?"

"Don't get many resources from Whitehall, less back-up. It won't cost much."

Mendham kept his response, which would have been to the effect that Seddall's idea of not costing much was likely to be different from other people's, to himself. Seddall came from a comparatively short line of military men, but one of them had emerged from years of African campaigning, including such seemingly unprofitable enterprises as the Ashanti Wars and the punitive expedition against the Emperor Theodore of Abyssinia, with a bad reputation and a large personal fortune. It was quite possible that some bauble from the treasury of the late Theodore would defray the cost of this lunch.

"How's Arkley?" Harry asked him.

"Mixed. Partly extremely pleased with himself, partly cogitating like mad about something. Asked me to lunch with him, as a matter of fact."

"What did you say?"

"Lunching with you."

"Good move. That'll worry him."

"It wasn't a move, it was a precaution. When Five and Six are in cahoots, you never know who's following you around. Why are we here, anyway? We can't talk much longer, lunchtime regulars will be in soon, bound to sit round the fire."

"This," Harry said munificently, waving a hand at the remains of Mendham's steak and kidney pie and chips, "is to thank you for making that phone call for me, putting your career at risk, all that."

"Oh, *super*, you shouldn't have, really, it's too much," Mendham said earnestly.

"Also," Harry said, "to let you know that, in the immortal words of John Paul Jones, of which young Gyseman reminded us, I have not yet begun to fight."

"I *say*, Harry. This is probably going to be the most exciting lunch I'll have all week."

"Piss off, Mendham. I'm feeling like a boy let out of school, that's all."

"Talking of immortal words, was it your wicked great-grandfather who said that thing you quoted, 'My commission is at Your Royal Highness's disposal'?"

Seddall looked at him; a not quite agreeable look. "You been looking me up, or something?"

"Before I took you up to the attic to play trains," Mendham said. "I know everything about you, Harry. Even then I was taking a risk."

Seddall was still looking at him, but the hardness was leaving his eyes. "You were indeed," he said. "No, that wasn't the naughty general, it was someone rather more famous, I think, and less notorious too. Can't remember. Where were we?"

"Reason for this meeting."

"Right. First to express my thanks, and second to tell you I am still in the fight, and third to ask you whether the same applies to you. I may not have to call on you at all, and I shan't call on you for anything spectacular and therefore dangerous to your good self unless we're coming down the straight and I need a touch of the whip, if you get my meaning."

"I don't quite get your meaning, but I get your drift, all right. If I think it's too dangerous I won't do it, my meaning being, that in such a case I'll leave you to sink or swim. *Sauve qui peut*, you understand?"

Seddall grinned at him rudely. "You're the most bare-faced self-interested coward I've met in this business."

Mendham allowed this compliment to go to his face, which was already in its immature mode since he was off duty, and he blushed. "I don't feel I really deserve that," he said skilfully.

"You're telling me you're still in, on the same terms as before. I take that kindly, considering how I fucked things up for you with your CIA contact, not to mention Ark-ley." Although it was Harry who was speaking them, while the words came out he looked as if he was listening to Mendham, instead of Mendham to him.

"You don't win wars if you give up as soon as you lose a battle," Mendham said sententiously. "Besides, you have this reputation for coming out on top."

"Yes, but you haven't," Seddall said brutally, and waited and watched.

Expressions shifted about on Mendham's face, showing first hurt and the desolation of other hurts remembered from other times, and immediately after that, like a defensive reflex, you could see him bring his thinking on to the thing that had hurt him and at once, then, understanding of why it had been said.

"You don't trust me," Mendham said. "You think I'm going to cross you."

"I don't trust you or not trust you, John," Harry said. "There's a small difference between you and me. You don't trust me, but you rely on me. You rely on me to do the best I can to make good on this thing. I don't really rely on you, because I know that when I ask you to put your money where your mouth is—and I grant that you've been very explicit on setting limits to what you'll do or not do—that when I do that you'll weigh up all the pros and cons and that you'll make your mind up after you've done that.

You're fast at it because you've that kind of mind, like you were fast the other night when I asked you to make that phone call. But I'm not the only one who doesn't know how you'll act when the chips are down; you don't know either."

"What are you saying, Harry?" Mendham picked one of the cold chips off his plate and ate it, in a meaningless symbolic act. "And try not to bare a chap to the bone, won't you?"

"You can do it to me any time you want to," Harry said, "but you won't want to. You don't have the need for it, you don't have the aggression."

Cinders fell glowing out of the fire basket and Mendham kneeled down and gathered them together with a shovel and put them back in the fire.

When he sat down again, his face bright red, he repeated: "What are you saying, Harry?"

"Damn it, John! That call you made for me, that got you in the shit with your CIA friend, don't tell me it didn't. So they'll be wondering why you did it, and like as not they'll be wondering in company with Arkley. You're exposed, Mendham, you're at risk, and you know it, because if Arkley gets the feel that you're ambitious for his job and are ready to make a move on him he'll break your life for you, you'll be out of the service with dirt on your name, any dirt Arkley cares to think up and throw at you."

"You think I'm too chicken to take that kind of risk." Mendham's face was no longer red, but it was pink, and not from the fire.

"Yeah," Harry said. "I think that."

"You're a shit, Harry," Mendham said. "I told myself after I'd sussed you out that if I was going to let myself get into dealings with you, then I'd have to put with this kind of garbage. You're lucky I don't walk out on you.

Listen to this, Harry: this is the news, read by John Mendham. After the big scene between Special Branch and the CIA I got back on to my Agency contact and told him how dreadfully sorry I was, that I had been assured they'd have a clear run at toting away the corpses from Mustell and washing off the bloodstains from the flagstones, all that, and that someone higher up had ordered the Branch to move in on them while they were at it. So, if they are in a secret deal with Arkley they are bound at least to have him on their list of people higher up who might have put in the double-cross; because not that many people could know about it.''

Seddall lit a Gauloise and let the first of the smoke trickle out of his nose slowly, while he kept his eyes on Mendham's. He knew there was more to come, so he just nodded.

"I pretended that *I* was set up to set *them* up, if you see what I mean. Well, I thought it might do, you know, I thought it might serve, but I didn't think it would go down as well as it did. So I sniffed around at it, said it was very mysterious and worrying, and that I found it was making me just a tiny bit anxious about what was going on at MI6 London station, and he fell for it. He said you and me both, brother, and I said what precisely did he mean by that, putting the tone in that said it was one thing for me to make cracks about my own service but it didn't give him any rights in that direction.

"So he said if I thought I was worried about what was going on in my neck of the woods I should try changing places with him, for Chrissake. What can you mean? I said. And what he meant, Harry, is that there has now developed an uncertainty about exactly who in the Agency set up their operation at Mustell and about what the hell it was for. What he does know, you see, is that it was set up from Langley; and that the clean-up party found one American body and two unknowns—one of them being the man you say was French—and there are two of their own men, sent over from the States for this enterprise, unaccounted for.''

A dungareed workman of the kind Harry thought had gone out with the hi-tech high-unemployment society arrived at the couch opposite with his girlfriend and began eating the same meal consumed by himself and Mendham.

Harry looked at them for longer than was polite and then did the same to Mendham. Then he looked round about him to make sure nobody was crouching behind them taking all this in.

''Ye gods,'' he said, ''what does—that sound like to you?''

''That, Harry, is why I am managing to be not chicken but terribly brave,'' Mendham said, ''and why I am willing to gamble for the sake of unadulterated ambition on the chance of seeing Arkley go, as our American friends would say, down the tubes.''

''All right,'' Harry said irritably, ''I was rude to you. What do you make of this stuff?''

''I'll tell you what,'' Mendham said. ''I'll buy the lunch. Then I won't feel so bad about your lousy behaviour. Why don't you tell me what *you* make of all this stuff?''

''Because I want to hear it from you. You work with these people, ours and theirs. I don't know them like you do.'' Seddall waved a hand about in a despairing kind of way. ''You know the pack you run with, damn it, you know their smell. If that's rude, too, I'm sorry.''

Mendham smiled. ''That'll be the day. You're like the Chocolate Soldier in that play, Harry. You never apologize. What I make of it, though what I smell is better,

because it's less definite, and I'm not definite about this:
what I smell is another"—he glanced across at the lovers
on the sofa opposite—"like our friend, a soulmate on the
other side of the tempestuous ocean, both of them running
a bit of business that's been kept extremely secret from
almost everybody, even perhaps from their managing di-
rectors, and even unknown, perhaps, to anyone at all on
the top boards of either of their companies. What do you
make of it?"

"That's the sort of thing I make of it too," Harry said.
"If it is something like that, you have to admire our friend.
He carries it off bloody well."

"He will make a dangerous opponent," Mendham said.
"I need a Scotch."

Seddall stood up and looked at Mendham's knees. "I
was bloody rude," he said. "I'll get these."

He went to the bar and came back with four large whis-
kies, bottles of soda water, and a large bottle of Malvern
water that had been taken fresh from the spring and spared
aeration. He made a clumsy encouraging movement of the
arms. "Dunno how you like it, Mendham, but there's the
makings."

Mendham, despite the going over he had just received,
was almost touched to see Seddall so vulnerable. "Dear
me," he said. "This is starting to look like one of those
days where it is wiser not to go back to the office."

The pub had filled up and was full of people and sound.
The couch facing the fireplace was now occupied by three
local worthies, who had jammed themselves into it with
unspoken suggestions of reproach at the two incomers who
were taking up their space.

Harry leaned towards Mendham and offered, close into
his ear, a further *amende*. "Do you want to see the knife
I took out of that Frenchman at Mustell?"

"Why not?" Mendham said. "Have you got it there?"

The knife was passed to him, wrapped in a piece of cloth. Mendham parted the folds of the bundle. "The death or glory boys use these, don't they? Why are you carrying it around?"

"That," Harry said, and touched the engraving on the blade. "I'm trying to work out what that dog's head means. If I carry it, it will speak to me sooner or later."

"Dog's head?" Mendham said. He snapped his fingers. "Got it!" he said.

"Got what?"

"That quotation you came out with about someone saying his commission was at HRH's disposal. It was Wolfe at Culloden, the man who took Montreal from Montcalm. He was a major at Culloden, I think. He was on Cumberland's staff, and the duke pointed to a wounded Highlander and said: 'Pistol me that scallywag,' or words to that effect."

"Jolly good," Seddall said, "and then Wolfe said: 'My commission is at Your Royal Highness's disposal.' By which he meant: no, I won't."

"Exactly so."

"What made you think of that all of a sudden?" Harry asked him.

Mendham turned the blade of the knife so that both of them could look at it. "The head," he said. "I think you're wrong about that being a dog. I think it's a wolf's head."

"Great godfathers!" Harry said. "Let's see that." He peered at it. "You could be right."

LATER THAT AFTERNOON, HARRY SEDDALL MADE HIS WAY to the Cavalry Club and looked up the Army List. An ancient toddled up to him as he leafed through the pages.

"Ah, Seddall," he said croakily. "I knew your father."

"So did I, sir," Harry said. "Oh, sweet Jesus!" he said immediately after, stared at the open page, and closed the book with a thump.

He left the club and walked briskly to the Defence Ministry, where he went to see an acquaintance.

"Hear you're in bad odour," the man said amiably enough. "Thought you were on leave."

"Right on both counts, Peter," Harry said. "Thought I'd look up some chums this weekend. Can you possibly tell me where I'll find this chap?"

He scribbled on a piece of paper and passed it across.

"I'll do it myself," Peter said. "Quicker," and departed.

He came back into the room with a curious care in his movements and an uncertain expression on his face. "I'm most terribly sorry, Harry, but your friend's dead. No chance of a mistake, I'm afraid. James Wolf, Queen's Own Highlanders, captain, attached to the SAS, killed on a routine exercise when a Wessex helicopter crashed into the sea in November. About twenty chaps bought it. No survivors. I really am most terribly sorry."

Harry looked thunderstruck. He had hit paydirt.

"I'm afraid there's no mistake. It's all there in black and white, well blue and white actually, on the print-out. Do you want it?" He fished in his pocket and brought out the crushed slip of paper, and made an embarrassed effort to smooth out the wrinkles.

Harry read it. "James Wolf," he said. "That's the man." He tried for the right sort of smile. "Thanks anyway, Peter." he said. "What the hell."

"Damn shame," Peter said. "I daresay the SAS chaps at Hereford could tell you more about it, except that they're so frightfully discreet about security up there they do tend to bring on this sort of bland smile if you ask them anything at all about what they do.''

''They might,'' Harry said. ''It's a nice thought, but it hardly seems worth it, somehow. These things happen, that's all. Well I'll get out of your way, then. Thanks anyway, Peter. So long.''

''Damn shame,'' Peter said again.

When the door had closed behind his visitor he went over to the window and spoke to the sky. ''Funny thing, that. Never knew Harry Seddall had so much feeling in him.''

14

SEDDALL WAS READING IN BED AT THE GREEN DRAGON IN Hereford when there was a light tap on his door. He sighed, laid down the book, picked up the pistol, and placed himself to one side of the door.

"Who is it?" he asked.

"Sorrel," said Sorrel.

He let her in, climbed back to bed and put his hands behind his head.

"Good grief," she said. "Are those your regimental pyjamas?"

"Don't be silly. Hodson's Horse never wore pyjamas. What's more, I'm well aware they don't do anything for me, and after the day I've had I don't care. I know what I look like. I look like something the cat brought in, so don't let's talk about me, let's talk about you. Why are you dressed like that?"

Sorrel was wearing leather trousers and a tight sweater, both of them chestnut-brown to match her eyes, with a belt cinching in the sweater to increase the prominence of her breasts.

"I think I look smashing," she said. "Oh, look. There's an electric kettle, I'll make us some tea. In fact, I know I look smashing," she said from the bathroom, where she was filling the kettle, "because he told me." She stood in the doorway and beamed.

"Who told you?"

She plugged in the kettle and sat down on the bed. Harry looked conscientiously into her eyes. "See," she said. "You have to make an effort to do that. You want to grab my beautiful body with your eyes, so you have to stare at me to stop them running over me. Lustfully. When you're old you'll be a dirty old man."

"I'm a dirty old man right now," Harry said. "Your kettle's boiled. Who told you?" His eyes abandoned the unequal struggle.

"No names no pack drill. The fella I spent the evening with. He's in the Army.'

"I'll bet he's in the Army. How much did you nick him for?"

"Don't be crude. It wasn't like that at all."

"OK," he said. "I'm just jealous. Now we've got that over with, what's this all about?"

"Here's your nice tea. How was dinner?"

"Dinner was a wash-out. Three hours of the kind of talk I like to have at dinner in the usual way, but when you're trying to worm something out of an SAS officer who insists on talking about how wonderfully Mitsuko Uchida plays the piano, and how tragic it is that the entire stock of Chateau Loudenne 1985 was destroyed in a fire, and quotes whole sentences at you from Burckhardt on the Italian Renaissance, then you realize he's seen you coming a mile off and is taking the piss."

"You poor thing," Sorrel said. "Still, I'm sure the dinner itself was nice for you."

"Well it was," Harry admitted sulkily, "but he got to eat it too."

Sorrel regarded him with suspicion. "Why are you playing that role?"

"What role?"

"That sulky stuff, like a little boy. That's what husbands do, I've seen them, to their wives."

"Oh, *that* role. It's because I'm hoping you'll begin to feel I am your husband and hop into bed with me."

Sorrel stroked his thinning hair. "It might happen one day, lover but this is not the night. Here, let me give you some tea your cup's empty, and I'll tell you what this nice man told me."

"Oh, Sorrel, can't it wait till tomorrow? What did he tell you?"

Sorrel, on the bed, hugged her knees and put her chin on them and said: "He told me that the senior officer on the helicopter when it crashed was Major David Marsham."

"Did he, by God!"

"He told me something else. He met David Marsham in the post office just across the road there," she nodded at the curtained window, "and Marsham was getting a parcel stamped to send abroad, to France. He saw France written on it. This was just before, a few weeks before, the chopper crash, and the last time he saw Marsham. So because of that, and because of what Marsham said to him, he remembered it.

Sorrel rubbed her chin across the leather on her knees. Harry waited. "He wasn't being quizzy about the parcel, or anything like that, I mean who would be? So the interesting thing is that Marsham came out with this off his own bat, that's how it seems to me, how it sounded to me, as if Marsham seeing this man he knew when he'd just posted the parcel off wanted to say something to someone about it and this man was there, so he said it. Does that make sense?''

''It could make sense,'' Harry said patiently, ''when I know what Marsham said to him.''

''He said: 'That's my last will and testament,' and he gave the other man a look he couldn't interpret, but it was strange, and seemed to mean something. My nice man took it to be one of those premonitions people get sometimes before they're buzzing off somewhere.''

''You've earned your cup of tea, haven't you?''

''Yes,'' Sorrel said. ''I rather think I have.''

''Move,'' Harry said. ''I want to get up.''

He walked up and down the room in his dressing gown, thinking. He drew back the curtains and he and Sorrel leaned out of the window and looked at the post office, at the cathedral as well, but mostly at the post office.

''That very post office itself,'' Harry said. ''My, my!''

''Do you want some real coffee?'' Sorrel asked him.

''Yes, I do, but it's pretty late. You'll have to coax the night porter.''

''In this gear? No problem.''

She came back followed by the man bearing coffee and ham sandwiches, and they feasted Sorrel's success.

''To tell you the truth,'' Harry said. ''I think you look smashing too.''

Sorrel laughed. ''I know you do. To tell *you* the truth,'' and the colour came up in her face, ''the reason I don't know the nice man's name is he wouldn't give it me. He thought I was a tart.''

The sandwiches finished, Harry leaned back in his chair and lit a cigarette. ''He was probably right,'' he said. ''It's not one of those things you learn, it's a thing you're born with.''

"Give me a cigarette," Sorrel said, and when it was lit: "That kind of remark, Harry . . . do you know what it is with you?''

"No. What is it?''

"It took me a while to get used to it. It's when you're feeling good you get cheeky. I've made you feel good, so it's your way of saying thank you.

Harry frowned. "If that's true, it's not much of a way of saying thank you.''

"It stinks," Sorrel agreed, "but it's what you do, and you're far too old to change, so we're stuck with it.''

Harry said absently: "I'm not that old. I met a man in the club yesterday who was older than me. Listen now. Tomorrow I'll get Mendham on to Marsham's next of kin. I can't go back to Peter Fulton on that, two queries on the same plane crash would look fishy to him after the way I approached him on Wolf. Mendham will have to get access to the the MoD computer somehow. He can do it. You and I, or one of us, depending on who it is, will do next of kin when we know who they are. Will you call Gyseman in the morning and get him to go through the files of *The Times* and the *Telegraph* for a week either side of that Wessex crash and see what he can come up with. I don't know what he'll be looking for so he'll have to do it with all his antennae out and listening. Can you think of anything else?''

"No. That sounds good." She yawned and stretched, and Seddall averted his eyes. "You're a bastard, Harry, but sleep well." She got up and kissed the bald patch and went off to bed.

* * *

Two nights later Gyseman opened the door of Seddall's house in Phillimore Gardens and Sorrel came in. Harry was on the floor of the drawing room playing with maps. She went round behind him to have a look.

"Albania," she said, "Yugoslavia, the Adriatic. You'll want one of France too."

"Yeah," Harry said. "You told me you'd got news. What is it?"

Sorrel threw her coat on a chair and settled herself along the chesterfield, pulling cushions about her. "This is a hungry girl," she said, "and what about a drink? What's that smell? It's those freesias, why all those freesias?"

"Dinner in half an hour or so," Seddall said, and got up to fetch her a drink. "This old dame at High Street Ken. underground was selling freesias, I took a fancy to them. Here."

Sorrel took the glass and swallowed. "Thanks. What's for dinner?"

"I'm cooking halibut," Gyseman said.

Sorrel raised her eyebrows. "Not again, Mick! Tempting Providence, aren't we?"

"Sorrel," Harry said. "You've got news, all right? Make a report, for pity's sake!"

"I like Jennifer Knight," she said. "I'm going back to see her again. One of those big farms in north Norfolk, flat flat country, all that sky. Don't like the husband so much. He's been farming there for thirty years and he's rooted out all the hedges, prairie farming, dustbowl stuff, dead keen on making money."

"Get down to it, Sorrel," Harry said, and immediately and illogically picked her up on what she had just said. "Jennifer lives off the money, too, doesn't she? Is she complaining about the hedges? Everyone up there was pulling the hedges out after the war."

"He's a pleasant enough man to meet, I admit it."

"You're getting notions, that's what it is," Seddall said gloomily. "It's incipient feminism. Soon you'll be no good to us."

"Roll on the day," Sorrel said sweetly. "Well now. David Marsham sent her a brotherly letter in the autumn. Mostly he sent postcards with jokes on them, not letters. This letter was rather solemn, she thought it was the sort of letter soldiers send before they go into action. He'd never done that before, that sort of letter. Also, she felt it was as if he wanted to tell her something but couldn't quite get round to it. That's the first part."

Mick asked her: "Did you see the letter?"

"No, she hadn't kept it. It was only after he was killed she began to think about it like that."

Harry thought. "That's not so much," he said.

"I think it is," Sorrel said simply. "She's a sensible woman and not the kind who dramatizes things. I understood her, the way she said it. I believe her."

"So what's the second part?"

"He had a friend, very close friend, French Army officer called Adhemar. Marsham saved his life once. Adhemar wasn't fascist enough at Algiers so he made enemies up above and got shunted into arms procurement. He was at a weapons display on Salisbury Plain when a rocket went wrong and Marsham spotted it before anyone else. Threw Adhemar off the observation tower they were standing on and jumped on top of him. There had been seven others in that group and three were killed and the rest lost arms and legs and things and were horribly burned.

"Adhemar told Jennifer this himself, Marsham took him up there one day to meet her. Adhemar told her he'd never seen a man move faster in a thing like that. She said you could tell there was a close bond between them, though they were both undemonstrative men. She thinks it is very likely that her brother would have written to Adhemar the same kind of letter he wrote her, but that he might very well have told Adhemar what he wanted to tell her but felt he shouldn't.''

"I get you," Harry said. "The parcel he sent off from Hereford.''

"Exactly, what he called his last will *and* testament, remember. I asked her about Marsham's will, and she said he'd made it years ago leaving everything, more or less, to her children. So that parcel wasn't his will in any ordinary sense. I wonder what it was.''

"So do I," Harry said. "So indeed do I.''

"So I presume we're going to spend some of your leave in France," Sorrel said.

"We have no choice, it seems. Where does Adhemar live, she did *know* where Adhemar lives?''

"Certainly she did. He lives near a place called Dieulefit in Drôme, about twenty miles east of Montelimar. France in May, what joy! I have the address, so you'll have to take me too.''

"You have done well, Blake, but surely not that well. All you had to do was go and talk to the woman. It was Mendham who traced her for us, and Mick here has really come up with something.''

"Is that so?" Sorrel said.

"Apparently I have," Gyseman said. "I thought it was a bit conjectural, but the boss has taken to it like a duck to water.''

"Hence all the maps, no doubt," and Sorrel heaved herself out of the sofa. "Show me.''

"I'll look after the fish," Gyseman said. "Nor rain or mud, nor shit or blood, shall stand between me and this halibut.'' He went off to the kitchen.

"First of all," Harry said, "we have this story about the Wessex helicopter crash into the Atlantic, twelve SAS lost and the rest aircrew. No names given, you'll notice, and I find that unusual. The SAS are careful about giving out names, certainly, but they usually identify their casualties. Right?"

"Right," Sorrel said. "Don't I get to read it?"

"You don't need to read it, I've just told it you. What you want to read is this." He gave her a photocopy of a news story, not about the Wessex. "Note that the Wessex story is dated Wednesday and this one Thursday, the day after."

Sorrel sat on the piano stool with the cutting in her hand. "Why would they not give the names of the SAS men who were killed?" she asked.

"Say it was Arkley who fed in that story, just let's assume it was Arkley, then he probably thought the less information there was about a phony story the less chance there was of someone taking a second look at it."

"If you have to tell a lie, keep it simple," Sorrel said. "Yes, that makes sense."

"Now read that," Harry said.

While Harry walked about the room sniffing at the freesias, Sorrel read the cutting from *The Times*.

ALBANIA CLAIMS ARMY
FOILED CIA BID TO
ASSASSINATE LEADERS

Belgrade (Reuters)—The Albanian Government stated today that an attempt by agents of the American Central Intelligence Agency to assassinate the country's leadership had been foiled "as easily as previous similar attempts whether by the ambitious

imperialist powers or the ferocious treachery of our
neighbours.'' This last is taken to be a reference to
Yugoslavia, since reports have appeared from time
to time in the Albanian press claiming armed Yugo-
slavian intruders had been shot while trying to land
on the Albanian coast.

The American Embassy here promptly issued a
rebuttal in which it described the Albanian statement
as ''characteristic of the paranoid imaginings of that
isolated country.''

The Albanian statement was issued in Tirana by
the official Albanian news agency ATA and said in
part: ''A clumsy attempt to murder senior members
of the Politburo of the People's Socialist Republic of
Albania, during a visit to the Vau i Dejes hydro-
power station on the Drin River in northern Albania,
was made yesterday by gunmen of the United States
Central Intelligence Agency. The eleven would-be
assassins were shot dead by the vigilant units of the
People's Army.''

The news agency goes on to suggest that the so-
called CIA men, who it said had landed by parachute
between Vau i Dejes and Shkoder (Scutari), had been
assisted by the Yugoslavs. Vau i Dejes is eleven miles
by road from Shkoder, which stands on the south
end of Lake Shkoder. The southern part of the lake
lies in Albania and the northern part in Yugoslavia.

''That's it, absolutely. The Wessex crash report gives
twelve and the Albanian reports eleven intruders killed.''
Sorrel let out a long, shuddering sigh, as if her breathing had been stopped by what she had read. She felt that
she was preparing herself for a shock, though she could
not see what that would be; they had learned much in the

past two days, but she had not had time to assimilate it all and make sense of it. All the same, she recognized a growing feeling of reluctance to meet a truth that was coming towards her, and she tried to stop her mind drawing the shapes of the pattern together.

Yet here was Harry Seddall, watching her with that close over-observant look that cats have, in those yellowy catlike eyes of his. "What do you make of it, then?" he demanded.

"It's too sudden, and for some reason I don't *want* to make anything of it." She handed him the cutting and stood up. "Can I get myself a whisky?"

"Sure," he said. "I'll tell you one thing. There's no way even this government would have landed the SAS in Albania."

Sorrel sat on the stool again and swallowed a large gulp of Scotch. "I needed that. The Albanians said they were CIA."

"I don't think I worry about that," Harry said, "in fact I know I don't. Official statements about things like that, and lots of other things too these days, are just versions of events."

"Very well," Sorrel said, and plunged in. "Let's look at it. We have twelve men reported killed in a crash and one of them was James Wolf. We think Wolf is still alive, though, and that he's going around killing people. We think he killed Blacklock, and a few days after that there was a form of CIA presence, jointly with a French presence of uncertain status, as Kenna put it, making an armed raid on Blacklock's house. We think the Franco-American group wanted to make sure Blacklock had left no bits of paper around that would expose a thing they didn't want exposed. We think that because that's what *we* were look-

ing for at Mustell, or that kind of thing, when they so
rudely interrupted us. All right so far?''

Seddall shunted the maps out of the way and leaned
back on his hands. ''Go ahead,'' he said.

''There are accidents people escape from and survive,
but a crash in the Atlantic in November is not one of them.
I mean no survivors were reported, and I mean you can't
rescue yourself from mid-ocean on your own. On the other
hand, if twelve men went into Albania and one survived
the firefight that the Albanians refer to, it is conceivable
that he could get away, especially if he is SAS. Whatever
the odds against it, it is conceivable, it could happen,
which is not the case with the Wessex crash.''

Harry got to his knees, took her glass, and stood up
with it and brought it back refreshed.

''Thanks,'' Sorrel said. ''Well, how are we doing?''

''You're doing what we pay you for,'' Harry said, making himself comfortable again on the carpet. ''Who could
ask for more?''

''Compliments,'' Sorrel said. ''Forward then, and we
come now to the question of what Colonel Seddall wants.''

''Oh, we do, do we?''

''Yes, my colonel, we do. Whether it is James Wolf who
killed Blacklock or not, what you want much more than
you want to catch up with Wolf, is to put the skids under
anyone up there in those high places of Whitehall who
deserves having the skids put under them, and in this case
we think Blacklock may have been one, that Arkley may
be another, and that there are bound to be others as well,
if they have in fact brought off this raid into Albania and
have been able to pass it off as a helicopter crash two or
three thousand miles somewhere else, if you see what I
mean?''

''Jolly nearly. It's time you had dinner, I think.''

"I may be a little bit juiced, Harry, but I know damn well how your prejudices work. We have to focus on Wolf, that's what we have to do, we don't even know if it is Wolf yet. The present you gave to that boy you dined in the Green Dragon to pass on to his CO, has there been any response to that yet?"

"No, not a word. That was only forty-eight hours ago, you know."

"That's two *days*! You should have shown the knife to the boy. If it meant anything to him he'd have reacted, and then you'd have known."

"No he wouldn't," Harry said comfortably. "He'd have taken it straight to the CO on his own account, if it did mean anything to him. And as to reacting, all he'd have said was that it made one think of the knife that put twenty wounds into Adam of Genoa for preaching against simony in fourteen whatever-it-was. That boy was so cool the ice in his Perrier didn't melt all evening."

"Perrier?" Sorrel looked at her empty glass, and set it down carefully on a piece of music lying on the piano behind her. "I thought you said he talked about wine."

"Oh, he did, but he wasn't drinking it. These SAS lads know when to keep their wits about them."

"Well, what do you know about that? I'm getting ticked off for drinking too much. Come on, let's go and see how Mick's getting on with the fish."

Seddall came to his feet and said. "Yes, I think it's that time."

The telephone rang and Seddall picked it up and gave his name, then said: "Can't tell you, I'm afraid. You don't have to think about that. Whatever needs to be done, I'll see it gets done."

He put the phone down. "Sorrel," he said. "It's Wolf all right. It was his knife."

Harry smiled. "All he said was: 'Where did you get it?' "

"That was the CO?"

Harry picked up a vase of freesias that he happened to be passing. "Let's have these with us in the dining room. I've told you all he said. He never said his name but that's who it was, all right, that's who it was."

15

AS THE BUS WENT DOWN THE STEEP HILL INTO CAUDEBEC the sun came out. Its light came and went through the trees that bordered the road and batted at his eyelids until he woke. He had a glimpse of the great church built at the wish of Henry of Navarre, and then the bus came to a halt and he got out. He stood blinking the sleep out of his eyes, getting his bearings, then walked down the rue des Templiers and round the corner to the street where he had left the car. As he passed the entrance to the hotel car park he saw it, a two-year-old Citroen DS he had bought at Christmas-time in Nyons. He walked on towards the river.

Christmas-time, he recalled Christmas Day at Adhemar's house in the Dauphiné, the snow a tearing blizzard outside and a huge fire of logs in the great fireplace with the feast on the long table, and just he and the colonel and the dog Bayard. He wished he had gone into that valley with David and the rest of them.

He came out of himself and found he was standing

stockstill in the middle of the pavement staring down at the ground. His face felt pulled in on to the bone and the emotions that were doing this to him touched him with unease, even with a sense of alarm. He set down his grip and rubbed his face with his hands and looked about him. No one was paying him any attention. He hefted the grip and walked round the corner of the hotel and up the steps to the front door.

Madame was at the desk, a strong, capable attractive woman near fifty, and she remembered him at once. "Your room is ready for you, the same room as before. For one night?"

"One night, thanks," he said as he took the key. "Thank you for letting me leave the car here. I hope it was not in the way—I meant to leave the keys with you so that it could be moved if necessary, but I forgot." This was a lie, since if for any reason someone had opened the boot and looked inside, there would have been trouble.

"No problem," she said. "You look tired—and what have you done to your face?"

He smiled. "A riding accident. But, yes, I *am* tired. I shall sleep this afternoon, and I shall be in for dinner."

It was the smaller of the two hotels standing almost side by side looking across the Seine, but the food was out of this world. He had already decided, standing there, that he would have trout tonight, among other things.

He went through the hotel and out at the back into the car park to examine the car. He opened the boot and lifted the rug and saw the machine-pistol and the box of ammunition, put the grip in there and closed it again. He went upstairs and fell on to the bed. He had taken care not to look in the mirror.

He slept for three hours and then lay in the bath, thinking it out. The letter Pruvot had written for him had been posted three days ago in Le Havre at the main post office. It would be in Paris by now, so they would be there tomorrow, perhaps only one of them, but with luck both of them, the Frenchman and the American. Yet it was the Englishman he wanted most. Pruvot had not known the Englishman's name, but perhaps the Englishman would come as well, and he would know him if he saw him from Pruvot's description.

It was a goodish drive to the house at Boissy–les–Anges where Pruvot had summoned them to meet him—to meet Pruvot. He smiled slightly; they would get a surprise. Then his face composed itself into its calm, almost blank, expression; the bleakness he had felt this morning out in the street had gone, for the time being at least, and now that he was aware of it lurking in him he would use willpower to keep it down until tomorrow was over. That kind of thing impaired efficiency.

Not that he expected too much of a hassle at Boissy. It was a house the CIA used for planning meetings, that sort of thing, and Pruvot thought there would be no more than two or three people there on a regular basis, apart from the French couple who looked after the place.

He got out of the bath, dried himself and dressed, and went shopping for shirts and underwear; bought a pair of cords and a sweater, the cords black and the sweater dark blue; bought toothbrush and toothpaste and walked slowly back towards the hotel. On the way there he sat by the river and smoked a pipe, watching a big freighter, then another one, come downstream under the high span of the bridge and pass him on their way to the sea.

For dinner he had trout as he had promised himself, and roast duck, and concluded the meal, since he was in that country, with bread and Camembert. While he was drinking coffee the proprietress came up to him and asked if the meal was to his liking.

"I was in ecstasies, and still am," he replied.

"You have rested," she said. "You are less fatigued."

"I am a new man, but it was your dinner that did that for me."

She laughed. "You will sleep well tonight, I think, and in the morning you will be wholly refreshed."

"It is a fact, madame, that I do not sleep more than three or four hours at night, but my nap this afternoon was a rare luxury."

"Ah!" she said. "Then you should not be drinking coffee."

"It is also a rare luxury," he assured her solemnly. "Now, since I am bound to wake early, I have it in mind to set off early, so may I settle my bill tonight?"

"Certainly, if you wish, but we are up early in this business and you could pay in the morning and have breakfast before you go."

He was prepared for that. "Sometimes when I wake and cannot get back to sleep I become restless, and if that happens I would wish to feel free to leave. It might be as early as four or five."

"That is early," she agreed, but having heard his explanation in advance, there was little surprise in her voice. "In that case, we shall make out your bill tonight and you can leave by the back door in the morning."

"Thank you, madame."

"For nothing," she said. "It is no problem for the hotel. What sleep you have, sleep well."

She went off to another table. He was content, now, that his early departure would seem nothing remarkable. Later, he paid his bill and went up to bed.

* * *

HE DROVE OVER THE BRIDGE WITH THE LIGHT OPENING
the eastern sky, and set off to the south. Mist hung over
the fields and crossed the road in patches, but he had plenty
of time and took his journey at an easy pace, watching for
farm tractors, used to having this time of day to themselves, to burst out on to the road with drivers probably
wearing earphones and listening to stereo at full blast.

After a while the sun rose and burned off the mist, and
soon he saw the bulk of Chartres cathedral rise over the
plain, its mass an incredible bulk scaled so to the land-
scape that it became a feature made by nature rather than
by man. After Chartres he stopped for coffee and brioches
in a village, and when he resumed his journey he moved
into a different mode, doing so by a deliberate act. He
watched the road before and behind with constant alert-
ness, noted the vehicles he saw so that he would know if
he saw them again, and after five or ten miles of this he
waited till he had a clear road and turned into a side road,
where he stopped the car beside a copse.

He went round to the back of the car and took a Walther
PPK and a Smith & Wesson from the boot identical to the
weapons he had carried in England and got back in the
car. He checked over both pistols and loaded them, and
then put the Walther in a shoulder holster and the revolver
on the passenger seat with a newspaper over it.

He got out of the car again and took the machine-pistol
from the boot and concealing it under his weatherproof
coat went into the copse. He found a decent-sized beech
tree and stationed himself about fifteen feet away. Through
the thin woodland he could see that there was no one moving on the side road; for the rest he knew that there was
always someone about in the countryside, but he shrugged.

He could see no one, and that was the best he could do. He fired a short burst at the tree, examined the tree, and fired another burst. The second burst hit the tree over an area between four and six feet from the ground; the first had been higher.

He took the machine-pistol back into the car with him, discarded the partly used clip of ammunition, laying it on the floor of the car behind him, and loaded the weapon. He laid it on the passenger seat with the newspaper over it and put the Smith & Wesson in the clip holster at the back of his belt, put the car back on the road, turned it in a field gateway and went back to the main road.

The sun was well up now and was making the day warm. He pulled the coat off the back seat and threw it on top of the newspaper covering the machine-pistol and opened the side window, put his arm on the window ledge and drove at a medium pace, again watching the traffic before and behind him, and also, now and again, watching the sky.

He came to Boissy–les–Anges and drove slowly but with no uncertainty through the town, taking inventory of the people he saw and the vehicles, looking for the unusual— or the familiar. When he had left Boissy behind, the road skirted a park on his left with a six-foot wall, and after he had been running beside the wall for almost a mile he turned the car away from the park and on to an unmetalled road that climbed steeply. At the top of the hill he looked down in front of him and saw a farm about a mile away, and no other houses except for those of Boissy on his right, even further off. He reversed the Citroen into another way-ward track which petered out after a hundred yards. When he got out he left the keys in the ignition. The car could be seen from the farm, but not from the road. So far, everything had been as Pruvot had said it would be.

He went around to the boot and unlocked it with a sec-

ond set of keys and took out the grip he had left there
overnight, and which had come with him on the bus to
Caudebec. He went out of the lane on the passenger side
of the car and took the coat and the machine-pistol with
him.

He did not return down the hill the way he had come,
but instead ran down the side of a field, vaulted the fence
at the bottom, crossed the road and scaled the wall in what
seemed to be one unbroken movement, having laid the
grip on top of the wall before he went over and now removing it as soon as he touched ground on the other side.

Pruvot had counselled him well. Fifty yards from him
was the chapel, a small building reflecting, so far as it
religiously might, the Second Empire style of the house
that stood a good quarter of a mile beyond it. As he came
over the wall the chapel sheltered him from most of the
house and when he was halfway to the chapel he was hidden from every window on the facade.

Once he reached the chapel a difficulty presented itself.
To enter it he must put himself in full view of the house.
The house on this side faced south and the chapel stood
parallel to it with the only door on its east end. He thought
that if he placed himself at the absolute corner of the little
porch and rolled himself vertically, as it were, round into
the porch and did it fast enough he would hardly be seen,
and if a glimpse of movement were noticed it might well
be taken for one of those illusions of the eye. It was doing
it fast enough that was the problem. The grip he carried
was heavy and its contents cumbersome, and if he carried
it there would be no chance of the swiftness of the act
deceiving any watchful eye.

He turned his attention to one of the narrow windows
that pierced the side wall. It was made of leaded squares
of glass in ecclesiastical shades of colour. That would do

it. It would not admit him but it would serve his purpose. He took out the Smith & Wesson as having the least sensitive mechanism, shucked out the cartridges, and tapped with the butt of the pistol at the leaded edge of the window. It conceded nothing. He struck three hard blows, but the glass was more firmly seated in the frame than he had expected. He reloaded the revolver and returned it to his belt.

He looked about him. Nothing but grass and widely spaced, majestic trees. Then the corner of his mouth twitched, he took off the weatherproof coat, laid it on the ground, and filled it with the small stones from the dry course that went round the foot of the chapel walls. Then he gathered it into a bundle and swung it at the window, which went in with a good breaking sound followed by the tinkle of glass on the floor inside. A sound, however, less calculated to attract notice than persistent hammering would have been.

He had trouble balancing the grip on the window ledge, and the task brought an expression almost of distaste to his face. When it was secure he put on the coat again, positioned himself close against the corner of the porch, hugged the machine-pistol to his body, and whisked round into the porch. The chapel door stood ajar and he let himself in, looked quickly around—into the organ loft, down the narrow stair that led to a boiler room—and when he was sure he had the place to himself he consulted his watch. He had three hours to wait. He cleared the fragments of the window from the floor and threw them down the stairs to the boiler room, and when he had done that was about to knock out one of the small panes of glass on the side facing the house when he saw it had been done for him already.

He stood on a pew and looked out. He had a clear sight

of the house. Smoke rose from two of the chimneys, but other than that there was no activity. He settled down to wait.

THEY CAME TOGETHER DRIVEN BY A THIRD MAN. THE Frenchman and the American then, and perhaps the Englishman? No, not the Englishman. The driver opened the rear door of the Mercedes for the other two, and followed them at a respectful distance into the house. In ten minutes they came out again in the same order. His preparations were made and he continued to watch them. As they approached the chapel one of the men waved backwards towards the driver, who was following them, and the man slowed uncertainly and then settled for strolling about on the grass.

When the two men entered the chapel they pushed the door to and looked about them. As they moved their feet resounded from the stone floor under the lofty roof.

One of them began to walk up the chapel and called out: "Pruvot!" He saw an object rolling towards him and panicked, running away from it, going for a gun under his armpit and calling out with half a voice: "Bomb!"

His companion had not yet registered the rolling object when the man who had been waiting for them emerged only three pews away with a machine-pistol in his hands. Neither of them had a gun fisted and ready to fire, and they stood as they were.

"Hands away from the body!" the apparition said. "Right up in the air!"

The object that was not a bomb was at their feet, and he made a momentary gesture of one hand at it, so that they looked down.

"Pruvot is here, gentlemen," he said.

The rest of Pruvot was under the sea, but his head was indeed here, the eyes mournfully closed but the mouth open and shouting at them, and the neck gouted with blood.

One of the men began to speak and the other fell to his knees retching, turning away from the horror on the floor of the chapel. When his gun came out the machine-pistol shot most of his shoulder off and the gun fell, the man was flung against the wall and slid down it to the ground leaving a shining smear of blood down the white wall.

"There is no time now," the man who had shot him said. "This is for eleven men you sent to be killed in Albania."

The bullets from the first burst tore into the chest and stomach of the man who had remained on his feet until then, and the bullets from the second into the man against the wall.

The man who had killed them went at once to the door, and saw through the opening that the third man, who had been running at the chapel, presumably on hearing the first shots, had correctly interpreted the two longer bursts of fire as meaning that he was hopelessly outgunned, so that he now turned and ran hell for leather across the grass towards the house. It was not heroic, but it was the best thing to do in the circumstances, and he lived to fight another day.

The killer first opened wide the door then dragged the two men, one after the other, down the chapel and heaved them in among the wooden pews. He went to the grip and took from it a can of petrol, which he splashed over the bodies, dead or still dying he neither knew nor cared, and over the wood round about them. He laid the can on its

side with the petrol still pouring out, on the far side of the
bodies from the door, and stepped back and lit a match
and tossed it into the petrol soaked area. The match went
out. He pulled a bundle of matches out so that they pro-
truded from the end of the box, lit them and threw the
whole box.

He was running for the door when the petrol went up
but even so he thought the flash of igniting vapour had
caught him and he threw himself headlong out of the door,
took the machine-pistol from where he had laid it and
thought as he did so it should have been left outside, worth
remembering that, and ran for the wall. As he topped it
he glanced back and saw two men on the steps of the house
looking towards the chapel, which had some smoke now
coming from the broken window and rising to the sky;
and he saw the white Mercedes being driven round the
side of the house out of sight. That man knew his stuff.
He was protecting his transport in case of a frontal attack
on the house.

Once over the wall he started at a good but unremark-
able pace up the hill and as he did so heard the petrol can
explode. That would hold them back, unless they were top
material. It would take a lot of keenness to run over open
ground at a machine-pistol and at a site where things were
exploding. He reckoned on fire engines but no more police
activity than an ordinary fire calls for: crowd control and
after the ashes had cooled the usual search for evidence of
arson. They'd find that all right, but not for a few hours
yet.

As he reached the car he heard them coming and he
climbed the bank of the lane and saw two fire tenders and
a police car go past on the road below. He got into the car
and drove down the hill and went after them, but by the

time he reached the entrance to the house they were already lost to view in the park.

When he struck the main road for Orléans he put his foot down and by early evening he was one among hundreds eating at a service station on the Autoroute du Sud.

16

"THIS IS THE PLACE," SORREL SAID. "LE POET-LAVAL. We should stop here so that I can have a look at the map. From now on we'll have a pretty warreny lot of little roads to negotiate."

"You mean navigate," Harry said.

"What do you mean, I mean navigate?"

"The word you want is navigate, not negotiate."

"You're an ungrateful hound, Harry. I've brought you this far. What does it matter whether it was navigating or negotiating? There's a car park under those trees, where they're playing boules."

He brought the Renault 25, hired at Lyons, to rest in the shade. "I like warreny, though," he said. "A good word. Let us go and make like tourists in yon café, while you negotiate with your map."

They sat outside in the sun. Sorrel ordered a *citron pressé*, and Harry asked for croissants, of which there were none; nor were there brioches, and he settled with a dismal countenance for bread and jam and coffee.

"I can get croissants and brioches all over bloody London," he said crossly. "Why can't I get them in bloody France?"

"You're too late, that's why," Sorrel said. "These places open at dawn. Eat your nice bread and be grateful."

Harry ate his nice bread. "It's ten o'clock," he said. "It is dawn. How's the map-reading coming along?"

"There's going to be some trial and error. It's not much of a scale, and since we can't ask the way I'm trying to work out how to cover the ground without looking too conspicuous."

"That kind of house, a *gentilhommerie*, we'll know it when we see it," Harry said confidently. "This valley seems to be all carved up into those peasant smallholdings that irritate the Common Market Agricultural Commission so much, with houses to match."

"Some quite big farmhouses."

"Only among the apple orchards. Apples seem to be where the money is round here, or was once, anyway."

"Why are you being so smug and professorial?" Sorrel asked.

"Yeah," Harry said, smiling a sardonic smile at himself. "That's because I don't know how to get Adhemar to trust me when so far as we know he's Captain Wolf's only ally, and I'm hunting Wolf."

Sorrel looked across the road at the men playing boules. "Can't you lie to him successfully? Tell him you're after the same people Wolf is after? It's partly true, isn't it?"

Harry lit a Gauloise. "This is not bad, you know. We should be here on holiday. Look at Adhemar's record. Dien Bien Phu in Indo-China; Algiers, where he tangled with the top brass because he didn't like it that the FLN were being tortured, not to mention their wives and sweethearts. He's a tough man, and he won't trust anyone lightly. He'll smell a lie, that's what I think."

"So what are you going to do, just drive up there and hope for the best? Or do you want me to captivate him?" She turned her head to the breeze and looked captivating.

"Well, no offence intended, but no," Harry said. "The opposite, I think. I want you to stay out of the way, if we can fix that. Wander about in the garden, or something, in an innocent way. We're both Army, he and I. I'll see if I can win any fellow-feeling out of that."

A big white Mercedes with tinted windows coursed through the village. It had luggage piled on the roof, a Deutschland plate on the back, and five or six dimly visible occupants.

"During the war," Harry said, "the Germans left this place pretty much to itself, the Resistance was strong hereabouts. Every now and then a column would drive in from Montelimar to Dieulefit up the road—where we'll probably stay the night—stood about for a couple of hours and then drove back again. The place made them nervous. Now they have holiday houses here. Adhemar was in the Resistance."

"How do you know all this?" Sorrel asked.

"Did my homework."

"You haven't met Adhemar yet, but you like him already, don't you? You imagine him as your kind of man. Why don't I just stay here and let you get on with it?"

Seddall frowned into the sunlight. The Mercedes had returned and pulled off the road under the trees. One of the tinted windows dropped and a voice called out to the men playing boules, who seemed not to hear. The door opened and a man got out and went over to the players.

One of them pointed back down the road, and the man re-
entered the car which set off in the direction from which
it had first come.

"The reason I want you with me," Harry said, "is that
I've a feeling things may start to happen around here soon,
and I don't want to divide my forces."

Sorrel drank the last of her *citron* and made, from one
cause or another, a wry mouth. "You put Mick out back
at—" she scanned the map to find the name "—Bégude-de-
Mazenc to keep an eye on the road. Does that mean you
think Mick can look after himself, but I can't?"

"Don't be an ass, Sorrel. I know quite well you can
look after yourself. I wanted that road watched and I want
you with me. Also," he added inconsequently, "I don't
much care what happens to Mick."

She had worked alongside Harry long enough to be almost inured to his habit of cynicism, and not always to
take it at face value. This remark about Gyseman, however, took her aback. She stared across the table at what
appeared to be a caricature of Seddall at his most unpleasant: the eyes bland and very open, the brow wrinkled into
corrugations so supercilious that they looked like a piece
of bad acting, and the lips held derisively and loosely apart
with tobacco smoke flowing out in a measured, histrionic
stream as if their owner wanted her to believe they marked
the entrance to the cave of the Oracle at Delphi. Harry
was being enigmatic.

There was nothing to be made of this, Sorrel decided,
and she shook her head and stood up. "Perhaps we should
get going," she said.

"Sure," Harry said, and put some money on the table.

Behind the village of Le Poet-Laval the high, wide valley in which it stood began to lift into the mountains whose
wild peaks and ridges, gorges and deep-set rivers, spread

in their confused mass to the great mountain ranges of the
Italian frontier. The search for Adhemar's house took the
Renault into a miniature version of this incomprehensible
terrain, and after more than an hour of exploration disen-
chantment set in.

"Nothing for it," Seddall said. "I'll ask this chap."

He left the car and went up to an old man who was
hammering nails through a faded notice board into a tree.
The board, which had not been repainted for ten years or
more, said on it: *"Chasse privée"*.

"Monsieur," Harry said. "Can you tell me where I
might find Le Poet-Grignan, M. Adhemar's house?"

"Ah! Bonjour, monsieur," the ancient said. *"Le Poet-
Grignan*, it's over there." He nodded over Harry's shoulder into an impenetrable mass of forest. Harry shrugged,
to convey that all he could see was the trees.

"Ah! Look, *monsieur*, I'll show you."

From the top of the bank on the other side of the road
he pointed again, and Harry saw the grey roof of a house
beyond the trees. They had a cigarette each, approved of
the weather, deplored the long winter and the unseasonal
coldness of the year up to last week, and Harry returned
to the car.

"We tootle along a bit and turn right," he said.

"I knew it must be round here somewhere," Sorrel
said.

They came to a break in the trees where the road turned
back on itself, and to two gateposts set in a crescent of
stone that curved away from the roadside. The gate was
open and the Renault entered the drive, which ran at an
angle for the corner of the house that rose behind a walled
garden. The car turned the end of the house and found
itself in a small courtyard, composed of the bulk of the
house, nearest the road, on their left; and in front of them

and on their right a building of smaller scale, rising to only two floors, which looked a good deal older than the four-storeyed wing on their left.

Beside Sorrel a carved doorway, long built into the wall of the house, was surmounted by a coat of arms and the date 1470. White roses were coming into flower about the door. She thought she would like to live here, probably forever.

As they climbed out of the car Harry was confronted by a man an inch or two shorter than himself, a small wiry man almost bald, with a greying moustache, a stern and serious face, but a pleasant enough smile. The man came out of a gate where the garden wall met the end of the house, with a liver and white spaniel at his heels.

"In what way may I help you?" the man asked politely.

You could explain to me, Harry said silently, why you are wearing a pistol under that sports coat. "My name is Seddall," he said. He gave the man his card, which gave his name and his own address in London. "I hope you won't mind our calling on you like this."

"Of course not," the man said without much meaning in his voice. "Colonel H. R. Seddall," he read. "I am Paul Adhemar. We have something in common, Colonel."

"I had hoped you would think so," Harry said frankly. "May I present Miss Blake."

"Sorrel Blake," she said as they shook hands.

"Sorrel," he said with a warming smile. "*La petite oseille*, we call it. A charming name, and well chosen."

Behind the courtesy of his manners, and behind the suspicion in his eyes, a lot of work was going on. He's trying to make us out, Seddall thought. We've come to the right place: Wolf has been here, is perhaps here right now. Adhemar knows we're the kind of people he'd get on with, in the normal way of things, but since he's committed to

Wolf—how far committed, though?—he has a problem on his hands.

"Colonel Adhemar," Harry said, "I have come to see you because we have a mutual interest in the survivor of a tragic event which took place in the autumn."

Adhemar turned to examine the morello cherry tree es-paliered against the wall beside him, where bees trafficked among the pink blossoms. The dog, which was sitting, looked at Harry when its master made this move, and grunted as if to say: Do not provoke us too far.

"Bayard," Adhemar said mildly to the dog, and smiled a little as he faced Harry again, and studied him now instead of the cherry tree, a man not much taller than himself and wearing a checked shirt and cotton trousers. "You are not armed, Colonel Seddall?"

"I have a pistol in the car. So does Miss Blake."

"Let us talk in the house," Adhemar said.

"I should like to talk with you alone, if I may," Harry said.

Adhemar looked at him. "We are alone," he said. "I am alone here, except for Bayard."

"I mean by myself, without Miss Blake."

"You wish to deny me the pleasure of Miss Blake's company? For what reason? She is not in your confidence?"

"She is completely in my confidence. I want to meet you as one man to another, as one soldier to another, if you like."

Adhemar, though he was still finding his way with this one, said with a glimmer of humour: "As colonel to colonel, perhaps. Unhappily, there are colonels and colonels."

"Sure," Harrry said, "and it takes one to know one."

Adhemar peered up at him, his brown eyes making a

close scrutiny of the other man's face. "What shall we do with Miss Blake? Leave her in the car with the pistols?"

"Dammit!" Seddall said. "You can have the bloody pistols. Do you think I would shoot my host in his own house?"

It was as if Adhemar, despite his upbringing and the generation to which he belonged, found this quaintly old-fashioned. "Stranger things have happened," he said. "Your point of view, if it is your point of view, has its appeal, but in realistic terms it is absurd. Miss Blake," he said, "if you would like to walk in the garden, Bayard will look after you, won't you, Bayard?" Sorrel thought the word he used to the dog meant guard, not take care of.

The dog stood up and looked at its master, who nodded towards Sorrel. She knelt down and Bayard went to her and sniffed her knees, and she turned down its ear, which was folded inside out.

The two men—the two colonels—went into the house, and she went through the gateway into the garden, fol-lowed, and then preceded, by the spaniel. The garden was walled on three sides and edged on its fourth side by a tall hedge of beech, beyond which was a lawn that ran along the face of the house. She found a bench in a rose arbour set halfway along a herbaceous border. The dog put its chin on the seat and she scratched it, and fondled his head. In front of her a path crossed the garden away from her, leading to a sundial in the middle of the garden, which was divided into four squares, part given to vegetables, part to soft fruit and flowers. At the far end of the path the ground rose gently almost to the top of the wall there. The slope was grassed and made a small orchard of apple and pear trees.

"Come on, Bayard," she said, and walked towards it

past the stone sundial, down the path bright with tulips and glowing with the deep colours of the wallflowers whose scent perfumed the air, through the old garden basking in the early heat of the year from the sun high in the blue sky, until she reached the orchard in its blossom.

"Let's sit on the grass," she said to the dog. The dog sat beside her, pleased with the heat above and the cool of the long grass under its belly. "Is that good, Bayard?" she asked it.

The dog, however, growled as she stroked its head and came to its feet facing the wall behind her. Sorrel turned and saw a man lying along the wall above her.

"Bayard, is it?" he said. "Hallo, Bayard. You're Sorrel Blake, Harry Seddall's sidekick. I'm—well they call me Sandy, probably best to leave it at that for now; no need for names; friend of Jamie Wolf's."

Pistols in the car, Sorrel thought bitterly. The dog growled again and whined as if about to bark.

"Hold on, Bayard," the man said hastily. "Friend of Jamie's but haven't seen him since September, Miss Blake, not since he left Hereford, you know, to go off on that . . . exercise."

"You're from Hereford?"

"One of the good guys, I promise you. Come to brief you and Colonel Seddall, if you could pass him my message when I've done." He cast a look behind him. "Do you mind if I come down off this wall? A bit visible up here."

Sorrel thought of Adhemar trying to assess herself and Harry Seddall. She rather took to this man on top of the wall, but what had that to do with anything? She made up at least half of her mind.

"All right," she said. "Come down but stay by the wall."

When he was down she and Bayard were twelve feet further away, near the foot of the grass slope. The dog bridled at the man's descending into *his* garden, but quietened to her hand on his shoulder. The youth, for he was plainly not far from his teens if indeed he had left them, sat with his back to the wall. He had that look of rediscovered innocence that young serving officers have when they have faced death and dealt it to others. He had brisk fair hair, grey eyes, white teeth, a tough chin, a good wide mouth and pink skin like a baby's or so it seemed from the distance of four yards.

"Can you *prove* anything?" she asked him. "Can you identify yourself?"

"Indirectly," he said.

"Then do it," she said rudely. "For all I know you're a KGB assassin. Russians can look pretty too, you know."

The pink in his complexion augmented itself. "Right. I know that Colonel Seddall took one of our chaps out to dinner at the Green Dragon and spent three hours trying to get something out of him. And I know that you set a floozie on to Sam—on to someone else—and that he got so carried away he told her about David Marsham sending a parcel off from the post office."

He stopped, noticing that the colour in Sorrel's face was reciprocating his own. "I say, are *you* the floozie?"

"I was the floozie," Sorrel said. "I'm not any more."

"I am deeply sorry," the youth said earnestly. "He said you were a knock-out but he said . . ."

"I can imagine the rest," Sorrel said. "Now that we know each other, so to speak, you can get down to cases, all right?"

"Quite right. First, a man called Arkley has been asking questions about Captain Wolf. Poor Jamie," he said with a grim set to the young face, "it sounds as if he might have gone over the top. Justified too, maybe, but over the top is over the top.'' He looked down at the ground for a moment and pulled a piece of grass to cover the moment, and began to chew it. ''That's one, right? Man called Arkley asking questions. Two is, someone burgled Mrs Knight's house—David's sister's house, that is. We thought they might have found this address. We know she gave it to you.''

''How do you know that, about the burglary?''

''We look after our own, you know, within reason. Jenny Knight phoned the boss at Hereford, you see, after your visit, and what with that and Seddall and you asking around among our blokes, we've had a few of the boys lying out at her place ever since.''

''Not much good, were they,'' Sorrel asked, testing, ''if they let the place be burgled? Whoever it was might have killed her, might have done anything.''

''No chance. The boys outside saw them go in and the boys inside were in the same room with them, all the time—the same rooms.''

''You were there, weren't you?''

''Actually, yes. It was my little show, till I got called off to come down here.''

''Are you allowed to play around like that?''

His equanimity was undisturbed. ''Jenny's house, that wasn't playing around. Useful little exercise, lying low all over the place. No one in Norfolk knows we're there— we're still covering the house—outside Jenny and her husband. Down here, I'm on leave. So is Colonel Seddall, I do believe.'' He said this last with a deliberately sly smile.

''My,'' Sorrel said. ''You do have your sources, don't you?''

''Believe you me,'' he said crisply. ''We need 'em in our business.''

"The fellow I went out with," Sorrel asked, curious. "Did he tell the boss, as you call him, that he'd told me about Marsham posting the parcel?"

"Absolutely. Got a bollocking. Knew he would, naturally. It was bloody careless. We don't *tell* anybody anything at all."

"Is he still with the regiment?" Sorrel was chewing her lip.

"Not decided, I think. Very likely to be out. Look here, don't you worry about that. You were doing your job, and rather well by all accounts, and he failed to do his. He won't hold it against you himself. Now, rest of story. We think it was MI6 broke into Jenny's house, and we think they'll very likely be around or send someone around, maybe some of those rather fast-and-loose Intelligence people they seem to go in for over here. So the message is, watch your step, and watch where you've just stepped the moment before, too."

"Yes," Sorrel said. "Yes, indeed. I take your point, and Colonel Seddall will take it too."

The youth stood up and flexed his body. "Time to be off." He put a hand on the wall, then took it off again. "The man you dropped off back down the road a bit—"

"You've been *trailing* us?"

"Watching you. Different thing."

"We never spotted you," she said mortified.

"Most pleasing. Just pass all that on to Colonel Seddall, will you? And the bit about the chap you left in that town back there. I suppose he knows what he's doing."

"What do you mean, does he know what he's doing?"

"No, truly, I think that's all to say about that."

He put his head up into a pear tree and looked out through the leaves and the blossom over the wall, as if he were waiting for something to happen out there.

"Is this all you came to do, deliver your message?" Sorrel asked.

"More or less," he said, still scanning the countryside beyond the wall.

"What about Captain Wolf?"

"What about him?"

"Don't you care what happens to him? If he comes here and MI6 and some French lot are after him? Don't you care about that? Damn it, we're after him too!"

He spared her a glance. "Colonel Seddall will treat him fair, the boss said. That's why he sent me here."

"What's fair? What can be fair for him now?" she demanded, astonished at her sudden vehemence. "A bullet through his head?"

"I know what's up with you," the very young man with the macabre innocence about him said. "You smell him near, on the way here. So do I. I wonder how close he is? Could be fifty yards, fifty miles. Hear this, lady: Jamie's a casualty already, he's gone from us. He's gone berserk, except that's what Vikings did; and Jamie's a Celt, a Highlander. Whatever Highlanders used to be, and not so long ago at that, that's what he's reverted to. Jamie will have to—time to go!"

He came out of the pear tree and stood against the wall, looking at her. "I remember the words he'd have used," he said.

"What words?"

"Jamie will have to dree his own weird," he said, and was gone.

"THAT MAN'S IN TROUBLE," HARRY SAID, WHEN HE HAD turned the car and started down the drive. "He says his phone's been cut and he thinks the house is staked out."

"That would make sense," Sorrel said. "I have lots of news." She passed on the report of MI6 activities in Britain given her by the pink young man from Hereford, and the conclusion that this part of France was likely, therefore, to experience an influx of Intelligence agents.

"That was very civil of Hereford," Harry said.

"How do they know all these things?"

"Even if I knew," Harry said stuffily. "It would not be for me to say."

"There's discretion for you," Sorrel said. "Turn left here, or have you forgotten we have to collect Mick?" The Renault turned on to the Montélimar road. "So how did you come out with Adhemar?"

"Badly. He gave me nothing at all, except that I can go back tomorrow night when he might be at liberty to tell me more. Means he's expecting to hear from Wolf, doesn't it? With the phone out, it means he's expecting a visit from him. If Wolf comes he'll walk into a trap."

"Can't we do something about that? Can't we at least do something about Adhemar? I don't like him sitting there alone with the phone cut off knowing that the place is surrounded."

"He doesn't know that, he just feels it, but I daresay he's right. What with your news and the phone off everything points to it. I suggested in a vague way he might like some company though that's not our business, you know, and I don't see myself exchanging shots with our own blokes from MI6 Paris station or wherever, so I did not sound enthusiastic. He pointed that out himself, in a way. He said he was a party to conspiracy to murder, and left it at that, except for saying that he had no reason to trust me, in the nicest possible way."

"So what do we do?"

"We hang about, that's what we do, and wait to see

how the cards fall. It's not our job to take a hand. Our job is to find out who's dealing the cards.''

He laughed suddenly.

''What's the joke?'' Sorrel asked.

''I was just thinking that Gyseman will have a pretty sore bottom by now.''

17

HE HAD LEFT THE CITROEN IN THE NEXT VALLEY TO THE south and he came now down the mountainside above Adhemar's house. From the crest of the mountain he had seen the sunrise about to break, but he moved down through the trees into a land waiting still for the dawn. He moved fast and straight, even where the trees were sparse, for he was above the early day's mist and if anyone was down there waiting for him, they were below it in the lingering dark.

He had telephoned the house the night before at two of the prearranged hours and both calls had met a dead line, which meant that Adhemar had neglected to pay his phone bill or that something worse had happened: worse was likelier. So he had driven past Montélimar and left the autoroute at Montélimar-sud, and taken the road round by the monastery of Aiguebelle where they made a liqueur, as he had learned from Adhemar and proved for himself, that gave Drambuie a good race.

He had found a good place to lay up the car, out of
sight of the road on a patch of land that looked untended,
and had slept for a few hours. Then he had started over
the mountains, a journey of ten miles or so, a good night
walk that he would have enjoyed except for the cause of
it. He had heard wild boar scuffling and the squeal of their
litter and had walked on with the hair standing up on the
back of his neck, since a wild boar with her young was a
dangerous beast. Sitting on the reverse slope of the mountain from the valley into which he was now descending,
he had watched the light break into the sky and seen cham-
ois fly, so it seemed, across the rocky summit.

The good walk was over now, though, and he had come
to his destination. He picked his place in his memory as
he came in over the mountains, for he had scouted all
these hills when he spent these months with Adhemar. As
he came down now above the house he found the place
and settled in it, waiting for the day to come to the valley,
and for the sun to burn off the mist.

He waited more than two hours. At the end of another
hour he had spotted three of them, and though he did not
suppose that was all, he decided it was all he would be
able to see from here. He noticed particularly the man
covering the kitchen door, which was set in the lowest and
oldest wing of the house. About thirty feet this side of the
house the ground dropped into a meadow and the drop
was a wall of about a yard in height. One of them was
posted in the meadow, harboured by the wall, but some
way to the side from the door into the kitchen. So far so
good.

He watched the house a little longer but learned nothing, and went back over the mountains to where he had
left the car. He had time on his hands and shopping to do,
so he drove round by Nyons, a market town a good way

from Dieulefit which was the smaller town that supplied the valley's immediate needs. There would be some of them at Dieulefit—whoever they were—and doubtless they knew what he looked like. Once he had acquired his simple disguise, he would probably be able to drive through Dieulefit without being recognized.

At Nyons he took a late breakfast, sitting not outside in the sun but at the back of the café. He ordered more coffee and smoked a pipe and read the local paper, and then went out to do his shopping. Fifteen minutes later he came out of a shop for women, carrying a large, a very large, paper bag with the shop's name written on it in flowing script. He went to the car, tossed the bag in the back, and left Nyons on the road for Dieulefit. He came to a picnic spot by a river where two families had spread themselves, and there he pulled the car off the road.

He planned to make a late afternoon call at Adhemar's house. For one thing, he had reasoned that by that time of day they would have had the thought that if he was coming today, then he must be waiting till after dark; for another, the weaker spirits among them would be getting fed up; and for a third, evening follows afternoon, and night follows evening, and he might be glad for the night to retreat towards, given one possible set of circumstances: namely, that he should come out of the house alive.

He lay on the grass, therefore, beside the car, and slept in the warmth of midday.

He woke to a cooling of the air and found he had the place to himself. He went down to the river and splashed water in his face then got into the car. He arranged the weatherproof jacket and the machine-pistol on the seat beside him so that he could pick them up clean with one hand. Then he took the paper bag into the front of the car and took from it a woman's huge straw hat, a scarlet cartwheel, and fixed it on to his head. They did not, after all, know what kind of car he was driving. All they would see was a woman in a straw hat driving up in a Citroen.

He drove down into Dieulefit, remembering it and liking it, and out under the long stretch of plane trees into the valley. No one he passed saw anything remarkable about his appearance. He had been right; no one would look for a man to be under such a hat.

When he came to the gates he turned in and drove easily up the drive and stopped the car at the door of the house. The door was open but no one was in sight. He paused for a moment, lifted the jacket with the machine-pistol inside its folds, got out of the car still wearing the hat and walked into the house. As soon as he was inside he drew the Walther from the shoulder holster and knocked the hat off his head with the back of his hand and let it fall to the floor.

Nothing moved.

He walked through the hall into the drawing room and found Adhemar lying in his favourite armchair, the centre of his body shot to pieces and splinters of rib bone sticking through his shirt. The face gave no sign of the violent death he had suffered. There was more peace on it than it had shown in life, as if Adhemar had found his rest.

The dog lying on the dead man's feet growled. "It's all right, Bayard," he said softly. "It's me." Bayard returned to his mourning, head on paws.

The man went round behind Adhemar and bending down, kissed the top of the dead man's head. When he stood upright again there were three men in the room, one who had come in by the door he had used himself, and two, standing together, who had come in from Adhemar's study. All of them had guns trained on him.

Who *are* these people? he thought. They're holding guns and they're not *using* them.

"Well, well!" one of the two men who were standing side by side said, in English. "Walk into my parlour, eh?"

The Walther was hidden by the back of Adhemar's chair. He lifted it and shot the man by the door and killed the other two with the machine-pistol under the coat on his arm. The machine-pistol, held in his left hand, jumped about all over the place and they were nastily torn up. The man by the door was alive and he asked him: "You English or French, or what?"

"French."

"Bastard!" the man said and shot him between the eyes.

This man had been wearing—was still wearing—a tie. He tore it off him and stuffed it in a pocket to make a tourniquet for his left arm which felt as if it had taken a bad one. It looked bloody enough. There was also a burning on his right thigh but that felt as if it would be all right till it stiffened up. He had got off lightly. The dog, he realized, had vanished. No wonder.

Time to go, to make the planned exit. Shouts from the garden and a man running straight for the window. He put two from the Walther through the window and ran through the house into the kitchen. He readied himself, the space of one second, at the back door, whipped it open and exploded out of it, sprinting for the top of the wall that dropped into the meadow.

He was halfway there before a shot was fired and he knew he had made it. He fell on to the meadow on his good shoulder, rolled once and brought up the Walther and fired three times at the bewildered gunman under the wall. The fellow was not at all cool. He scrabbled with his heels at the turf and with his hands at the wall behind him and there was time to holster the Walther and shift the machine-pistol to the right hand to finish him off.

Along the wall keeping low, then along the trees till it was time to set a line for the woods on the hillside. They would see the blood on the floor and they'd come after him when they had calmed down and got their minds sorted out.

Once in the wood he got out his knife and cut away the shirt sleeve, and when he saw the size of the lump the bullet had taken out of his arm he knew it was bad indeed. It would hurt like hell in a minute, and it was starting now. All this while he was binding the tie above the wound and trying to make a knot of it with one hand and his teeth. He got the knot set and twisted the scabbard of the knife under it until it was tight enough. He tied the hand-kerchief over the scabbard to help hold it in place so that he could use his good hand to reload the Walther and the machine-pistol. The Smith & Wesson was still on his belt. He was carrying half a bloody ton of metal.

Last and hardest thing, but it might save his life for him: he lifted the wounded arm and edged the sleeve of his weather-proof jacket on to it, and then worked the rest of the jacket on. He slung the machine-pistol on his right shoulder and went up the hill among the twisted, stunted oak trees, moving towards the top of the mountain and towards the evening: looking for a place to hole up before night came, because there was not much mileage left in him, and he knew it.

18

"I CAN TELL YOU," HARRY SAID, "I DON'T LIKE THIS ONE little bit."

Sorrel and Gyseman had been all through the house and found it empty.

"What do you think?" Gyseman asked him.

"I think there's been mayhem, and a clean-up done. That's not the chair he was sitting in when I saw him yesterday. I mean that's where he was sitting, but it's a different chair. It was the chair he *liked*, you know how you can tell. And this window is new, fresh putty round it. It looks to me as if they've got Adhemar for certain. If they got Wolf as well, if Wolf came to their trap and they took him or killed him, we're up a gum tree.

Sorrel found the pictures conjured up by this speech unpleasantly reminiscent of the strange atmosphere at that other house in England, where Lord Blacklock had been murdered. There as here flowers had stood in bowls and the old furniture had shone with the polish whose smell coloured the air. Except that in this room, by Harry's way of it, it was the intruders, whether they were assassins or kidnappers, who had taken this dismal care to make the room as its owner would have liked it, after they had used on him whatever violence the need to remove his favourite chair suggested.

The whole feeling of it was repellent. "I'm going outside," she said.

She went to the garden where she had walked before and settled herself this time not in the rose arbour, but on one of the stone benches set round the sundial in the centre. She looked up at the sky, as blue as yesterday's but fading now as evening came on. There was a hawk up there and usually she was pleased to see a hawk, but today she was unduly sensitive. "Go away," she told it. "Leave the poor little buggers alone!"

The hawk paid her no attention, but a sound came from under the bench she sat on, a kind of groan followed by a whine, and the liver and white spaniel emerged and looked at her sorrowfully, and with doubt.

"Bayard!" she said. "You poor man!"

The spaniel gazed at her for a while and then put his nose up on to her knee and she stroked his head. Six months' quarantine, she found herself thinking, or is it four? If one colonel's gone, my lad, you might as well go to the other. You wouldn't like to live in my flat, but he has a garden, and Holland Park just next door, and he spends a lot of time down in the country. What do you think of that?

Not much, obviously, but Bayard was too forlorn to respond to much of anything. Adhemar *is* dead, and he knows it, or he wouldn't be like this. I wonder when he last had something to eat.

Sorrel stood up and moved towards the house. "Come

on," she said to the dog, but he sat down and seemed ready to lower himself under the bench again. Probably sat here with Adhemar in the evenings. "Come on, Bayard," she said, "time for supper." How did you say come to heel in French. *"Viens!"* she tried, and the dog almost moved. "Bayard!"

The dog followed her into the house, and she went to the kitchen and found some cold meat which she put down for him. There was a dish for water but it was empty, so she filled that and set it down beside the other. Bayard took little of the meat but he lapped up a fair amount of water. Then he went to the back door out of the kitchen and asked for it to be opened, so she let him out.

She leaned in the doorway and watched him ramble about, and looked up at the tree-covered hills on the south side of the valley. The green of them was fresh in the late sun. The dog was sniffing at the corner of the wall and jumped inelegantly down out of sight. When she saw him again he was nosing across the meadow. She had begun to feel responsible for him so she called out to him to come back, but he simply halted where he was and barked at her. She thought he was whining but she couldn't be sure at the distance.

She went over to the wall where he had jumped off it and went down after him. She had taken three paces when she saw the blood on the grass. "Dear God!" she said, and looked desperately at the dog on one side of her and the house on the other. "Stay, Bayard, stay!" She yelled hopefully, and climbed up the wall again and ran into the house. From a window in the passage that ran to the front of the house she saw Seddall and Gyseman by the car, apparently ready to leave.

When she reached them, she said. "The dog's on a trail.

Adhemar's dog—he's on a scent. And there's blood on the
grass at the back, out at the back there.''

"It could be," Harry said. "It just could be," and he
ran round the end of the house down to the meadow, with
the others behind him. They saw the dog far across the
meadow and still on the scent.

"I'll get the first-aid kit from the car," Seddall said.
"Mick, get some bits of food from the house, chocolate,
whatever, it's all guesswork this. Bring water. Sorrel, get
off after that bloody dog and if you can catch him that'll
be good, but keep with him!"

There was a back road along the foot of the hillside and
she caught up with Bayard there, casting back and forward
at a loss for the scent until he picked it up again in the
woods that clothed the mountain. By that time she had
taken the silk scarf from her neck and got it under his
collar. She let him keep going up into the trees but slowed
him down to let the others catch up.

Bayard led them on a long slant up the slope. A fit man
running, Seddall thought, would have gone straight up.
This is how a wounded man would go or an old man,
winning some height but taking the easy way. Which of
them, Adhemar or Wolf? How well did the dog know
Wolf? If I was a woodsman or the Last of the Godamned
Mohicans I'd be able to tell if anyone else had gone this
way after him, whoever he is.

The sun had gone down and the light in the wood was
fading when Bayard took Sorrel down into a hollow floored
with dead leaves. The dog whined and scrabbled and they
found him bedded under the leaves.

"Bayard," he said weakly. He fired the Walther once
but the bullet went into the earth two feet from the muzzle.
At the sound of the shot the pigeons lifted out of the oak

trees with a great fluttering, and Harry lifted the weapon from his hand.

"Just as well, maybe," the man said with half a voice. "Who are you?"

"Seddall. Harry Seddall."

"Seddall. I know that one."

And he fainted away.

Harry began to do what he could for the arm. "Sorrel, fetch the car up on to that road we crossed. Mick and I will bring him down as best we can. Then I'll have to make a phone call."

He made the call from the café in the village, leaving the Renault in the dark of the car park under the trees with Sorrel and Gyseman watching over the wounded man. When he was back in the car he said: "We'll use Adhemar's house, why not? We'll have a doctor here in one hour or two. We're to bring a bed downstairs so we'll put it in the kitchen, and Mick and I will sleep there and you can sleep in that maid's room over the kitchen, Sorrel. We'll use the back of the house only and we'll tuck this car and the doctor's well into the forecourt. I want no sign of life to show out of the front of the house. When the doctor's in we'll secure the gates at the entrance, so that if any of Adhemar's friends call they'll think he's away."

Gyseman said: "What will we sleep on?"

"I don't give a fuck what you sleep on," Seddall said. "All you have to do or think about is what I tell you to do. Now shut up and let's keep the tension down. I want this man to live." In a few moments he said: "There'll be a blood drip and God knows what all, so before we settle him on it we'll leave space either side of the bed and we'll put it near a power point." Then he said, thoughtfully and to himself: "Why all the detail? Either I'm growing old or this business is getting to me."

Sorrel thought this business must be getting to all of them. Gyseman's asking what they were to sleep on, coming from that apparently self-sufficient quarter, had struck her as idiotic. She had questions herself about the wisdom of using Adhemar's house—anyone could turn up, gates or no gates—but where else could they take their patient, or prisoner, or whatever he was? He was too close to death to be toted about the countryside. So she kept her questions to herself.

The doctor arrived in a special stretched Citroen fitted out as an ambulance but with no markings on the side. He had the patient medicated, the wound dressed and blood going into him before he even introduced himself.

"Hawkins," he said curtly.

"I'm Seddall," Harry said. "How is he?"

"Don't be an ass," Hawkins said, "and don't light that cigarette."

He was a trim light man a little taller than Seddall with pale skin and eyes and a thin, scholarly face.

Harry put the cigarette back in the pack. "I don't know the difference between prognosis and diagnosis, doctor," he said, "but I know that 'Don't be an ass' is neither. Might he live?"

"He might live, and he's more likely to die." His eye fell on a mattress on the floor. "What's that for?"

"We're going to sleep in here," Seddall said. "I don't want the front of the house seen to be occupied."

"I'll sleep with my patient," Hawkins said. "Nobody else will. I'll need a nurse. The boy can do it, he looks strong enough. If he gets better there will be bedpans and so forth to see to."

"I am strong enough," Harry said, "and I'll be the nurse." He moved closer to Hawkins, who looked to him as much of a boy as Gyseman, and said in a quiet and unpleasant voice: "We shall have to stop this role-playing, Dr Hawkins. We don't have a situation here where any of us can parade about like an admiral on the bridge of his flagship with battle ensigns flying. We need to be calm and sensible, and where we have differences of priority we need to discuss them. I want that man to live and so do you, but there are other people who want him to be dead, which is why he got this way in the first place, so your requirements and mine will simply have to harmonize."

Hawkins and Seddall regarded each other. "You're quite right," Hawkins said at last, with no change of countenance at all. "There must be a room upstairs. Those off duty can sleep up there, we need hardly be prudish about having a mixed dormitory when a man's life is in question, I take it?"

Harry nodded.

Hawkins walked down the kitchen and looked about him. "We cannot cook in here, but I see an electric kettle, a microwave oven and even what is called I believe a toaster-oven, and these can be taken upstairs and used there. A bathroom?"

"There is a bathroom upstairs too," Sorrel said.

"We may manage very well after all," Hawkins said. "Now it is time for visiting hours to end, so if any of you want food will you take it upstairs and eat it cold, for tonight. I shall expect to be alone with my patient in five minutes, and I shall act as night nurse. Objections?"

There were none.

Upstairs, with Sorrel on the bed, Harry and Gyseman roughing it on the floor, and the dog lying in his basket between the men and the woman like a sword, Harry said into the darkness: "I don't like his manners, but I'm inclined to think he knows his stuff."

19

HAWKINS KNEW HIS STUFF.

Five days later Sorrel drove the ambulance, with the doctor and his patient in the back, down the autoroute to Cannes. The Renault 25 followed from far back. During the five days the doctor had hardly left his patient at all; his manner had not become in the slightest degree more sociable, but as a doctor he would have been hard to beat.

From Cannes they drove up to a small villa in the hills near Grasse, where Harry decided it was time for the doctor to be eased out of his lordship over the wounded man's destiny.

For a start he would have to change the ground rules, since the doctor was not only in the full manifestation of his professional power, he was, more or less, in his own home. Hawkins lived here, the staff who had cooked the dinner they were about to eat, and the staff who had begun to serve it, worked for him; the two male nurses, one of whom was sitting in the patient's room at this moment, worked for him; the gardener who kept the grounds worked for him. For so young a man in his profession the doctor lived in a grand manner, and he was, here, on his own ground. His confidence, therefore, would have to be disturbed.

Harry's objective was to have private speech with the doctor's patient, but he came at it obliquely.

He ate the mousseline of salmon without a word, and then said: "Delicious. Doctor, do you realize that your patient, in the state of health to which you have now brought him, is quite capable of taking the gun off that man of yours upstairs and trying to shoot his way out?"

"Rubbish," Hawkins naturally responded, since that was his character. "The wound is far from healed and in any case neither you nor I could deprive William of his weapon."

"Even I could deprive William of his weapon, doctor, and that man upstairs could do it with one hand tied behind his back, which is the extent of his present incapacity, in practical terms."

Hawkins leaned back in his chair and the shadow of a smile moved on his mouth. "You must not presume to teach me my business, Colonel Seddall."

Harry let his eyes drift across Sorrel's face with a particular expression in them and she excused herself and left the room. The table-maid provided a distraction by removing the dishes.

Sorrel came back into the room as Hawkins was about to carve the *boeuf Wellington*, and laid a Colt automatic in the middle of the table. Hawkins understood at once, which was very quick of him; and he went white, which Harry found deeply interesting, since it suggested that the doctor had a great deal of his personality invested in own-

ing control of his environment. The carving knife and fork
found themselves returned to the tablecloth.

"What is the purpose of this charade?" Hawkins uttered these words in little more than a whisper.

A mortified William burst into the dining room and
Hawkins for a moment closed his eyes.

"Who is with the patient?" he demanded when he had
opened them again.

"No one. The girl . . ."

"You mean Miss Blake," Hawkins said admirably.
"You do not leave the patient alone, and you do not come
into this dining room. Return."

He picked up the knife and fork and began carving. His
colour was coming back. "What is it you want, Seddall?"

Seddall acknowledged the man's resilience with a wry
smile. "I can see why you run this place, Doctor. I will
want to start interviewing the patient tomorrow, privately
and alone."

The carving, which was deft, was not interrupted, but
Hawkins said: "I cannot have that. The man is by no
means out of the wood."

Harry helped him self to spinach and new potatoes.
"He's my prisoner as well as your patient. And here is a
piece of news. This is a private contract, and the contract
is with me."

Hawkins was so interested that he neglected to be defensive. "It is? But since the call came from . . ." He
looked at Sorrel and Gyseman and since they were under-
lings, named no name. "I naturally took it that the agree-
ment was with him, with his organization."

"Sure, why wouldn't you?" Harry said.

"I am entirely at your command," Hawkins said, with
the fluency of a robot that had responded instantly to being
re-programmed, and fell upon his beef with all equanimity

restored. Harry understood this perfectly. Hawkins had
been reassured that he was in complete control, subject to
the requirements of his employer of the moment. All that
was unusual was that the employer was here in person.

Sorrel said: "What if he doesn't want to be inter-
viewed?"

"I'm not going to torture him," Harry said sourly.
"That guy has been going around helping people to shuffle
off their mortal coils for a reason, and the killing's over
now, he knows that. The passion has gone out of him.
He'll want to *tell* someone about it now."

"What do you think, Doctor?" Sorrel said to Hawkins.

"Colonel Seddall may be right, Miss Blake, though I
do not know enough of the patient's recent history to form
a definite view." As if to offer them the opportunity,
should they so choose, to supply this lack in his knowledge of the patient's background, he took up his wineglass
and regaled his eye with the rich red glow of the Aloxe-
Corton that accompanied the beef, touched his lips with
his napkin, and let the wine mature in his mouth before
he swallowed it.

Finding that he was not to be enlightened, he continued: "Whether some passion to kill, that you apparently
know of, has gone out of him, I cannot say. Certainly he
is quiescent: apathetic, perhaps, though in truth I have no
real knowledge of his state of mind. His physical state I
can speak of, and I am definite in the opinion that you
should not interview him tonight, so soon after his journey
here. Tomorrow if you must, and the optimum time would
be the morning, at about eleven. He is at his best then,
his most alert; in the afternoon he becomes somnolent."

"Very well," Seddall said. "Eleven o'clock tomorrow
it shall be."

When the *boeuf Wellington* had been followed by rum

Malakoff, and the rum Malakoff by coffee on the terrace, Gyseman said: "Well, Sorrel, shall we go and inspect our rooms?"

"Inspect our rooms?" she asked with surprise. "That sounds incredibly rude, Mick, as if we had come to a hotel."

There was a silence on the terrace, though the night sound of the crickets rose from the grass. The three men exchanged looks of perplexity, so that Sorrel felt non-plussed and without knowing why, a little cross.

"Well, what is it?" she demanded.

"It's not important at all, really," Gyseman said, "except that I thought you knew. You and I are not staying here. We're in a hotel, in Grasse."

"My fault," Harry said without much suggestion of apology. "Should have told you.

"Goodness, it doesn't matter," Sorrel said, which certainly it did not, though why she felt so strangely displaced, by such a minor event, from her position as Harry Seddall's right-hand woman, she could not explain to herself.

"I have only the one spare room," the doctor said, "what with the quarters for the household staff and the two nurses, and the medical section of the house, indeed, which includes an operating theatre."

"Doctor, if that is an apology, there is absolutely no need," Sorrel said brightly, "especially after such a dinner. I shall be very happy in the hotel. It will be rather like being off duty." Which was a bit of a snap at the boss, she thought.

"Be off duty," Harry said, "until after luncheon tomorrow, if you like. Unless you count looking after the dog being on duty. He's taken to you. You and Mick can take the car, I shan't need it."

Bayard, it was true, was lying under Sorrel's chair, and he departed with Sorrel and Gyseman as if that was what he would have expected.

Dr Hawkins walked down to the gates to let the car out and to lock up again after it.

Harry watched the Renault's tail lights turn on to the road and said to the moon: "That went off quite well. She feels left out so he feels in, secure. Childish, really."

He did not say it out loud, however, because you never knew who was listening, even when you were footing the bill yourself.

He thought he would have one more cup of coffee, and then go upstairs to interview the patient.

HE LIKED THE ROOM, TALL AND WHITE AND COOL, LIKED the crisp white sheets around him and the white Traviata-gauze curtains at the lofty window. He liked even William, his nurse and warder, and thought it was a pity he had been shamed by that girl, taking his gun away from him. He had wondered, not for long, what that was about. Not for long, because nothing held his mind long, here in this room. It was the perfect place to have ended up, this aseptic neutral white way-station to where, perhaps, to no-where? It was of no moment to him. He had no volition and no will. He would be nowhere for long, now, which explained to him why his mind was operating on the short-stay principle. A thought here, and then blankness and peaceful suspension for a while in this white room, and a thought there. William was reading to him from a book called *The Hussar on the Roof* by a man called Giono, a native of the same part of Provence as William, fifty miles or so north and west; a writer unfairly stigmatized as fas-cist, William said. Dear me, too bad, such a shame, who cared? He liked the idea of this hussar living up on the roofs above the town, whatever it was, but he had lost the thread some time ago, and took his contentment from the slow quiet voice in which the reading took place.

The buzzer sounded its signal, apparently correctly, for William went to the door and opened it, heavy soundproof door, and the small colonel person came in, Seddall, bearing a tray. He ousted William and when they were alone together with the door locked again the small colonel person said: "Doctor says it's allowed, and I thought you might like a weakish whisky and soda."

"That's Glenmorangie. My grandfather came from near there, from Tain, where that comes from. Came from Strath Conon."

"Do you think I don't know that, Jamie? It occurred to me that you might have, well, an affection for the taste."

Wolf put his good arm behind his head and watched Seddall pour the whisky and fill the glass with soda from a siphon, not one of those piddling bottles with the wrong taste in them.

"Can you heave me up a bit, organize the pillows?"

"If you promise not to strangle me or break my neck with one hand, I might manage that."

"Not funny, that, Colonel. But I promise."

They ended up with Wolf comfortable, the whisky glass resting on a flat place on the bedcover with his fingers round it, and Seddall on a chair near the bed with his own glass of undiluted whisky on the bedside cupboard.

"I don't think I'm allowed to smoke," Seddall said.

"Smoke, what the hell. The room's air-conditioned, and I don't mind tobacco smoke."

Seddall lit a Gauloise and took up his glass: "To Marsham," he said, "and to Adhemar."

Wolf looked down at the glass in his own fingers and

let it stay where it was. "What's your first name, Colonel?"

"Harry," Seddall said.

"That's right, you're the Harry Seddall man. You're pushing me the wrong way, Harry. You want me to tell you things and I'm willing to do that, but don't make jokes about me breaking your neck and don't offer toasts to people who were close to me and got killed."

"Understood," Seddall said, and drank some whisky. "There's no ashtray."

"Use that saucer under the carafe. Ask me something."

"I'd like to make a tape of what you tell me. Would you mind that?"

Wolf swallowed some of his whisky and soda. "Yes," he said, "I do have an affection for the taste, even through all that soda water. If you want to tape it, is it to do some people down?"

"That's what it's for."

"What people? It must be the people who set us all up to get killed."

"Is that what they did? I didn't know that. But yes, those are the people."

"That would be good. Who do you work for?"

"On this one," Harry said cheerfully, "until I got sacked, I was working for the Prime Minister, one of those three-person ad hoc committees for handling a top secret crisis like you."

"Why did you get the sack?"

"I was coming close."

A smile touched the thin mouth on the long solemn face. "Close to MI6, or SIS, or whatever they like to call themselves? So they put it over on you, did they? They put it over on us, that's for sure."

Seddall took the tape recorder from his pocket and

raised an eyebrow at Jamie Wolf. Wolf nodded. Seddall laid the instrument on the bed and started it running.

"What made you think of MI6?" Seddall asked him.

"That was David Marsham, He saw a man he knew coming out of that MI6 block in Vauxhall Bridge Road, then he saw the man lunching in the club one day with Blacklock. David knew from the boss that Blacklock had authorized the operation; and that man David saw lunching with him had once done a blueprint for a demented plan to spring a coup on Enver Hoxha, used to run Albania, man who died. David said there was some kind of romantic hook into some of the old guard in Six and in the CIA about destabilizing, that's the word of the month these days, the regime in Albania. You'll know about that. They had a couple of goes at it that went off at half-cock. Well, David didn't have much to go on, and anyway it wasn't till later on that he began to think there was something funny about the op, and then he remembered that, about seeing this guy with Blacklock. Can I have a bit more Glenmorangie?"

"Sure. You hungry or anything? Would you like tea, or coffee, or something besides whisky?"

The long face looked at him, not just the eyes, the face itself seemed to bear on to him as if trying to recall some elusive sense that its owner had mislaid. It was a face out of Goya, stark and fierce but with the life hollowed out of it, and an unappeasable defeated knowledge waiting in the eyes, like a curse to be completed.

"Whisky's fine, thanks," the face said.

When they were settled again, Seddall said: "That wouldn't be very smart, would it, lunching together if they were cooking up a dirty deal?"

"It was smart, really. Blacklock's real job was defence procurement and this bloke he was with was on an Intelligence committee looking into how to spiffy up their computer system."

"I'll want the name," Seddall said.

The name went on the tape.

Bad night for Arkley, Seddall thought.

"To cut a long story short," Wolf said, "David put together all his suspicions and bits of facts on paper, and he sent it off to Adhemar in a parcel with a great deal of money." He stopped and the eyes went adrift for a space. "The money was for me, to help me clean the slate for David and the rest of them."

He lifted his glass and watched the bubbles come up towards him, then he took some and let the glass rest on the bed again and looked at Seddall, who said: "What were you doing in Albania?"

"What we were told we were doing was rescuing a senior NATO official whose plane had gone off course and crashed in the mountains. We were told the Albanians had given out he was dead along with the rest on board the aircraft, but in fact had him prisoner in a house in a valley. We were to go into the valley and get him out. He was supposed to know things about NATO's first-strike options that it would be very bad if the Russians got to know."

"That's not a bad plot, except for the notion that the government would send the SAS into Albania like that."

"Oh, we weren't going as SAS. We went in dressed like the local peasantry from over the border in Yugoslavia. They're always accusing the Yugoslavs of landing, or rather trying to land people on the Albanian coast, and we had weapons to suit. That was when I first began to think it was all a bit strange on my own account—David didn't tell me his worries until we were *there*, actually on the edge of the valley."

He shook his head, remembering.

"What was strange?"

"We were shipped off at short notice, I mean we all knew we were going, but one day we just *went*, no personal belongings, nothing, just straight off to this special camp prepared for us; run by the Americans. We were there two weeks, so the Yanks supplied us with everything. Clothes, toothpaste, the lot. We all went to the dentist on the camp too, to make sure no one would get toothache or had an abscess in the making, they said. *That* was what was strange, really strange. They gave us general anaesthetic. I was in there for over an hour and when I came out felt as if my teeth had had a real going over. Not painful, but they felt worked on. Bloody weird, but I couldn't make anything of it."

"Can you make anything of it now?"

"No."

"What happened after that?"

"Oh, after that we went." He sipped from his glass. "Look, can I have a straight shot of this stuff? I know it's not what the doctor ordered, so to speak, but this gnat's piss—I need something stronger for the Albanian bit."

Seddall poured him a neat whisky, and another for himself.

"Now tell me the Albanian bit."

Wolf told him.

The new moon hung like a scimitar over the valley. Its pale crescent was no threat to the men hiding under the tamarisk trees on the edge of the oakwood. The night above them sparkled with stars, but the starshine and the moonlight did no more than soften the darkness where they lay.

Before them rose mountains, invisible until the eye reached the jagged line of peaks and ridges that ran across the glittering sky. The mountains curved in to right and left, enclosing both ends of the valley which waited for them, down there in its rocky cradle, like a black and secret lake.

A mile from the men and three hundred feet below a light shone out of the blackness. Since they reached the top of the slope, four hours ago at dusk, a watch had been kept on the light. Nothing had moved across it.

Two of the men went back down the hill a little way. "What d'you think?" the major said.

"I don't know. I don't know at all."

"Yes," the major said. They spoke with their heads close together. Soon the major said: "I remember a time in Africa when we fought the Kikuyu. They were plainsmen and we drove them up into the mountains. It was the wrong climate for them and they got ill with bronchitis. We could tell when they laid an ambush for us, by the coughing."

There was a silence, as if the two men were listening for the sound of coughing; there was no sound but the crickets in the grass, and a beetle that droned past the younger man's ear and smacked into a tree.

"What do you hear?" the major asked him.

"Not enough, I think," the man said.

"That's what I think too." The major sighed. "You'll be cross about this—I want you to stay back and watch." He felt for the other man's shoulder and put a grip on it, to keep him quiet. "I want you to keep out of it and see what happens, and that's all I want you to do. If it goes wrong it will go wrong altogether, so I don't want you coming down there to help us out. It would be a waste of time, you know that."

There was no answer. The hand on the shoulder gripped it tighter and shook it a little. "Yes, I know that." But the tone was dubious and even sullen. "So what do I do—if it goes wrong?"

There was a foul taste on the major's tongue. He swallowed the bile that rose in his throat and sat up. "For now, go back to the river. Turn north to the mountains. When you have that light in view again stop and wait. See how we make out. You've got an hour to get there. We shan't move till the ground mist starts to rise, but in any event I'll give you the full hour before we go in. If it goes wrong get out to Greece or Yugoslavia."

At this point there was a hesitation, and when the major spoke again there was embarrassment in his voice. "Go to France, to Lyon. You'll find a poste restante letter at the main post office."

"What is this?" the younger man exclaimed. He lay on his back and looked through the oak leaves at the stars, while he heard what the major had said. Then he went on coldly: "Why the melodrama; what do you know that I don't? And why me—why not Saxon? Saxon's fast on his feet, he'd get himself across the border."

"I don't know any more than you do, not for certain. It's just that I've got a feeling about this one: the way things were said, the way a man looked at me. If I tell you now you'll say I'm being paranoid."

"What would it matter what I say? Tell me."

"No. Wait and see. And Saxon? He'd get away all right, but I've picked you for it. You're a vengeful man."

"Vengeful!" He lay still and taut, as if something had moved in the wood.

The major smiled to himself in the dark. "Yes, vengeful. Don't you recognize that? Don't you know yourself?"

"No," he said, and stretched himself limber again. "Go on."

"If we've been set up," the major said in a new voice,

casual and without stress, "if we've been led, then I would think someone ought to do something about it, wouldn't you?"

"Meaning what? Tell the headman?"

"If you like, and if you can do it safety. But I'm not sure you can—not safely for him. Anyway, chew it over for five minutes." The major stood up. "I'm going to see George. Move left."

The major went back up the slope, and the other man put his ear to the night and listened. Then he came to his feet and moved some way along the hillside, noiseless on his feet and feeling his way past the low branches of the scrub oaks. At the new place he lay on the ground and listened again, for any difference in the night. He saw a man's bulk loom against the sky and waited until the major spoke a word and then answered him. Then major made his way along the hill. For a while he did not speak, and then he said: "George Saxon's not happy. Says he has a hunch."

The man thought about Saxon's hunch. He thought that he had heard fear, earlier, in the major's voice. He thought that the major had been around and had perhaps been in this game too long, but his nerve was still good. He thought the major was wily, and that if the major thought there was something to be frightened of, he was probably right.

At last he said to the major: "You mean that if it goes wrong, I should find out about it myself. On my own."

"That's it, yes."

"And the letter at Lyon—that's because you think I'd be safer in France than in England."

"That's it," the major said again. "If twelve men are supposed to disappear and one of them turns up walking around, who will quite clearly know there's been a double-cross—well, I doubt if he'll live very long."

"Yeah," the other man said. "I doubt it too."

"So lie low in France. Hibernate. Start in the spring, when this one's off the books."

"Right. What will I do with what I find out—" his next question hung between them before it was spoken "—with the ones I find out about?"

A small wind stirred the trees. The major felt a leaf touch his face. "The weather will turn soon," he said, "autumn's coming in. If this thing goes wrong, it will be up to you, won't it? Whatever you find out, trust nobody with it unless you can absolutely trust them, nobody at all."

"So with the ones I find out about, and if I can't trust anyone, what would you expect I'd do?"

"Well I wouldn't expect you to bloody lie back and think of England," the major said angrily, his nerves breaking out at last. "If it goes that way, it'll be because me and ten of ours are killed down there, and what I would do is I'd bloody expect you to do something about that."

"Sure," the other man said in a tone that was suddenly emphatic. "It's what I'd expect me to do myself, but I wanted you to lay it on me. I wanted you to know."

The wind pushed at the trees again. The major looked up and saw the clouds draw in from the sea towards the mountains, putting out the stars as they came. "Here comes the weather," he said.

The two men stood up as if the clouds had brought a message to them both.

"Time to go," the major said. "We don't know how clever they might be. If they're clever you're inside the cordon already, so you take care, Jamie. And when you get out, watch your back."

"I think you're wrong, David. I think we'll be meeting at the get-out."

"No, you don't, but thanks anyway."

"Break a leg, then."

"Right. I'm off," the major said, and came back again.
"It's been good," he said.

"It's been good all right," the younger man said.

He set off downhill through the wood, and the major
climbed up to join the men waiting on the rim of the valley.

*The river was not yet in spate, but the September rain had
sent enough water tumbling down the watercourse to cover
the sounds of the man's passage through the wood. There
was too little time in hand for him to move with complete
stealth, and he was almost sure by now that there was no
encircling ring of men to trap him. All the same he took
what care he could. He did not follow the river bank but
kept a constant distance from it, and every so often he
stopped and went to the ground, and looked and listened
into the night. He did this again, now, for he had come to
the end of the trees.*

*He lay there for a while, trying to get a sense of the
ground in front of him through his night glasses. He lay
longer than he would have wished, for the hour the major
had promised him was certainly past, and then he made
up his mind. He ran out blind into the dark, and took the
upward slope of the hill pasture in long high-stepped
strides, stumbling on molehills or tussocks of grass but not
falling, until an instinct slowed him to a walk and he found
he was looking down on the valley, looking down on the
single light that marked the target of the major and his ten
men.*

*The wind at his back was rising and he put himself over
the crest into the lee of the hill. Above his head the clouds*

flew across the sky, showing only glimpses of the moon and stars.

He hunkered down and took chocolate from his pocket and began to eat it. When he had last seen the light in the valley—when he and the major had been watching it together—it had shone bright out of the blackness. Now it glowed soft and yellow, so the mist was up.

"One for our side," he said to himself, and began the waiting.

He waited until he knew they must be there, closing in on the house that was marked by the light, before he let go of his patience. He thought the major must be taking his time, like a fox sneaking up on a henhouse it has taken chickens from before. The man spoke softly to the valley.

"Come on, David!" he said. "Come on! Get in and get out!"

Suddenly, watching the light glow steadily out of the valley, he knew the major was right. The thing would go wrong. The tension of it leapt in him and stopped his breathing for seconds before it happened.

A radiance burst out in the mist below, a perimeter of light round the single light. It was as if a bud had blossomed into flower before his eyes.

The pent-up breath came out of him in a strange sound between a groan and a shout, and before the first shot was fired he had pulled himself, flat to the ground, over the crest behind him and rolled downhill on to the meadow, back into the blackness of the night.

He came to his feet and while the harsh clamour of automatic fire and the thud of explosions beat up at him from the valley he checked his equipment: the Uzzi on its sling; the pistol in its holster and the silencer for that in its pocket; the ammunition clips for both; food, medical kit and amphetamines; and the Yugoslav compass—most of all, now, the compass.

Then he went to one knee and scoured the darkness around him, while the explosions in the valley stopped and the concentrated mass of shooting broke up into hard short bursts, into triplets, and at last into single, isolated shots, and silences between them, and then one very long silence ended by a shot, and then one silence that went on forever.

When the clouds parted for a moment to let the moon look down, it saw a strange thing, a man standing on the edge of the valley who held a knife before his face and kissed the cold steel.

The clouds hid the moon again, and the man set off northwards into the mountains.

20

Gyseman was up before the hotel was awake. In track suit and running shoes he passed through the empty lobby and when he was outside began running at an easy pace through the streets of Grasse in the chill hour before dawn. When he was out of the town he had some five kilometres to go and when he approached the villa he was warm. A 3 Series BMW came up the road towards him and as they passed each other the driver gave him a friendly wave.

Short of the villa's grounds he saw a white piece of cloth caught in the hedge that ran beside the road. When he came level with it he stopped running and jogged in place like an athlete not wanting his limbs to stiffen, and while he did so he turned slowly to see what, if anything, was going on around him. Satisfied that the coast was clear he ran back to a break in the hedge, vaulted the gate there, and went back down the inside of the hedge with his eyes on the ground.

He came to two bundles lying on the damp grass. One consisted of a heavy wool sweater and trousers with a thermos and a bar of chocolate wrapped up in them. He pulled the trousers and sweater on over the tracksuit and put the chocolate in a pocket, but the thermos flask had not survived being thrown over the hedge into the field and he heard the glass rattle inside when he picked it up, so he tossed it in among the hedge roots.

He went over to the other bundle which was wrapped in plastic and frowned when he felt the thinness of the wrapping inside. He tore it open and took out a light sporting rifle. He went over it carefully. It seemed to be unharmed: it was a .22 Mossberg auto-loader. There was also a Mossberg telescope sight and a screwdriver, and he sat on the plastic sheeting and fixed the sight on the rifle and put the completed weapon to his shoulder.

Something blurred at the end of the scope and he followed it and found himself looking for a moment into the eye of a magpie. The white feathers of the piebald bird shone in the light, and he realized that for it the sun was up, though it had not reached him yet, down there on the ground.

He loaded the weapon and stood up. With the rifle on its sling over his shoulder he walked up the field to the plane tree he had chosen and climbed into its branches. When he was about sixteen feet up he had a clear enough view of the shuttered window, and was able to achieve a comfortable stance for aiming the rifle. He settled himself there to wait, and breakfasted on the chocolate.

He hoped that they kept hospital hours at the villa and would be up and about early. Dinner had been over by eight the night before, which encouraged him in this expectation. The sun was up now and he was warmly clad, but he had little opportunity to keep his muscles and sinews mobile, up in that tree. And in any case he wanted to get it over and done with.

The first sign of life was the appearance of a woman going into a shed at the back of the house carrying one of those scoops that hold fuel for a stove, and returning with it filled and going out of sight again as she returned to the house. Soon after that a plume of smoke came out of a chimney, as the stove was opened to ignite the fresh load of anthracite or whatever it was they used in it.

Not long now.

He thought he was well hidden in the leaves of the tree, but when the shutters on the window were thrown back and a man leaned out to hook them to the wall of the house he held himself very still. He had not seen the man before, but knew it must be the other male nurse, who alternated duties with William. When the man went back into the room he put the rifle up and his eye to the telescopic sight.

It was almost as if he were standing immediately outside the window. He watched the man assist the patient to sit up, arranging the pillows behind him, exchange a few words and then leave the room again, presumably to fetch breakfast.

The man on the bed turned and he found he was looking at him face to face. He flinched at this, which was ridiculous, because he knew he was invisible to the other man. He did not like the guy. Even relaxed into exhaustion, and perhaps by medication, it showed the lines of the over-intense Celtic obsession with matters remote from reality—feelings, ideas, beliefs, inherited or imagined from the past, and distorting the present. To Gyseman it was a kind of sickness. Look what the guy had done, for Christ's sake!

But Seddall seemed to have some kind of half-baked relationship with him, and Sorrel Blake had an odd look in her eye when the guy was mentioned, as if she felt some far-out mystical or maybe sexual connection with him. To Gyseman he was some kind of dinosaur, which he was about to despatch with a small calibre rifle.

The trouble was, he didn't want to do it. The face smiled into the telescope.

Gyseman took the rifle down from his shoulder, wiped his forehead with his sleeve, put the rifle up again and sighted on the heart. He fired three times and knew it was done.

He reached up and lodged the Mossberg securely in a fork of the branches, scrambled swiftly to the ground and ran towards the road. He saw the red BMW slowing as it passed along the far side of the hedge and he went over the gate and along the bank to where the car had come to rest. He had a glimpse of a woman's headscarf in the back. As the passenger door opened he put a hand on the roof of the car and let himself down and in, and the car leapt off in a fast start that threw the door to even as he reached out to close it.

He'd made it. He was clear.

"Morning, Mick," the driver said, and inside himself Gyseman shuddered. It was the wrong voice: Seddall's voice.

He felt a cold pressure of metal under his ear for a moment before it was withdrawn. "Be still," Sorrel Blake said. "I'll use it. Believe me, I'll use it."

"You set me up," Gyseman heard himself saying. He sounded aggrieved, unjustly treated. "You set me up," he said again.

"Everybody's doing it these days." Harry turned the car into the driveway up to the villa. "It's what started this. It's what they did to Wolf. Got him, did you?"

Gyseman said nothing to that. The car stopped at the door. "What happens now?" Gyseman asked.

Seddall got out of the car and put his head back in. "Dr Hawkins will have a point of view about that. I think I might humour him, up to a point. He has a vigorous attitude about his patients getting bumped off; bad for business. Why don't we go and see him?"

They went upstairs to the doctor's office, past the door behind which, presumably, Wolf lay unbreakfasted and dead. The male nurse Gyseman had seen through the telescopic sight was standing against the wall. The doctor was leaning on his desk, waiting. He came a little way forward and nodded to the man against the wall, who went up to Gyseman and taking his left arm by the wrist pulled up the sleeves of the sweater and track suit. Gyseman had not begun to struggle before the doctor put the needle in, and he felt himself begin to go. The nurse swung a hospital trolley against his back and they tipped him on to it, and he passed out.

When he came to again he knew at once where he was. He was lying on the table of an operating theatre. His head felt surprisingly clear, no muzziness or sickness, but he had the same sense of wonder about what they had done to his body that comes after an operation, though the apprehension was with him immediate and vast, since he had no idea what he had been brought here for.

The apprehension moved to panic: his arms would not move, his *legs* would not move.

Dr Hawkins appeared at the side of the operating table. "Relax," he said. "You are unharmed. I am a doctor, after all. But you are covered with plaster of Paris. For how long depends on you. Colonel Seddall has something to say to you, which I will not stay to hear."

Seddall took Hawkins' place, except that he pulled over

the trolley and hoisted himself on to it, and sat there swinging his legs and smoking a cigarette. Gyseman felt an absurd instant of outrage at the very thought of smoking in a surgical theatre.

"To me, Gyseman," Seddall said, "you're just a little shit. You're quite a clever little shit, but all that means is that you're quite clever. You were planted on me at that recruiting meeting, and that makes you MI6, so you don't have anything very much about you that I would like even if you hadn't been cheating me from day one."

"Yawn, yawn," Gyseman said.

Seddall looked at the cigarette in his hand. "Shit," he said softly, and shook his head, then he ran a finger nail along his throat.

The male nurse appeared right above Gyseman, behind his head. He grabbed him by the hair and pain sang along Gyseman's neck, a small and exquisite pain. Gyseman saw a straight razor lift out of his sight with the kind of flourish a barber makes when he's shaving a customer.

"Thanks, Renand," Seddall said. "Do you think we can heave this lump on to the trolley? I want him over by the window."

That was very disagreeable. They rolled Gyseman on to the trolley so that he lay there with his head over the end, face down, while the waxed linoleum floor passed under the trolley's wheels. Then they turned him over, with a lot of difficulty, and Seddall opened the window so that he could look out.

"It's going to be a nice day," Seddall said. "You can't see that much, but you can see the sky, pretty blue sky I would say. Those birds, see 'em. You can see the tops of those trees, good time of year for trees, the leaves are still fresh into their green, aren't they, Gyseman? What time is it? Not ten o'clock yet, my goodness. I could do with an espresso, and then a couple of hours after that a man could start on his luncheon. Life is full of days, Gyseman, and if you don't tell me what I want to know so that I can have it on my little magic tape recorder, Gyseman, you will have no more days, you'll have no more of this day, Renand will cut your throat as soon as I leave this room because it's going to cost me a pile of money *not* to have Renand cut your throat, Gyseman, since your killing Wolf is a very bad thing for his business and he reckons it would be the best sanction against it happening to him again.

"So *I* won't be killing you. I won't feel tender about it or guilty, all I'll feel is not so poor as I will be if you tell me what I want to know, because then I'll buy your life from Hawkins. I must congratulate you, meanwhile, on that very delicate line across your throat. It has only just nicked the epidermis, very little blood. It will be easy for Renand to kill you here without messing the place up. All he has to do is wheel this trolley on to a rubber sheet, of which there are two or three stacked across the room, turn you over and put a bucket under your throat and pull your head up to stretch your neck and slice it open.

"Do you hear that tractor, Gyseman, good country sound, better than hearing your own blood fall into the bucket? A dog barking, Gyseman, whatever next? Do you want to have your throat cut at ten in the morning with the sun shining and you only in your thirties? Think of all the good days you could have before you're forty or fifty, Gyseman, and tell me you'd prefer to die here, today, now, on this nice sunny day in Provence and become just number ten or eleven on Renand's list."

Renand said something.

"That's disappointing" Seddall said. "You would only be number three, Renand says. Who's behind you, Mick? Who planted you on me?"

"Has he killed two men? How do I know that?"

"I've killed more than two myself," Seddall said, "but not in the way of murder. Renand's a cold-blood murderer. Tell you what—Renand, let the man have a look at you."

Renand stood beside the trolley and put his hand under the back of Gyseman's head and lifted it a little, the pain running along that line on his neck, so that they could stare into each other's eyes. Renand seemed to get quite a kick out of this and his expression was jovial, which made an appalling impression on Gyseman.

"If I tell you, and I can't see why the hell I shouldn't, I mean I would hardly be dying for Queen and country, would I, so if I do, what happens to me?"

Seddall said: "I'll have bought you from Hawkins, so he'll look after you on my account. He's a very commercial man. He'll keep you here for two weeks, but you won't have all that plaster on. He'll keep the plaster on both your legs, so that you'll be less tempted to walk out on him. He'll cut it off before you leave."

"And then what?"

"Then away you go, into the wide blue yonder. You can go back to Six, if they'll have you. They well might, those people. Just don't come into any of my favourite bistros, that's all."

Gyseman fixed his eyes on the wide blue yonder. He did not feel good. "I'll tell you," he said.

ARKLEY'S TABLE WAS AT THE REAR OF THE RESTAURANT facing the door, the chair he sat in at the mid-point of the back wall. He looked like a *capo de mafia* bitter with vengeance, his face a monument of cold rage, imminent with power. His presence exacted an extraordinary deference from the space around him. The room was filling, though since it was not yet noon there was still open choice of where to sit. Such tables near him as had been occupied when he arrived were still untenanted, and no table adjacent to his had been chosen by any of the newcomers.

He wore a pale grey suit and a hat that matched it sat across from him on the white linen cloth. He had coffee and a glass with brandy in front of him in the manner of a Spaniard preparing for the day.

Seddall had seen this portent from the bar and had got himself a drink to carry into the dining room. If Arkley was going to upstage him, at least he would provide himself with props to even the balance. He sat down and put Arkley's hat on a chair, and gathered in an ashtray for himself from a neighbouring table, since Arkley was plainly exercising an exclusive right over the one on which his cigar, resting in a careful horizontal, smoked.

"Hi," he said, knowing that Arkley would not respond to such a low-life mode of address. "It's all over bar the shouting, Arkley. The jig is up."

Interlopers seated themselves at a neighbouring table. Arkley stared past Seddall's head, Cesare Borgia seeing the dukedom of the Romagna slipping from his grasp.

"There's a red BMW 3 Series in the car park," Seddall said. "One of your Paris lads is in the boot. He was alive when I put him in, but he should be got out of there." He tossed the car keys on to the table, and they clinked against the ashtray with the cigar on it. Arkley took up the cigar and drew on it then studied the living coal at its tip as if there was a thought to be found there.

Arkley spoke. "What will you do now?" he asked. His voice was like the corncrake, and his eyes soaked into Seddall's as if they were laying a curse.

"I thought I'd go back to London. I thought I'd go and

clean your house out for you, metaphorically speaking,"
Harry said.

Arkley began nodding slowly, up and down; the cigar
held level, beside the face going up and down. "I could
kill, you know," he said.

"*Who* would you kill, Arkley? It's your goddamned department." Arkley said nothing.

Harry crushed his Gauloise to destruction and stood up.

He left Arkley sitting there, his fiefdom shrunk now to
his own solitary table, and went away.

21

An east wind, cold and unseasonal, blew upon the cherry trees of Brunswick Gardens, so that they began to shed their blossom before it was time. A little drift of the pink flowers built up against Seddall's foot as he locked the car; released again when he set off for Mendham's house, they scampered with him along the pavement.

He stepped out of this exuberant tide and walked up the path. The door was opened by Jane Mendham. She no longer had the fringe and the straight hair flowing down the shoulders of those '60s Kensington girls. Her hair now was cut short, an acceptably styled middle-class version of punk. She looked also younger, and more dynamic.

"John's up in the attic, with his trains," she said. "You just keep climbing until you get there. I'll be going out soon, so if you want tea or coffee it might be best to make it yourself. John seems not to do that sort of thing successfully."

As he went up the stairs Seddall tried to leave behind

him the fibrillations she was putting into the air around her, and to remember the cherry blossom, which had felt rather jollier to be with, instead. Other people's lives: sometimes he envied them, and at other times, of which this was one, he wished he might have been spared their intimations of discord.

As he put his head up through the trapdoor he heard the Leningrad express leave Paris, or maybe it was the Flying Scotsman pulling out of Edinburgh. Whatever else was going on in this house, the trains were running on time. Mendham was successful at that sort of thing.

"Hallo, John," he said, but he said it to the Carnegie zig-zag, which had won an undying place in his affections.

"Harry," Mendham said, allowing no more than a glance and a nod to interrupt his preoccupation with the requirements of running two trains on limited track availability; for though he had two trains pounding the rails, there were two others on the system, one standing at a station, and the other stopped at a signal.

"Windy out," Harry said, looking round for an ashtray. It was getting harder to smoke these days. Nobody cared any more.

"Use this," Mendham said, and slid an empty coffee mug on its way.

This seemed rather seedy for Mendham, but then Mendham was being at home, wearing an old jersey, one of those ancient garments of which a man can grow so fond that he feels friendship even with the holes. At the office Mendham looked like an advertisement in the Sunday papers, not the colour supplement ones, the ones in the black and white bits. That security you get from clothes: Harry wondered what kind of security the old jersey was giving Mendham now.

"Not such a good trip, then," Mendham said, having

programmed his miniature network to his liking. Turning, at last, to attend to his visitor, his face was amorphous to the eye, suggesting two accounts of itself at once, the volatile open child version and the contained version of the functionary, emotionless and practical.

"Wasn't bad," Seddall came back at once.

"Oh," Mendham held his elbows, and put two fingers of his right hand into the hole at the left elbow of the jersey. "I thought that with Wolf being shot like that, you didn't get the goods on . . . you didn't find out what it had all been about."

"How did you hear about Wolf?"

"Oh," Mendham said again, but his face changed and he unwrapped his arms and put his hands in his jacket pockets, all emotionless and practical, except that his jacket was downstairs in the wardrobe. He used his trouser pockets instead. "One does get to hear these things at the office, you know."

"Sure," Harry said, "I know one does."

The signal dropped and the third train started to run. Despite himself, Harry felt part of him grow excited. Three trains going at once, golly! Mendham was not the only one who regressed to the nursery; chastening stuff.

"Do you know what I first thought was odd? I mean, I thought so later, I didn't notice it at the time."

"What was that, Harry?" Mendham was frowning at the three trains, at a stopwatch, and at the control board in a continuous sequence.

"When you came up with Kosovo at that dinner party," Harry said. "It was a damn nice evening, by the way. I hope Monique wrote to thank Jane."

"Yes she did, much appreciated," Mendham said, and then added illogically but with some extraneous meaning hidden in the words: "Not that Jane would care that much anyway."

Harry found this sinister undercurrent in the Mendham household unfortunately timed, and babbled usefully to win free of it. "I'm glad Monique wrote. I always get the woman to do it if I can. When I do it myself I always forget until it's rather later than is polite."

There was still a bit of silence to be got through, but the trains filled it quite well. Harry looked into the coffee cup and saw dregs in it. He dropped the smoked-down Gauloise in it and heard it sizzle. He longed for home.

"At the dinner table," he ploughed on. "When they were talking about minorities, you knew that Kosovo was where the Albanian minority in Yugoslavia is centred. It seemed an odd thing to know."

Mendham was having a big problem. His face cleared as he solved it, and did something to the control board. He was like an otter watching his cubs disport themselves in the fast flowing river.

"Kosovo? I'm in the Foreign Office, Harry, we know these things."

Seddall stared at him. "The Foreign Office? That's all eyewash, John. You're in MI6."

Mendham stared blankly at the trains speeding round the tracks, and at the maze inside his head that showed him a continuous forecast of their destinies. "I mean at that dinner. I was being a man at the Foreign Office. I always do that in the social line." He smiled a very little as two of the trains vanished into the tunnel under the zig-zag from opposite ends. "It's my cover, Harry."

Seddall watched him carefully. This was Never-Never Land, this was. "What I mean, John, is that you're not a diplomatist, you're a spy man."

"I know that," Mendham said comfortably. "I was just

explaining. I think Jane's going to leave me; I wish she wouldn't."

They had been beating about the bush for so long there was nothing left of it but twigs. "It might be for the best if she does leave you," Seddall said. Christ, this was raw. "Wolf told me all he knew before he died, and what is a good deal more to the point, John, Gyseman talked to me so that he wouldn't die."

"Well then," Mendham said, "I don't see why it would be better if Jane leaves me. If I'm in trouble it would be better if we were . . . if we were still together. Or perhaps not. Not the way to use it, is it?"

"Use what?"

"Love," Mendham said.

He moved a switch on the control panel and one of the trains went out of circulation into the marshalling yard. Mendham watched the two other trains run their separate courses for a while and then took one of them out of play and left the remaining train to run round and round on its own.

He stood up straight and examined Seddall closely for a long moment. His face had stopped wavering, and was as intelligent as a face could be on a man trying not to register unnameable terrors within.

"Twelve men dead," he said, and then listened to the sound of it. "You want to know why."

"Yes," Harry said. "That's what I'd like to know."

Mendham sat on the floor with his back to the wall, the platform that carried the railway lines over his head like a roof. He pulled up the sleeves of the old jersey and bent one knee and clasped his hands round it.

"Those talks between East and West," he said. "The great détente, all that. The Russians tried to take advantage of it, down in Albania. When Hoxha was alive he wouldn't look at Russia, you know that. He was in cahoots with the Soviets for a bit after the war, ditched them, and got along with China for a bit, and then he settled for being autonomous, Albania on her own, no ties with anyone else, a hermit among the nations. Not a bad idea, in some ways, though I suppose in the circumstances the comment is subjective.

"The Russians would like Albania in the Warsaw Pact, down there on the Mediterranean, what wouldn't that do for their naval strategy, never mind anything else. Foothold in the Mediterranean. They don't have Greece, they don't have Yugoslavia. Obviously more reliable than Libya. They've always wanted Albania. So they decide to take advantage of the détente, on the basis that America wants the détente this time, the West wants it, there's a second-term presidential election coming up in America and the President is counting the votes already on his détente platform. So if the Russians do something low-profile and discreet the Americans won't get to hear about it and if they do they dare not react in any useful way or they'll blow the détente and the President loves his second term."

Mendham interrupted himself and got irritated. "Why don't you take that damn recorder out of your pocket, Harry? I'm not exactly a babe in the woods about this sort of thing, you know. Put it out on the floor and get yourself a nice clear tape of this."

Seddall acknowledged this with a lowering of the head, and felt himself ungainly as he wrestled the tape recorder out of his coat pocket.

"That should be babes in the wood," Mendham said, and chewed his lower lip. "Two babes in the wood, never just one. That's how it is now, though. Take your coat off if you want, I mean take the gun out as well, nobody's going to *mind*."

Seddall couldn't handle that one and shook his head. Mendham had suddenly turned real, and Seddall couldn't catch up with him this fast. Mendham started off again:

"The Albanians like being on their own. They're safe that way. The Russians won't let the Americans move in and the Americans won't let the Russians move in. So far as power-politics goes, Albania is in balk. At least, that's how it has been up to now. After Hoxha died the leadership accepted a few overtures from western countries, but there was no great broadening of diplomatic relations. Still much as it was, but with the leadership no longer the dogmatic authority of one man, differences of view, that sort of thing."

Seddall, relying on the tape to record this preamble, allowed himself to be fascinated by the train's recurrent passage over Mendham's head. It had come to appear to him as Mendham's familiar, an associative spirit that spoke to a secret part of Mendham; even a reassurance to Mendham that he, Mendham, was truly there. He took the pistol out of his pocket without thinking what he was doing. He did it because his hand was becoming sweaty on the butt, and since he had done it, he simply laid it on the shelf beside him, where Mendham's familiar spirit would see it every time it passed.

"So the Russians," Mendham said, "got one part of the Albanian leadership to agree to a secret meeting in Albania. Thin end of the wedge, of course. The other part didn't want it, but what could they do? If they held out against it they risked the Russians beavering away at their more sympathetic colleagues and getting set to go the whole hog when the time was ripe. So they spoke to the French."

Harry was startled. "The French?"

"Well, of course. The French can talk to anybody. They

have this style of inflexible logic and flexible politics. When we want to insult them we call it pragmatic. The French told the Americans these talks were going to take place and *some* Americans thought these talks were just not going to take place, and then they thought some more, and came to us.

"They had actually fed scenarios into their computers, to work out what would do the business: what would tell the Russians they must call off the talks in Albania, but would not provoke any kind of escalation: what would let Moscow know that Washington would use armed force if it had to, in order to prevent Russia getting a naval base in the Mediterranean and getting a hook round the southern flank of the North Atlantic Treaty countries."

Seddall, who had a deep fondness for Italy, frowned. "What about Italy?" he said.

"Come off it, Harry! What *about* Italy? A new government once a week and have you looked at the size of its NATO contribution? Now, what the Americans came up with was this: that to let Moscow know they would not be afraid to use force if they felt the need, what they should do was make an extremely small, almost invisible, show of actual force; and by actual force they meant an armed raid. Not on Russia, that would be out of the question, that would mean goodbye to the great détente and it would mean a lot more, because the Russians would have to respond in kind."

"Albania, then," Harry said.

Mendham liked this suggestion of dialogue. "And just where in Albania?" he asked, like a schoolteacher with an apt pupil.

"I'll be damned!" Harry said. "They decided to shoot up the talks."

"That's right. They decided to shoot up the talks, only

no one was to be hurt. A lot of fireworks round the house and bits of the house knocked off, selected windows in empty rooms—rooms with no lights on—shot to bits.

"Then the Americans chickened. They could not use real Americans to shoot at Russians, they decided. The computer told them that might be too much, but they could use phoney Americans, get the same message across, and avoid escalation."

"The President was in on this?" Harry asked.

"Don't be naive. Washington was in on this. Not the White House, not the Pentagon, but Washington. Say, someone on the National Security Adviser's staff. Officially, the President could not even know about the Russian move on Albania, or how could he meet the General Secretary of the Soviet Communist Party. It was vital for neither of the boss men to 'know' about any of this when they were meeting face to face."

"So then what?"

"So then these particular Americans approached us, not the Prime Minister, and not the Government. The CIA approached me."

Mendham, amazingly, looked pleased, as if at the recollection that the right people had understood his value at last. "Because Dundas is out of it, which is called being ill. Because Arkley is only a stopgap as his deputy although Albania is his section at Six, which was good for me, because I could build it in, to be on the safe side if anything went wrong, that Arkley had handled our end of it."

"It had me going for a bit," Harry said amiably, beginning to be apprehensive that Mendham would suddenly change mood and stop telling the tale.

"It did, didn't it?" Mendham was looking pleased again. He was enjoying this bit. Presumably, the way the story was going, he would not enjoy it for much longer. "And they chose me because they knew I had the nerve for it and could work it, which I damn well did, too. Lastly, because I met Blacklock quite a lot over defence procurement because I'm on a committee for that, and they thought Blacklock could be got to authorize it."

Seddall asked, "What about Glaisher?"

"They arranged that. When Glaisher was over in Washington they put something in his food that gave him a terrible pain in the gut, whisked him off to Bethesda Naval Hospital in Maryland and when he came out of the operation told him he'd had acute peritonitis. They took out his appendix, poor Glaisher. It was beautifully timed. The other Ministers at Defence were out of the country too— all we needed was a couple of days—and Blacklock signed the order and it went down through channels and was secreted into oblivion and the SAS boys were out of Hereford and on to an American base and the operation was on."

"And at the base they Americanized them. Wolf told me that. Their teeth and everything."

"Absolutely," Mendham said cordially. "Toothpaste, soap, anything that might be found on them. The food in their stomachs. There would even have been traces of Coca-Cola. Working with the CIA can be quite rewarding. They're much more thorough than we are."

"Was it CIA?" Harry asked bluntly.

A thought came to Mendham, the first return of doubt, the move towards the intolerable outcome. But still he held it away. *Carpe diem,* Seddall thought to himself, and after that, will he go mad? Is he mad now?

Then Harry realized that by accepted standards, the behaviour of people in Intelligence was imbecile. He began to have doubts of his own, watching the little miniature locomotive and its train of coaches whipping over Mendham's head; he began to wonder whether the fact that he had identified the train as Mendham's familiar meant that he had a like voice in himself, waiting only to be heard.

"The first contact was CIA, but after that I think they were CIA men who had retired. That tremendous American mania for not saying to yourself what you're doing out loud, Harry? You know? The French were the same, not that I had direct dealings with them, but I gather they were using ex-*SDECE*."

Seddall thought he wanted to get this over with, even if it risked Mendham clamming up. He needed to be shot of this unhealthiness of Mendham's, that was beginning to infect him, in which Mendham was explaining to himself how reasonable the whole exercise had been.

"Surely to God, John," he said brutally, "you can see that they were setting you up just as you were setting up these SAS boys?"

"No, I was *not*. I was not setting them up. It was a secret operation and there were bound to be some casualties, they know that when they go on an operation, the SAS, they expect casualties. There were going to be just one or two, just what they would expect, Harry, what they would expect!"

You could see something within refusing to let him lose his temper with Seddall, not the man himself controlling his anger but the anger being controlled before it reached him. Keeping it nice, Harry thought. Bloody marvellous.

"So what went wrong?" he asked.

"It was the Albanians, not the Americans. The Americans were straight with me. The whole thing was set up, too late to call them off, when the Albanians told the French they had decided all the . . . all the men . . . well all the men, you see, now, do you see? All of them?"

Seddall got a cigarette out of the pack and flicked his lighter and nothing happened. The flint was gone. This was bad. Mendham was going to pieces down there on the floor, he would be blubbering any minute now.

It was all out now, anyway, but there was something Seddall needed to ask Mendham.

He went down on to his toes, to be more on a level, and picked up the tape recorder and turned it off. "What was it for, John?"

"For?" Mendham looked up, looked up hopefully at the relic of a friendship he had wanted even when he knew he had started it himself to cheat the other man.

"Yes. Why did you want to do it?"

"Well *goodness*," he said like a little boy, "so that they would *know*, that was what it was *for*."

"Who's they, John?"

"They, just *they*, just so that they would know how good I was. I was good," he said, and the tears came down his face.

Harry stood up and put the recorder in his pocket. He picked up the pistol and had a great wish to shoot the hell out of that absurd train as it went over Mendham's head, but it was too late for that.

He looked at Carnegie's zig-zag and thought what a good thing that was to have made; not just of Carnegie, but of Mendham too.

He lowered himself through the trap in the floor, and left the two of them together, the little train scuttling round above its master's head; and went down past the silences of the house.

AUTUMN

22

SEDDALL LOOKED OUT AT THE TREES IN GREEN PARK, AND
said hallo to Arkley, who was established on the battered
leather couch under the window. He had designed psycho-
logical barriers to prevent intrusion by any chance acquaintance: *The Times* crossword was on his knee, the
gold pencil in his hand, and a schooner of sherry sat on
each end of the table in front of the couch.

As Seddall sat down Arkley threw the paper aside and
took up his glass. "Good!" he said, by way of welcome.
"La Ina," he said, of the sherry. "If it's not what you
want . . ."

"It's what I want," Seddall replied. "It's what I very
much want, but I don't know that I can handle so very
much of it."

Arkley was delighted. "Your generation drink sherry
out of thimbles. You drink sherry in a club as if you were
in a woman's drawing room."

"*My* generation," Harry said, "is not that distant from yours."

"You are middle-aged," Arkley said with contentment, "and so you think you have grown old."

Arkley had never been a man who would go gently, when his time came, into that long night. He was a man who held the present at bay, never mind the future and far less, what came after it. His expression now declared that the best men, grown old, become giants and quite possibly, if they work at it, immortal.

This was a different Arkley, too, from the enraged herd bull at Cannes who had seen his pre-eminence about to be snatched away from him. This was Arkley come out on top, Arkley knighted, Arkley no longer deputy and acting head, but confirmed chief of his department. This was Arkley happy to grow old, and to feel himself at harmony with the great men of all antiquity.

After they had lunched on adequate food but a claret to which Harry had never tasted the equal—a claret which to be at its best must have been decanted many hours before, a sign that Arkley had gone to some care to manifest goodwill towards his guest—they settled with coffee and cognac in a corner of the smoking room.

"That was very fine, Arkley," Seddall said. "But until we met at that memorial service for Dundas we had not spoken to each other all summer, not since France."

"Poor Dundas," Arkley said, though with something hilarious behind his face. Arkley at ease with the world was something to see. "You are wondering," he drew on his cigar and studied it, as if to be sure it was not suffering, "about the occasion for this meeting."

Seddall lit an unsuccessfully constructed Gauloise, which went up like a torch and sparked tobacco seeds about the place before it calmed down. "That's what I'm wondering," he said.

"Aha!" Arkley said, jocose as anything. "I am in your debt, Seddall, and I shall not forget it. I may come to resent it, as men will, but so far my mood towards you is one of uncorrupted gratitude."

A man in this style of eloquence needs no encouragement, and Seddall drank cognac, brushed ash off his suit, and waited for the rest.

"When you unmasked Mendham," Arkley said, first looking around him to be sure there was no one in the vicinity, "it seemed to me like disaster, for the department and for myself. I do not know which of you, at that juncture, I disliked most. Soon after my return to London, however, it transpired that our Russian friends, whose embarrassing delegation to Albania had in any case packed their bags shortly after the fireworks in which all these good men of ours died, let Washington know that they had abandoned any designs they might have been suspected of having to extend their sphere of influence into that, quite amazingly beautiful, you know, little country.

"The stroke, therefore, devised by all these seedy fellows who live in the half-light of the Intelligence world— American, French, and our own Blacklock and Mendham— and who do not live in the real world where you and I live, Seddall: the stroke they devised had been, it therefore turned out, a success, despite the appalling means they had employed. Those responsible in Washington, accordingly, felt it safe to claim the credit for it, which they received, and thanks then came from Washington to London on a very private line, if you take me?"

"Oh, I do," Seddall said. "I do indeed."

"Quite so," Arkley said, and cherished his cigar, and gave himself some cognac, and smiled a cold, reflective smile. "This occurred, as I say, not long after I, and yourself too, of course, came back from France. I was being asked, in fact, what we were being thanked for, at about the same time your report would be going in. It seemed to me, Seddall, that I was in very deep shit indeed, one way or the other, so I had nothing to lose. So what did I do?"

Seddall was extremely curious to know. "What *did* you do, Arkley?"

"With one bound, I leapt out of the latrine. It was exactly like that, I assure you. I imitated the instigators of the plot in Washington, and claimed credit for it myself. Mendham, I said, had been working to my orders. It was a horrendous gamble, like backing a horse that had never jumped a hurdle to win the Grand National: I simply did not see how the Government could accept even so useful a result, with regard to our international relationships, when it was based on the deliberate sacrifice of the lives of twelve British soldiers. But as I say, I had nothing to lose. I expected Downing Street to take the dark view of the whole business, but whether they took the dark view or the rosy view, unless I claimed responsibility for it, then it would have happened under my nose, without my knowing anything about it, while I was running the department. Hopeless. That would have been hopeless."

While he leaned forward to turn the ash on his cigar on to the ashtray, Arkley said: "When I was made head of Six you kept quiet, Seddall. You could have made a stir, if you had chosen to. That is why I count myself in your debt."

"No problem," Seddall said. "You can pay some of it, if you like. Just tell me how you got rid of Mendham."

Arkley smiled like a pterodactyl watching its shadow sweep across the earth. "I told him to get out, or I would destroy him. He's doing industrial espionage in the States now.''

"Gyseman?"

"Vanished. Gone to ground. Perhaps he is shooting kangaroos in Australia. Your own Miss Blake, Sedall, is she retired too?''

Seddall put his cigarette out clumsily. It took a long time. "We're neither of us retired, Arkley. Sorrel's visiting a friend in East Anglia.''

"Ah, yes. The good Mrs Knight, in Norfolk, I believe.''

Seddall stood up and thanked Arkley for the meal. Arkley stood up too, and said not at all. Seddall told Arkley he would find his own way out, and Arkley said he would stay to finish his cigar.

They did not part, but looked at each other. A smile turned Seddall's mouth and went away again.

"Yes?" Arkley said.

"I was thinking," Harry said. "They'll have a strange opinion of you in Downing Street.''

Arkley stared, and then his face cleared. You mean Arkley the ruthless mastermind. All these dead men.''

"That's what I mean. Don't worry about it, Arkley. You'll grow into it," Harry said, and went out of the club into St James's Street.

SEDDALL WENT TO BED EARLY THAT NIGHT, AND READ FOR a bit. He fell asleep with the light on to the sound of the November rain beating at the windows.

When he woke he heard Monique singing in the shower, and looked at his watch: not quite midnight. The shower stopped but the singing went on, a sad song in a sweet clear voice, a tune which Harry recognized but could not

identify. He put a name to it at last. Sh Springsteen's "My Home Town," with ple choly as if in Nevers or Limoges, or where nique came from, they shared the same sa small-town America as small-town Ameri this soulfulness about places she didn't kno

When she came out of the bathroom, he

She dropped the towel and looked care flection in the pier-glass, turning slowly, wh "I only sing the song," she said. "Not th

Looking at her, he sighed enormously. he said.

"It's a sad song," she said, nodding, a kissing him as she arrived. She lay acros stroked his face. Then she frowned, and sat right up against the bedhead with her f her on the pillow. "What is that?" she d

There was a huffling sound and someth up out of the bed.

"That's Bayard," Harry said, as the peared. "He's a countryman of yours. quarantine today.''

"You could have told me," Moniqu to stroking the dog's head instead of H back into bed and hugged Bayard, w amorously.

"He is a beautiful lover. I will Monique said. "Then where will you

"I'll be over here, waiting" Harry man, when something's worth waitin

Downstairs in the drawing room slept on Seddall's chair, and dream

J.K.
was
watc

smile. "This occurred, as I say, not long after I, and yourself too, of course, came back from France. I was being asked, in fact, what we were being thanked for, at about the same time your report would be going in. It seemed to me, Seddall, that I was in very deep shit indeed, one way or the other, so I had nothing to lose. So what did I do?"

Seddall was extremely curious to know. "What *did* you do, Arkley?"

"With one bound, I leapt out of the latrine. It was exactly like that, I assure you. I imitated the instigators of the plot in Washington, and claimed credit for it myself. Mendham, I said, had been working to my orders. It was a horrendous gamble, like backing a horse that had never jumped a hurdle to win the Grand National: I simply did not see how the Government could accept even so useful a result, with regard to our international relationships, when it was based on the deliberate sacrifice of the lives of twelve British soldiers. But as I say, I had nothing to lose. I expected Downing Street to take the dark view of the whole business, but whether they took the dark view or the rosy view, unless I claimed responsibility for it, then it would have happened under my nose, without my knowing anything about it, while I was running the department. Hopeless. That would have been hopeless."

While he leaned forward to turn the ash on his cigar on to the ashtray, Arkley said: "When I was made head of Six you kept quiet, Seddall. You could have made a stir, if you had chosen to. That is why I count myself in your debt."

"No problem," Seddall said. "You can pay some of it, if you like. Just tell me how you got rid of Mendham."

Arkley smiled like a pterodactyl watching its shadow sweep across the earth. "I told him to get out, or I would destroy him. He's doing industrial espionage in the States now.''

"Gyseman?''

"Vanished. Gone to ground. Perhaps he is shooting kangaroos in Australia. Your own Miss Blake, Sedall, is she retired too?''

Seddall put his cigarette out clumsily. It took a long time. "We're neither of us retired, Arkley. Sorrel's visiting a friend in East Anglia.''

"Ah, yes. The good Mrs Knight, in Norfolk, I believe.''

Seddall stood up and thanked Arkley for the meal. Arkley stood up too, and said not at all. Seddall told Arkley he would find his own way out, and Arkley said he would stay to finish his cigar.

They did not part, but looked at each other. A smile turned Seddall's mouth and went away again.

"Yes?'' Arkley said.

"I was thinking,'' Harry said. "They'll have a strange opinion of you in Downing Street.''

Arkley stared, and then his face cleared. You mean Arkley the ruthless mastermind. All these dead men.''

"That's what I mean. Don't worry about it, Arkley. You'll grow into it,'' Harry said, and went out of the club into St James's Street.

SEDDALL WENT TO BED EARLY THAT NIGHT, AND READ FOR a bit. He fell asleep with the light on to the sound of the November rain beating at the windows.

When he woke he heard Monique singing in the shower, and looked at his watch: not quite midnight. The shower stopped but the singing went on, a sad song in a sweet clear voice, a tune which Harry recognized but could not

identify. He put a name to it at last. She was singing
Springsteen's "My Home Town," with plenty of melancholy as if in Nevers or Limoges, or wherever it was Monique came from, they shared the same sad nostalgia for
small-town America as small-town Americans. Why all
this soulfulness about places she didn't know?

When she came out of the bathroom, he asked her.

She dropped the towel and looked carefully at her reflection in the pier-glass, turning slowly, while she thought.
"I only sing the song," she said. "Not the words."

Looking at her, he sighed enormously. "Come to bed,"
he said.

"It's a sad song," she said, nodding, and went to bed,
kissing him as she arrived. She lay across from him and
stroked his face. Then she frowned, and gave a yelp and
sat right up against the bedhead with her feet tucked under
her on the pillow. "What is *that*?" she demanded.

There was a huffling sound and something followed her
up out of the bed.

"That's Bayard," Harry said, as the spaniel's head appeared. "He's a countryman of yours. I got him out of
quarantine today."

"You could have told me," Monique said, and turned
to stroking the dog's head instead of Harry's face. She got
back into bed and hugged Bayard, who licked her face
amorously.

"He is a beautiful lover. I will prefer him to you,"
Monique said. "*Then* where will you be?"

"I'll be over here, waiting" Harry said. "I'm a patient
man, when something's worth waiting for."

Downstairs in the drawing room the black cat Sacha
slept on Seddall's chair, and dreamt her evil dreams.